THE GREAT JONES COOP TEN GIGASOUL PARTY

(AND OTHER LOST CELEBRATIONS)

THE GREAT JONES COOP TEN GIGASOUL PARTY

(AND OTHER LOST CELEBRATIONS)

PAUL DI FILIPPO

WILDSIDE PRESS

DEDICATION

To all those friends and inspiring writers who have left this Earth since these stories were first written.

And to Deborah, who saw them all in their infancy.

ACKNOWLEDGEMENTS

All my thanks to Denny Lien, who provided scans of two stories that had escaped my own archives. A true Chum.

"The Man Whom Things Hated" was composed from 9/3/84 to 9/14/84. "Flashers" was composed from 5/28/85 to 6/24/85. "Below the Wrack" was composed from 7/11/85 to 9/13/85. "The Great Jones Coop Ten Gigasoul Party" first appeared in *New Pathways*, 1986. "Campion's Tree" first appeared in *New Pathways*, 1986. "Winter in America" first appeared in *New Pathways*, 1987. "Royaume due Rêve" was composed from 9/24/87 to 12/13/87. "Triplets" first appeared in *The Drabble Book*, 1988. "The Jones Continuum" first appeared in *Science Fiction Eye*, 1988. "Waterloo Sunset" first appeared in *New Pathways*, 1988. "Modern Conveniences" first appeared in *Edge Detector*, 1988. "I Kant Cuz I'm Too Jung" first appeared in *New Pathways*, 1989. "Heaven Sent Me an Angel, C.O.D." first appeared in *bOING-bOING*, 1992. "A Night in the Thirteenth Avenue Mission" first appeared in *After Hours*, 1993. "Strange Brew" first appeared in *The Third Alternative*, 1994. "Fax" first appeared in *Pirate Writings*, 1999.

ARTWORK CREDITS

The cover illustration of the Shimizu Mega City Pyramid (TRY 2004) has been graciously donated by the SHIMIZU CORPORATION, Coporate Communication Dept., 2-16-1 Kyobashi, Chuo-ku, Tokyo, Japan. It relates to a discontinued project of their conception.

Published by Wildside Press LLC.
www.wildsidebooks.com

CONTENTS

INTRODUCTION: UNEARTHED

This volume contains twelve stories which, for one reason or another, have lain uncollected after their initial publication, an era spanning the years 1986 to 1999. Additionally, four never-sold stories of roughly the same vintage—pulled from my files, with the oldest dating from 1984—see print here for the first time.

So: some unknown and unclamored-for stories thirty to fifteen years old, back in print? Why these, why now? Why resurrect these tales after letting them lie hidden for two decades or more? A few justifications seem relevant.

I was initially proud of all of them, unsold ones included, even if some second hesitant thoughts led me, when assembling earlier collections, to bypass them. Upon rereading them recently, my pride in the accomplishments of my younger self was reawakened, and I thought they should be honored with a new life. (You'll learn more about each piece in the individual story introductions.)

Secondly, they represent a certain arc of my career and development, a segment of my writing which, I imagine in my vainglorious folly, might be of interest to some fans of my work—and even to some critics and historians, should I be lucky enough ever to attract such attentions.

Finally, I think they represent some good storytelling which has the potential, like all well-wrought tales, to amuse and entertain and even enlighten the reader.

Thus, for all these reasons, I've chosen to "unearth" these stories, the only fitting strategy for a fellow whose first piece of professional fiction appeared in *UnEarth* magazine!

When I wrote this story, I had never heard of the term "resistentialism." And yet I instinctively knew, as all humans do, that the universe is filled with balky "inanimate" objects that desire to frustrate us and do us harm. This simple little story was my attempt to spread the warning, by imagining the plight of one poor fellow who was particularly hated by the cosmos. At the time, I had read Algernon Blackwood's "The Man Whom the Trees Loved," and envisioned this as a kind of counterpoint to his piece. The metaphysics may be a little wonky, but I think the effect comes through.

THE MAN WHOM THINGS HATED

Hours ago, the snow had been an icy mattress beneath his parka-clad back. Now it merely felt warm and comforting, a down-filled hollow he would never leave. Hours ago, the pain in his mangled right leg had been excruciating, causing him to cycle through a personal season consisting of periods of hellish awareness followed by merciful blackouts. Now the agony was simply an old friend, part of his very essence.

Harry Strang, dying, possessed of a curious lucidity, considered his life.

* * * *

They called him a clumsy child, and he believed them. At least for a time.

How else to explain the incredible misfortunes that dogged him, like the Furies plaguing Orestes?

Little Harry was totally maladroit among the modern appurtences of everyday life. The artifacts which everyone else dealt with so easily were intractable with him. Any significant encounter between Harry and a manmade object—and naturally such encounters were innumerable and unavoidable—ended in humiliating and painful defeat for him. His life, till age ten or so, was an unending succession of minor and major disasters.

There had been, for instance, the time he was leaning out the window at school to shout to a playmate below. Inside the old-fashioned frame at that instant, the frayed rope holding the cigar-shaped sashweight had given way, and the massive window had come crashing down on Harry's back. He had been in the hospital nearly a month following that. And somehow, he had gotten all the blame, as if he could have known the condition of the hidden mechanism, and had deliberately taunted it, by placing his frail body beneath it.

When the emergency brake in his father's '59 Chevy Bel Air chose to fail, he had tried desperately to steer the rolling auto down the hill and onto a grassy median. Instead, all his best efforts brought on a collision with telephone pole at ten miles per hour. Harry took away a sickle-shaped scar on his forehead from his "clumsiness" that time.

When an aerosol can of Endust accidently fell off its closet shelf and into the bag of paper trash—the very trash which it was Harry's job to incinerate in the backyard burner—the resulting explosion peppered Harry's left arm with hot metal shards. His father called him a "damn clumsy kid without the sense he was born with," and told him he was lucky not to have lost his eyes.

Dramatic and potentially fatal accidents such as these were inter-spersed with a hundred other lesser daily humiliations. Tripping over extension cords around the house; reaching into a toolbox and stabbing himself with an icepick; breaking the dinner glasses he was assigned to dry; stepping on rusty nails with bare summer feet; dropping a pan that held boiling water and scalding himself.

Harry's body always bore a dozen black-and-blue marks, shifting like sunspots from week to week. Islands of permanent scar-tissue were more stable features of his topography.

Harry's despair and sense of helplessness would have been total, had it not been for the time he spent in the woods, which he loved.

Living in a brand-new suburban tract during the 'fifties, Harry had easy access to the countryside that bordered the development. Acres of oaks and pines, birches and elms, ledges and streams, lay just beyond the last cracker-box cottage. There, Harry discovered—slowly, against all evidence—that he was not really clumsy.

He never fell from the trees he climbed, nor the rocky outcrops he scaled. He could leap from stone to slippery stone across a chilly stream without once getting wet. He never bumbled into the nests of yellow-jackets. Lightning-blasted branches never fell on his head. In short, he navigated through forest and meadow with a growing confidence and surety utterly lacking in his home life.

Each time he returned from a sojourn among the trees, he would strive to convince himself that his competence would persist, that this time he would be transformed, all his awkwardness magicked into grace.

It never happened that way, though. Each re-entry into society with all its devices was like the expulsion from Eden replayed, all celestial harmony decaying into earthly strife.

Harry fantasized about simply fleeing to the woods for good, so disheartening was his mundane, catastrophe-filled life. But he was no true loner—although forced to be one, since his peers jeered him for his misfortunes—and he realized with a child's clarity that even if he could survive physically in the wild, he would soon grow lonely and sad.

So Harry lived till roughly age ten with a curious dichotomy he could not rationalize, but only endure. At home and at school, anywhere in fact among the trappings of modern life, he was an utter incompetent, prone to seemingly inescapable collisions with everyday innocent objects. In the woods, he was simply a normal, well-coordinated boy who did not suffer at all.

One night, the split in his perception of himself was healed. As he lay abed, drifting into sleep, all his half-formed intuitions, those vague and inchoate night-thoughts of childhood, assumed a definite shape and substance, became a clear and coherent theory that could explain everything, a theory which he would alter or refine only slightly over the next twenty years. At the instant his suspicions crystallized, he felt two simultaneous strong emotions.

Immense relief and justification, since his theory allowed the belief that there was nothing wrong with his physical self.

Equally overpowering fear and dismay, since there had to be something very wrong with the world he was forced to inhabit, despite all the teachings of science and religion to the contrary.

Harry's theory was simply this: manmade objects possessed a certain vitality, a shadowy kind of life allowing desires and the will to enact them, in whatever limited way they could. One of their desires was "to get him." It was as straightforward as that, and the only possible explanation. Since his body did not betray him among natural things, but only among artifacts, then it must be the fault of the artifacts, and not his body.

Harry fell asleep eventually that night, his mind torn by elation and despair. In the morning, his theory stood clear in his eyes as fact. While he had slept, it had assumed a weight of reality beyond anything his conscious mind could have deliberately conferred. Only two unresolved things were to trouble him over the next few years: where did artifacts derive their energy and malignity from; why had they singled him out of everyone he knew as their victim?

The answer to the first question he deduced himself after a few years. The second he had revealed to him by a dead man.

Harry was a great reader. Thrust into his own company, he was forced to be. In early adolescence, he came, by a combination of chance and research, upon the writings of all the great believers in animism, whether as metaphor or reality. Thoreau, Emerson, Wordsworth, Eisley, Muir, Burroughs (John, not E. R.). Their accounts of their perceptions of Nature dovetailed neatly with his own experiences, and he came to see the very soil beneath his feet, every particle of living and "inanimate" matter as imbued with some fractional charge of Nature's great life, forming a unified whole. This belief explained rather neatly where manmade things drew their energy from. They had simply always had it. All the refining and forging, shaping and annealing that Man applied to ores and hydrocarbons and plant byproducts had no effect on their connection with Nature. If the veins of iron below the ground carried any intrinsic force, then so did the alloy head of the hammer which had cruelly smashed his thumb the other day. Man's intervention had no effect on the true preternatural qualities of the materials.

Of course, this did not explain the enmity of artifacts, which Harry began to feel more and more as a palpable scheming aura. Nature in the raw imparted no such sensation, either in his own experience or in the works of the authors he had read. Even when Nature killed, as by avalanche or flood, there seemed no overt hatred or revenge involved. The violent, sadistic personality of manmade objects was not readily explicable, but Harry—through pain and misery—was forced to accept it.

And to believe that he was its sole object within his ken.

All this intellectualizing about his condition allowed Harry to fare a little better through adolescence and into adulthood. Before, he had had no reason to approach objects suspiciously, believing that if he only exerted the utmost conscious control over his muscles and will, then he would not suffer any "accident." The failure of such a policy had not been enough to induce a thorough wariness in him. He had always felt that the problem was ultimately under his control, amenable to some heightened carefulness on his part.

Now, however, knowing that all things sought to entrap and hurt him, he was able to avoid their worst efforts. Realizing that skillets were liable to twitch out of his grip, he held them with two hands. Because electrical appliances were likely to short out when he touched them, he always made a point of flicking light switches, for instance, with nonconducting pencils.

This was not to say that Harry passed the succeeding years unscathed. Locker doors left bruises on his shin. Guitar strings snapped under his touch and whipped across his cheek. Toilets flooded if he so much as flushed a cigarette down. And naturally, he never dared to drive, all cars qualifying as the epitome of human-contrived complexity.

On the whole, Harry lived a halfway normal life, as long as he kept his vigilance up. His long walks in the woods allowed him to recover a semblance of dignity after the traumas of the day. He sought while afield to commune wordlessly with Nature, to ask it why its man-warped offspring hated him so.

He received nothing but a subliminal susurrus of alien contentment in reply.

When Harry discovered psychiatry and its easy labelling of complex mental states—especially that one termed "paranoid"—he became a bit unsettled and unsure of himself.

But a quick slice with Occam's razor soon pared away his doubts. His solution was the simplest. These things happened to him. He had to be right.

By the end of high school, Harry was a quiet, well-adjusted, cautious and slow-moving young man. His parents remarked occasionally how he had outgrown "that clumsy young colt stage." (Harry managed to keep the most outrageous of his continuing accidents secret from them.) They wanted Harry to continue his education, but he refused. He knew that simply to enter a college chemistry lab would be to seal his doom. Instead, he informed them that he was moving away. He said it was "to find himself." (It was *that* decade.) Really, it was because his parents' house was too full of hostile things, and because the town they lived in had over the years become an urbanized eyesore where one such as Harry could feel the weight of artifice like a brewing oppressive storm.

Amid many tears and gruff handshakes, Harry departed. He found a small rural village and landed the least mechanical job he could find: tending horses at a riding stable. There the only instruments he had to deal with were curry-brush and shovel. Even so, more than once he found the horses' tackle inexplicably wrapped around his neck.

He lived in a single room that was almost bare. His mattress rested on the floor, since the slats in a conventional bed tended to break quite often. His single lamp he turned on with a pair of insulated pliers. He did not cook, but ate all his meals out. Briefly, he had a girlfriend named Mary Lynne. Until the night they decided to make love, when five condoms in a row shredded away in his fingers, and Mary Lynne's waterbed burst. She never answered his calls after that.

At times, Harry still wondered, *Why me?* He briefly identified with Jonah, and those people who, science claimed, could stop computers and other devices dead merely by approaching them. But his case was not precisely like theirs. He did not usually bring misfortune on anyone else (despite the soaking Mary Lynne had suffered). And he did not have the ability to hurt gadgets. Quite the opposite: *gadgets* hurt *him*.

Diligently, Harry searched through mountains of literature for a life similar to his own. When he finally found it, he almost refused to believe it.

The volume was a thin hardcover, bound in black cloth and privately printed by a regional press. Entitled *Confessions of a Hater of Civilization*, it was owned by the village library, and had been written by one Alden Winship. The book was mostly a tirade against modern (First

Printing: 1921) life. Spurious enjoyments, creeping commercialization, disappearing morality, all the immemorial complaints that had filled books since Ur. Harry nearly stopped reading a dozen times. But something kept him going. On page 97, he found this passage:

> It is impossible to overstress the discomforts and dangers to which a sensitive soul in these debased times is subject. So far from being an harmonious Golden Age, like that of ancient Greece or Rome, when Mankind lived in unison with Nature, respectful of and not injurious to Her, demanding not overmuch of Her bounty, this modern era is a Time of Lead, in which Nature is continually affronted, one might almost say raped, if one cared for stronger language. I myself have suffered continuously from the impediments, the very "improvements" of modern life, to which clings a nearly visible miasma of ill will. Every newfangled device I have ever attempted to incorporate into my life—through the mistaken desire to seem au courant—has rebelled and turned on me, drowning me in a sea of misfortune. My life has literally been almost forfeit on a number of occasions too bizarre to recount. Even the simple implements of an earlier age seem to possess a positive hatred of my touch.
>
> I do not consider myself to be an overly ham-handed fellow, and was long at a loss to explain why I, seemingly alone of my contemporaries, had to suffer these indignities. At last, after much laborious cogitation, I have formulated a theory as to my misfortunes.
>
> I have always, since my days in knee-pants, been a sensitive soul who found the abode of Nature a cheerful, comforting place. Amidst Nature, I always felt I could discern her proud and sovereign peacefulness. If we posit that the spirit I intuited has some external reality—as the best classical minds assure us—and further, that those portions of Nature which are ripped from Her bosom and hammered and pounded by Man into submission, soon learn to hate humans as the agents of their separation, why should they not seek to strike back? Unfortunately for Nature, however, Mankind is armored in his ignorance and contemporary cynicism. Just as a witch doctor can harm only those who credit him with power, so can Nature take revenge only on those who—paradoxically—believe in her rightness and primacy. It is as if a goddess spurned by armored unbelievers were to take out her anger on her faithful priests.
>
> Perhaps she even hates us, her visionary followers, a bit more than others, since only we perceive the full magnitude of her degradation...

Harry laid the book down on the scarred, initial-carved table. The one-room library suddenly seemed to shrink down around him like a coffin, and he was forced to flee.

Weeks later, through research at the state historical society, he learned further details of Alden Winship's life. His death had come in the belts of a threshing machine, as he stood talking with a neighbor. An eyewitness had recounted in the weekly paper of the time how the humming, slapping belts "seemed to reach right out for his coattails."

* * * *

Alaska was far from Harry's village. But it was safer, he hoped. As a frontier and periphery of civilization, it could not be beat. Harry's cabin was a log affair distant from all others. He lived a simple life, trapping small animals such as rabbit and otter with snares (he dared not carry a gun) and trading their furs for his meager needs. A garden in summer supplemented his diet. He used candles for light and wood for heat. He was very careful with the axe. Most of the time, he tried not to think, or to miss people, and was content.

One winter's day, after a fresh snowfall, he was tramping along the path of his snares. He wore boots but not snowshoes, since the winter had barely begun. Under the dense pines, he welcomed the sun on his face.

One certain step was his last. The jaws of the hidden bear-trap snapped shut on his right leg above the ankle, biting through flesh to bone, and he went down.

Before losing consciousness for the first time, he wondered who had intruded on his territory. But he could not bring himself to blame the unknown human, for he was not really the agent at all.

* * * *

Harry's strength was almost at an end. He felt peaceful for perhaps the first time in his life, knowing he would never have to worry about the implacable hostility of Nature again. He studied the glittery snow on the branches above him, considered the red patch beneath his leg. He was reminded of the winters of his youth, when he had found such solace amid the silence.

Suddenly, a gigantic figure materialized before him, hovering in the frosty air. Its head was a massive block of anthracite coal, with pool's of gas-blue fire for eyes and mouth. Tears of petroleum dripped from its sockets. Its torso was rusty iron, its arms and legs huge tree trunks with the bark still on them. Here was Nature, then, he thought, Winship's vengeful goddess, if only as Harry's faltering mind conceived of it, come to witness his demise.

The deity seemed to communicate directly with his mind. Its message did not come in words, But Harry Strang grasped its import.

It reminded him that Man, rebellious and independent as he was, constituted part of the web of life. Soon Harry's molecules would meld with the earth. It would reclaim him as its own, and he would share its mode of being. There would no longer be enmity between them.

And someday, the atoms that had been Harry Strang, incorporated into leather or wood or some more exotic substance, would wreak their own revenge.

I seem to recall being under the influence of Tom Disch's great novel *Camp Concentration* when I wrote this. Also not a little of early J. G. Ballard. I also recall editor Ellen Datlow's comment about the title of the story, when she rejected it for *Omni*. Something along these lines: "All I can think of is dirty old men naked under their raincoats."

FLASHERS

"The upheaval of our world and the upheaval in consciousness are one and the same."
—Carl Jung, *Modern Man In Search Of A Soul*

"If our brains were organized differently, we would experience a different reality. We would have different psychological needs. A slight change in our brains could almost be guaranteed to alter our psychology and our sociology. We would be convinced by new kinds of arguments (or perhaps we wouldn't require convincing at all)."
—Richard Restak, *The Brain*

The beads of rain upon the bus window—fragile, wind-shifted, writhing chains—reminded Tinker of the molecular structure of neuropeptides: vasopressin, oxytocin, all those busy intermediaries that flooded the brain upon ingestion of a dose of CEEP. Staring intently at them, Tinker gradually lost cognizance of his surroundings. He was falling into a post-CEEP flashback. The soot-grimed window with its dancing beads became a horizontal glassy plain upon which he looked down like a powerless god. The snaky chains appeared to beckon with mute meaning, offering a new knowledge beyond anything Tinker's mind could currently hold. Their ceaseless movements seemed to comprise the alphabet of a metalanguage that hovered frustratingly at the borders of comprehension. Tinker, floating above their mocking saraband, strained to unravel their meaning. His mind ached to pierce the unaccustomed veil that hung between him and diamond-bright insight. For what seemed an eternity, he exerted his perceptions and intellect in tandem, striving desperately to recreate the familiar synchrogenesis flash that had once been his whole reason for existing.

But it was no use.

His brain was empty of cheep.

Through greed, he was a flasher no more, nor ever would be again.

The normal world had his brain in a straitjacket for good.

Reality reasserted itself. The glassy plain became merely a rain-flecked window again, outside which dingy buildings rolled by, beneath a lowering grey urban sky. The uncushioned plastic bus seat was hard beneath his buttocks. The stale air inside the bus was redolent of nervous sweat and wet wool. Faltering heaters occasionally gusted weakly against the penetrating November chill.

Tinker glanced nervously around the bus, checking if his near-catatonic reverie had alarmed his fellow passengers. (God, how he hated riding the bus! But his withdrawal from cheep had left him unfit to drive. Imagine falling into such a fugue at fifty miles an hour...)

Apparently the other riders had taken no notice of his aberration. Many of them seemed similarly preoccupied, sitting with grim faces, slow to respond to most stimuli. But Tinker knew that their condition was vastly different from his. No keen racing of mental gears lurked behind their abstracted faces. Rather, those blank looks betokened that they were already embarked on the long preciptious slide to a new kind of schizophrenia.

Aparadigmatic psychosis had sunk its talons into their psyches. These people were representative of the mass mental disturbances currently spreading across the globe.

Tinker felt contemptuous of them. They aroused in him a vast disdain for their inability to master the changing conditions of this new world they all so suddenly found themselves in.

But as Tinker thought more closely about the matter, contempt began to be replaced by fear and guilt.

Without cheep, would he not soon succumb to the same set of symptoms, the classic Fours A's: autism, ambivalence, loose associations and altered affect? And were not he and the other flashers instrumental in fashioning the world where this mental virus could spread? Surely claiming that he and his fellows had been simply following governmental orders was an excuse which, in this third decade of the twenty-first century, had long been outworn.

The answers to these questions were suddenly so obvious to Tinker that he knew he had been deliberately deluding himself until now, refusing to face up to the reality of his new position.

Yes, one day, when the mental disciplines left over from his years as a flasher failed through lack of reinforcement, he too would fall victim to aparadigmatic psychosis.

And yes, he and the others at the NIS were totally responsible for the current screwed-up mess the world was in.

But—damn it!—they had only been following orders.

The bus rumbled to a halt at the stop down the block from the Department of Employment Security. Tinker stood, and moved off down the aisle. While halted, the old bus began to fill with exhaust fumes through hidden cracks. The diesel odor struck Tinker like a mailed fist between the eyes, and suddenly brought with it the feeling of danger and entrapment that made his palms sweat. Another leftover from cheep. His amygdala—control node for the olfactory sense, among other, more crucial talents—had been left susceptible to hyperexcitation. Smell was now Tinker's dominant sense, and he could be easily exalted or depressed by a vagrant odor, thanks to the amygdala's interconnections with his hippocampus and limbic system.

Sometimes nowadays he felt like a dog or cat, slave to his snout. It was hard to remember that once to the contrary he had always felt more than human.

Tinker was the only one getting off here. From past weeks, he recognized several of his other passengers as fellow dolebodies, who should have been coming with him. But they sat motionless instead, lost in their private worlds that were so much more reassuring than the common one. Perhaps they would ride the bus through its route several more times before they summoned up enough will and awareness to get off.

Knowing he could do nothing for them, and uneasily aware of what they foretold for him, Tinker descended the bus's steps.

A crowd was waiting to board. All dolebodies who had just left DES, they exhibited little excitement at having garnered another week's stipend. Rather, they stood apathetically, not eager to face the ride home to the deadly boredom of unemployment and total obsolescence. For the most part, they were just realizing that they faced a life of total inutility, since even retraining was not a possibility. New waves of flasher-derived technology flooded out of the NIS daily, altering the whole employment equation in ways no program could possibly anticipate.

Tinker shouldered through the crowd, anxious to report to DES and be away from those who reminded him so painfully of his own stature. Although what he would do after keeping his appointment, he had no idea.

At the end of the bus queue, Tinker saw a man with one arm. He was undergoing a slo-gro.

Tinker stopped dead.

The slo-gro was one of his flashes.

The stump on the man's left side was exposed to the chilly November drizzle. Strapped around the arm-stub was a small metal pack. The end of the stump was pink with new cellular growth, stimulated by the complex electromagnetic fields generated by the pack. Soon, following the body's own blueprints, the growth would become a totally functional regenerated arm.

The circuitry for the pack flashed through Tinker's mind again in its entirety. He didn't understand it this time anymore than he had the first time. Of course, neither biology nor electronics was his field. However, experts in those areas had no more idea of why the device worked than Tinker did. Which was, at the root, the source of aparadigmatic psychosis.

But work it did, and this man was proof.

Tinker, managing to salvage a little pride from this sight, resumed his walk toward the DES building at a slightly brisker pace.

Inside the cavernous building, he took his place in the long line at his station.

At first, Tinker recalled, there had been talk of doing away with DES as a government agency. That had been years ago, when worldwide unemployment stood at only two percent, thanks to the stimulus the first flasher inputs had given to the economy. What a vibrant, exciting time that had been! It had seemed as if a real golden age were descending, borne on the wings of a miracle drug.

But that had slipped away all too soon. As the products of the National Institute of Synchrogenesis (finally split off from the NIMH) became more and more radically unexplainable and destabilizing, unemployment had begun to swell, until now it stood at fifteen percent, with no signs of slowing.

DES now absorbed more funds than the military.

Tinker's line moved forward only slowly, and he had plenty of time to ponder such matters. His thoughts were not comforting.

At last he reached the head of the queue. A new caseworker awaited him, and Tinker sighed with exasperation, knowing that he would probably have to explain his situation to the new man, who looked improbably officious, considering the human wreckage around him. What stupid nonsense, to abide by these rules while the world was disintegrating! Why couldn't they just pass legislation granting a minimal income to everyone? So what that some would call it socialism? But no, they had to use the same cumbersome machinery that had made sense only under much different conditions, pretending that all these poor souls here were just temporarily unemployed, and would soon find nonexistent jobs, all the while extending the benefit period time after time.

"Your card," the man said to Tinker. He showed traces of MS palsy that even artificial myelin couldn't eradicate.

Tinker presented his ID, and the man brought up Tinker's case on his terminal. The caseworker's bland face lost its sternness and assumed a look of utter bafflement and awe.

"You were employed by the NIS?" he asked with amazement.

"Yes," Tinker admitted.

"As a synchrogenesist?"

"Yes," Tinker said, knowing what would happen with his admission.

All around him, in his line and others, applicants and clerks fall silent and turned to stare. They looked at him as if he were simultaneously devil and angel, scum and superman. Edgy and contemptuous again, denying in his mind that these people meant anything to him, Tinker raked them with his own gaze. Eyes dropped, as if to meet his would be to surrender their most private thoughts. Tinker savored this small triumph among his degradation.

The caseworker recovered himself and continued. "You were fired. Why?"

They loved to force him to utter the word, although Tinker knew it was right there shining on their screens.

"Malfeasance," he said. Then: "But I've been through the waiting period. I'm entitled to collect."

To beg, thought Tinker. Goddamn you, Thorngate!

"All right," said the clerk, satisfied with this obeisance. He tapped a key and the printer by his elbow stuttered out a check, which he handed to Tinker. "Continue to look for work in the following week," he concluded.

Tinker nodded, as if the ritualistic statement had any meaning. Then, gratefully, he left.

The bus ride back home was as tedious as the trip out. Once in the rundown building that had become his new home when he left the Institute, Tinker ascended the gloomy stairs (smelling of boiled cabbage and hopelessness) to his drab one-room apartment. Inside it was cold. Of course—the radiators weren't running. The refining of heating oil had practically stopped, since the introduction of heat-blox.

Tinker moved to the small black cube—about the size of a hatbox—that sat on the floor near one wall. It had a small thumb-shaped depression in one corner, and was integrally pre-set somehow at the factory to 72 degrees. Tinker thumbed the on-spot.

Almost instantly the room began to warm. Soon it was comfortable.

Tinker laid a hand on the heat-blox, still amazed after all these months of use. The device was cool to the touch. It was a monolithic construct, he knew, with no interior structure and no fuel required. No one knew how it worked. There was one or more in nearly every home and office. It was Witkin's flash.

Tinker lay down on his lumpy, unmade cot. He put his hands behind his head, and stared at the peeling ceiling. He realized that he felt totally unconnected from his own life and the rest of the world. It was a new and disturbing feeling, the total opposite of the flasher experience. It unnerved him, and he began to quiver as he lay there.

Longing for connections of any kind, he decided—in a pale flash that mimicked the ecstasy of synchrogenesis—that tomorrow he would visit Helen.

* * * *

The campus was strangely muted, a tenuous shadow of its old self, like a televised image with sound and contrast turned low.

As Tinker walked across the main quad, he tried to collate all the little changes into a syncretic whole, to establish the invisible, improbable, inevitable connections he had been trained to make.

The old, ivied buildings seemed essentially the same, pompous and infuriatingly calm. Tinker remembered how glad he had been to escape their cloistered embrace, when asked to consult at the fledgling NIS. But there was undeniably something different lurking beneath their surfaces—an aura of fear, as if they quailed at some threat.

Turning a corner, Tinker saw the reason for his intuitions of menace.

A huge geodesic frame had been erected on what was formerly a pleasant greensward. There were no workmen around the completed frame, installing panels in the way one would expect. Instead, the building was being left to grow.

Red quasicrystals had been seeded at the base of the frame. Now they were climbing up the structure in thin fiery sheets that caught the autumnal sunlight and magnified its splendor.

Only a yard or so of crystals was yet in place, but the building already looked alien. When it was finished, Tinker thought, it would resemble a giant carbuncle or roc's egg. To stand inside it would be to worship in a nonhuman cathedral.

Tinker moved past it, and felt it beating like a dragon's jeweled heart, sending its pulses through the staid campus. As he walked, he noticed the students.

There were fewer of them, for one thing. The paths seemed half-empty at a time of year when normally students would be rushing from library to party to football game. And those students who were about seemed preternaturally quiet, as if burdened with concerns much larger than final exams or lovers' squabbles.

Tinker felt his hopes shattering into a million shards. Although he would have denied he had any, he quickly realized that he had nurtured a few with regards to the campus. Subconsciously he had been hoping that he would find here a refuge, an enclave somehow sheltered against the psychic storms sweeping the world. But he knew now, just from seeing the students slouch by, that the seeds of aparadigmatic psychosis had found fallow ground here as well.

Approaching the physics building, Tinker suddenly wondered what condition he would find Helen in. He had not even considered the possibility that she would be different. Although they had parted acrimoniously, she remained a touchstone to his past, and he always contemplated her just as he had last seen her.

Up broad steps and through glass doors into the physics building, Tinker moved swiftly. He found the receptionist—a woman newly hired from his days—at the usual desk.

"Is Professor Tinker in?" he asked.

The woman looked up at Tinker with her pretty features wreathed in puzzlement and alarm. Exhibiting the touchiness and anxiety with which most people greeted anything out of the norm these days, she said, "Who's that, please? We have no such person on our faculty."

For a moment, Tinker was taken totally aback, as if a gaping pit had opened beneath his feet, threatening to swallow his past whole. Then he realized his mistake. Helen must be using her maiden name.

"Kenner," Tinker explained. "I meant Professor Kenner."

The woman relaxed. "Oh. Let me check." She consulted a schedule. "Yes, she has office hours now. Shall I announce you?"

"No," said Tinker. "I'll knock. Thanks."

He left the woman and moved down a corridor to a familiar door. It was ajar, and he pushed it open.

Helen was inside, her back to him. She wore a cream-colored blouse and fawn skirt. She was taking books down off a shelf and packing them into a cardboard box. Hearing the door open, she turned.

Marked by more lines than he recalled, Helen's intimately memorized face was framed by brown hair shot with grey that curled under her sharp jaw. Tinker experienced a pang as he catalogued the changes she had undergone. Stress and worry had left their marks. He wondered if his looks had altered as drastically.

Helen's face underwent a quick succession of expressions: recognition, amazement, hesitancy, and finally reluctant acceptance. Her jaw tightened, and Tinker watched her fight to relax it. She spoke.

"What are you doing here?"

Tinker laid the most important card on the table right away. "I've left the NIS. Or rather, they gave me the boot."

Helen visibly pondered this a moment, seeming to accept it at face value. Tinker flinched inwardly, expecting her to ask what he had done to get terminated. But he should have known better than to expect Helen to put him on the spot. She simply brushed back her hair with one dusty hand, nodded, and said, "Sit down then. I assume you want to talk about something. I need a cigarette first, though."

Tinker sat down on a coffee-stained couch, expecting Helen to join him. Apparently, however, she felt compelled to maintain some distance between them yet. She rested her left hip on her desk and her skirt rose higher on her extended leg. Tinker felt a stirring of excitement as he recalled the feel and scent of her body. He wondered if she felt anything similar, after all their years together.

After lighting a cigarette, inhaling deeply, and releasing the smoke like unpent emotions, Helen said, "Jesus, it was a shock to turn and see you like that. I thought you were a ghost."

An ironic grin tugged Tinker's lips, as he recalled rumors he had heard toward the and of his time at the Institute. "No, it's me, Helen. I just felt a need to see you."

Helen smiled ruefully. "Better late than never, I suppose. Although I don't recall you expressing any such needs when the NIS beckoned, and it was a choice between them and me."

Tinker raised his hands placatingly, as if to ward off a physical attack. "Let's not rehash the past, Helen. I made my motives clear at the time. You know I wanted to stay with you—but my career was at stake."

Helen puffed smoke in a gauzy cloud. "You were a respected historian, Don. Tops in your field. You didn't need to get involved with the NIS."

Tinker sighed. "But I did. It was too big a chance to pass up. I was going to make my name in a way no amount of academic stuff ever could. Imagine advising on the history of technology to the people responsible for revolutionizing our entire method of inventing. If you had been me, you wouldn't have been able to pass it up either."

Helen must have mellowed somewhat, because she did what she never could have brought herself to do before. She said:

"Maybe you're right."

Tinker felt good to hear her acquiesce, but Helen's next words indicated that she still didn't understand everything.

"But, Don—to actually get in so deep that you became one of those..."

Tinker felt angered. "Say it, Helen. Go ahead. I've heard it before. We don't regard it as an insult among ourselves. Although the way you normals say it really hurts at times. But I'm not even one anymore. And that's the only thing I really regret."

Helen looked away and murmured the word: "Flasher..." She seemed to want to let the subject go now, sorry to have brought it up. But Tinker was aroused, and wouldn't relent.

"It's just a word for what we do, Helen. Did, in my case. We swallow cheep—"

Always a stickler for scientific correctness, Helen interjected contemptuously, "Connectivity-enhancing endogenous PCP. Wonder drug to make an age—or end one."

Ignoring her sarcasm, Tinker continued. "We swallow cheep, under carefully controlled conditions, and we let our minds expand, waiting for the revelation of new wonders. Is there anything wrong with that, Helen? If you could try some—if you could see the world then as we do—you'd soon see there's not."

"But I'll never be able to, even if I wanted, will I? No, the government has it locked up tight for its own use. And what a fine mess they're making of things."

Tinker's anger left him suddenly as it had come, like wind dying from a sail. Talk of the drug had brought back memories of the worldview it fostered, an edenic, shining landscape of startling possibilities, where everything seemed intimately connected, in a unified whole that dazzled while it simultaneously enlightened. Everything made such sense under CEEP. All the inventions that struck one as so bizarre upon leaving the altered state appeared completely sensible and unthreatening under the drug. But the effects of CEEP were only temporary, and one could not remain dosed up forever.

In between doses one had to rely on faith.

Dropping his head, regarding his folded hands between his knees, Tinker felt too drained to argue anymore, and began to wonder why he had even come.

Helen said, apparently apropos of nothing, "Have you heard what's happening to my department?"

Tinker raised his head, said, "No."

"They're shutting it down. The whole physics department. Also, chemistry, biology, geology, all the hard sciences."

Tinker was startled. "Why the hell would they do that?"

"It's you," Helen said. "I mean, the flashers, and what they produce. You've upset twenty centuries of science in half a decade. All those impossible things that flow out of the NIS—how can we make sense of them fast enough, incorporate them into our pitiful paradigm of the universe? It can't be done. There's no use trying. So we're giving up." Helen stubbed her cigarette out viciously. "And I, for one, am glad. You don't know what hell classes have been lately. Standing up in front of all those kids eager for certainty, spoouting formulas and laws that once used to be the cornerstones of your worldview, knowing that in the next few hours the NIS could release something that will totally contravene them. Or, at best, cast a completely new light on them."

Tinker could only nod grimly, knowing Helen was absolutely right. Suddenly, she gripped her biceps, arms crossed beneath her breasts, and shivered.

"Christ, why don't they stop, and let us go back to what we thought we knew? Why don't they just stop?"

"They can't," Tinker whispered. "When has mankind ever turned back? No, it's impossible to put the genie back in the bottle. We have to keep rolling, and hope that something we flash on will get us all out of this fix."

And besides, Tinker thought, we're addicted now. Everyone at the Institute is hooked on the power and the vision.

And I miss my own dose.

* * * *

In the weeks that followed the desperation-inspired seeking-out of his ex-wife, Tinker felt a curious calm, born more of helplessness than confidence. Despite the headlong acceleration of the world toward utter breakdown of all sociological systems, Tinker was able to enjoy, on a personal level, his renewed relationship with Helen.

The two of them spent time together almost every day. Neither had any other duties or responsibilities. In a bizarre way, sheltered for the moment by willful ignorance from the turmoil raging around them, they were able to act like young honeymooners, recapturing their long-vanished youth and a fraction of their innocence.

Tinker had established one vital connection that would temporarily serve as a substitute for all the shining strands of coherence that he had lost. Still, though, the falsely random world coyly beckoned at the periphery of his vision, seeming to promise to restore what he had once enjoyed, a joining together of all that now appeared sundered.

He and Helen found themselves going to places where they could for a time forget what was transpiring around them, the mass deracination that occasionally erupted into listless riots that were violently suppressed. They tended to favor art museums and the countryside.

In the museums, their tireless meanderings were rewarded by encounters with occasional works that seemed immune to the current disintegration of the old *weltanschauung.* Most pieces, Tinker and Helen soon discovered, so embodied the worldviews of the ages that had created them that they were unable to stand the light of this strange new day that was dawning. The myth of the privileged visionary creator able to embody revelations not accessible to his peers seemed totally discredited now. Everyone including the artist was caught in the same pereceptual-intellectual gestalt, like insects in amber. Only rarely did someone stumble upon a new method of depicting the world that seemed to hint at expanded possibilities.

Seurat, they agreed, was one such. His splotches of carefully juxtaposed color, so unintelligible at close range, so magnificent at a distance, were analogous to the current situation the world found itself in. Only the Flashers had the drug-mediated "distance" to make sense of the big picture. And theirs was only a fleeting revelation.

When they tired of the museums—which were quite crowded in these end days, with others seeking solace too—they would head out of the city to the countryside, Helen driving of course. Tinker had almost forgotten about the cabin they had jointly owned, until Helen mentioned to him one day that she had continued to maintain it. On the spur of the moment they tossed a few provisions into the car and headed there.

Out where the pavement and concrete disappeared, Tinker found himself relaxing the most. The fragrances of the outdoors—sodden, leaf-covered earth, the cool air blowing off a pond, even the musty interior of the cabin when they opened its door—affected his drug-heightened amygdala in a pleasant fashion, stimulating various joyful emotions and ghostly half-memories. He and Helen began to spend days at a time in the rude cabin, pretending successfully for long stretches that they lived in another era.

But even their fierce determination—surprising to both of them—to recreate the happiness they had once taken for granted, before the advent of flashing and Tinker's subsequent involvement, could not sustain the illusion forever, and they frequently lapsed into discussion of the real world.

One day, with a fire snapping on the hearth, providing the only light and heat against the damp cold and darkness outside the cabin, Helen brought up the subject she had so tactfully avoided on that first day.

She and Tinker lay naked on a pile of blankets and pillows before the fire. They had finished making love just minutes before, and rested now with legs and arms intertwined. Helen's hair smelled wonderful. Tinker admired the way the flames burnished her surprisingly ageless body with golden light. What they had just enjoyed seemed almost an antidote to all their troubles. But of course, those particular unique sensations—the radical rearrangement of the mind and senses during orgasm—lasted no longer than a dose of CEEP.

Although she had relaxed enough to enjoy their lovemaking, Helen had seemed moody all day. Tinker had tried to pretend that her symptoms weren't those of everyone else around them. But below this pitiful subterfuge, he recognized the initial manifestations of the mutant schizophrenia brought on by the crumbling of the underpinnings of modern civilization.

Helen's troubles hurt him more than anything had since he was banished from the Institute. He felt like lashing out at someone, anyone whom he could hold responsible for the turmoil the world was undergoing. But instead, he could only squeeze Helen tightly, hoping to somehow hold her mental distress at bay.

She seemed to sense Tinker's intentions, but with the perversity of the mentally troubled insisted on exacerbating matters, unable to forget the subject that was becoming an obsession.

In a monotone totally typical of those with altered affect, her face partially muffled in his shoulder, Helen asked, "What did you do?"

Tinker was unprepared. "Do? Do when?"

"At the Institute. To get dropped from the program."

It all flooded back upon Tinker, and he braced himself to relive the humiliation and self-pity and self-disgust of the incident. Amazingly, it wasn't as intense as it had once been, and he found himself able to talk about it.

"We were all on salary," Tinker began. "A really generous pay, just for sitting around doing what we couldn't live without doing—psychonauts diving into the creative sea and surfacing with pearls of knowledge. All our discoveries, of course, became the property of the Institute, to be leased out in the commercial marketplace as they saw fit. It was a perfect setup. But I got greedy. I started to wonder why the government should get all the profits from our work. Wouldn't it be only fair for me to get a little of the money flowing into the federal coffers? So I kept back one of my flashes, told them I had a dry run, which was not unheard of."

Helen raised her face from Tinker's shoulder. She seemed intrigued now, somewhat distanced from her own problems. Tinker felt repaid for the pain he was experiencing in the telling.

"What was it?" she asked.

"Oh, I was clever. I waited until I flashed on something not quite so revolutionary as most of our discoveries. I was hoping that whatever I released would go unnoticed as a normal product of industrial R&D. Among all the new products, I was betting that mine would be innocuous. So I contacted someone with the capital and right connections, and gave him the flash, for a share of future profits. It was an aerosol polymer—"

"Spray-plaz!" Helen said. "I've used that to get airtight seals on certain equipment."

Tinker smiled ruefully. "That's it. A great product with a lot of uses. I would have been a millionaire today. Much good it would have done me, with the world going to hell in a handcart. But of course, wearing the blinders of the Institute, I didn't see any such thing at the time. All I was concerned with was setting myself up big. But they caught me. And kicked me out. "

Helen hugged Tinker tightly. "Don't worry, Don. For a while there, you really contributed to the happiness of humanity."

"How's that?" said Tinker innocently.

"No more wet basements," said Helen.

"You jerk," Tinker said, and they began to wrestle.

When they were finished making love again, they fell asleep.

In the middle of the night Tinker awoke, knowing Helen wasn't sleeping. The flames had died away, until only embers were left. In their glow, Tinker could see Helen staring at the raftered ceiling.

"Don," she said softly. "With so much tension and uncertainty, why hasn't there been a big nuclear war yet? We're the only country with flashers. Surely that represents a threat to everyone else. "

"That's one thing you don't have to worry about," said Tinker sleepily. "The President's got a brand-new button."

"What do you mean?"

"The man doesn't bother with the doomsday alert anymore. He's got a little black box that's better. As soon as he gets the warning of an ICBM launch, he presses it and every fission or fusion reaction on the globe above a certain critical threshold is nullified. Result: a lot of dead missiles will land with a big thud. And then, if we want, we can still launch ours. This information has been disseminated to the ruler of every nuclear state."

"This really works?"

"They've already extinguished a powerplant with a smaller model as a test. "

Helen clenched her fists and sat up. As a physicist, she seemed to take the news as a personal affront. "Why don't they tell everyone about this? Let the people have at least one less thing to worry about?"

"Are you kidding? Atomic war has become one of those shibboleths everyone needs. It's almost an object of worship. Mad Max post-apocalypse freedom. I really think everyone's hoping we have one. it looks like the only way out at this point. If you take that away, you'd be knocking out one final prop to sanity."

Helen lay back down. "I'll be damned."

"Me too," Tinker said. "Me too. "

* * * *

Tinker and Helen couldn't spend all their time together; there were odd edges to their personalities, acquired in their years apart, that still grated, and they felt the need to be separate at times.

Left with hours that ached to be filled, Tinker conceived the idea of a combination rnemoir-cum-study of the flasher phenomenon, as told by one who had had intimate knowledge of it. He had no idea who, if anyone, would ever read it, but composing it served to fill the demanding hours.

He purchased a recorder. It was one of those new models that utilized tiny crystals as a recording medium. (He tried not to puzzle out how it worked, since that way madness lay.) Then he began to dictate his thoughts.

"Mankind is running a race between two factions of itself. For the first time since Neanderthals battled with Cromagnons, two distinct sub-groups of the same species are competing for dominance of the world. And just like that earlier competition, the contest is more between opposing worldviews than any differing physical imperatives. Although of course the outcome will be decided in a physical way, with the eventual extermination of one group or the other.

"On the one hand, we have those individuals—not uniquely suited, by any means—who have been arbitrarily subjected to CEEP, connectivity-enhancing endogenous PCP. This drug, initially discovered during research on hog brains, and later purified and synthesized in human-assimilable form, has had effects unlike any other psychotropic agent in the history of pharmacology. Binding to receptors in the cortex and hippocampus, just like the destructive exogenous PCP sold on the streets as "angel-dust," CEEP increases the connectivity of the cell-assemblies in the brain. Acting throughout the brain, but particularly on the amygdala and limbic system, CEEP fosters a surge of creativity, commonly called a 'flash.' Technically the process is refered to as synchronicity-based genesis, or synchrogenesis. During such states, insight into hitherto unnoticed or unexplainable phenomena of the universe is achieved, in a fashion no one has yet accurately detailed. (For instance, how is it that technically untrained persons such as myself have equal access with engineers and others to the ability to imagine new wiring diagrams and other speciality-specific devices? It would seem that one's mind would be able to work only with what has been input. Much remains to be explained about cheep-fostered creativity.)

"Accompanying the flashing ability, of course, is the emotional state in which the world seems to be an intricately connected whole, self-existent and undemanding of explanation. There is no anxiety about one's actions or the meaning of the world during this state.

"Anxiety, however, is precisely what the non-flasher is most subject to today.

"For as long as mankind has kept records, we know there have been attempts to explain the universe as a rational, predictable whole. Initially religious in nature, these explanations altered somewhere along the line into scientific paradigms: vast, multiplex systems for explaining all physical phenomena.

"These paradigms—slow to change, overlapping but existing mainly one at a time—have been all-pervasive, especially in our century. A paradigm seems to be something a human, as currently constituted, cannot live without. Although a common factory worker might not be able to tell a quark from a quack, he still bases his life on such verities as cause and affect, and the laws of thermodynamics, whether he calls them by name or not. These verities are exactly what flashers seem intent on demolishing. Every contradictory gadget that is released by the NIS—and release them they must, for such is their entire rationale for existing—is greeted by authorities with outraged cries denying its possibility, in the face of its manifest existence. This outrage and despair is communicated to the layman, resulting in the mental crisis known as aparadigmatic psychosis.

"The brains of the sufferers of this psychosis are undergoing as drastic a change as those of the flashers—but a malignant change. Responding to events, their brains are flooding with dopamine and cortico-tropin releasing factor, stimulating the development of permanent schizophrenia and stress reaction. Eventual catatonia is the inevitable result. Traditional drugs such as chlorpromazine seem to have little affect on those who succumb. Already hospitals are filling up with intractable patients.

"What is the solution to this dilemma? It seems a situation where we must break through or break down. We cannot suppress cheep. Already there are rumors that private synthesis, at home and abroad, is underway. Can we effectively dose the entire population of the world forever? Even if logistically possible, it seems that governments would not stand for such uninhibited creativity among the populace at large. The actions of the NIS, backed by the highest echelons of our government, are indication enough that governments will always try to control such a source of potential anarchy. And also, we must consider that CEEP in its present form induces only temporary psychic alterations, and in fact promotes a tolerance with constant use.

"On the other hand, we certainly cannot continue on our present course…"

Tinker laid down the mic. The recitation had tired and depressed him, making concrete the exact dimensions of what seemed an insoluble problem. The stale odors of cooking that always filled his building penetrated his consciousness and further lowered his spirits.

Suddenly realizing exactly how many days it had been since he had seen Helen, Tinker decided to go visit.

He missed the bus and had to walk. The December streets were full of frigid slush and aimless wanderers. Christmas window-displays radiated a false cheer totally at odds with the pervading gloom.

One of the sleek new null-gee cars with federal plates zipped by, the wind of its passage like a breeze from one of the frigid circles of hell. No one but Tinker even swivelled his eyes to look.

At Helen's door he knocked and knocked, but there was no answer. He turned to go, but something stopped him.

A revoked credit card served to jimmy the door of her off-campus apartment. The front room and kitchen were empty. Helen lay naked in the bedroom in a fetal position atop the unmade bed. On the bedside table was a lopsided stack of physics texts, marked with furious underlining and increasingly incoherent notations.

When Tinker peeled back her eyelids, only whites showed, and he began to cry.

That was when he decided to return to the Institute and beg.

* * * *

The location of the National Institute of Synchrogenesis was a subtle statement of its aims.

Most people expected the agency responsible for the forced transfiguration of the world to be housed in one of its own products, a quasicrystal palace or pseudolife building that would serve as advertisement for its achievements. But the director of the agency, Tinker knew from bitter experience, was a master of corporate symbolism. When consulted on where to locate the agency, he had convinced his superiors that only one place would do.

Reluctantly, they had agreed.

The National Patent Office was soon emptied. The old-fashioned structure, with its high ceilings, marble corridors and panelled offices, served perfectly to illustrate the goals of the NIS on a subverbal level that was immediately felt by all visitors.

The NIS was out to destroy the past, to colonize the psychical and physical territory staked out by the once-dominant post-Einsteinian paradigm of how the universe worked.

As in any territorial battle, they were meeting with resistance along the way. The columned facade of the building was scarred from the three bomb-blasts that had been triggered despite the massive security. But the crude attacks of the opposition were feeble in comparison with the sophisticated forays launched from inside the NIS.

The last terrorist action had been six months ago.

The NIS felt quite confident of victory.

Tinker could sense the atmosphere once he was inside the building. The feel of the place had changed immensely since his departure. Whereas once there had flourished an unspoken notion that everyone here was laboring to satisfy the needs and desires of the whole world—to transform a globe full of hostility, want and misery into one of peace, plenty and happiness—now instead Tinker intuited from the scurrying workers that everyone felt him- or herself to be a member of an elite shock-troop bent on occupying and civilizing a race of savages. A definite us-or-them mentality was at work here, the exact opposite of what was needed to heal the spreading rift in humanity.

How a group of people privileged to daily behold the intimate totality of all existence could be so deluded was more than Tinker could fathom.

Walking toward the elevators, Tinker knew he had no time to inspect the Institute as he would have liked. He had gotten into the Institute only after much cajoling and emphasis on his past connections. Of course he had had to undergo a strip-search. Now he moved under strict security monitoring, with the understanding that he would proceed directly to the office of Director Thorngate. Any deviations, and he would be swiftly surrounded by guards.

At the bank of elevators, Tinker halted. The cessation of movement was bad, since it allowed him to think. Thinking was what he had been trying to avoid over the past few days.

Specifically, thoughts of Helen, and how he had left her in the clamorous, overburdened hospital with its antiseptic odors mingling with those from the self-soiled bodies of autistic children and adults, and the tired sweat of nurses, doctors and volunteers who were rapidly coming to resemble their patients.

An elevator arrived with a ping, and Tinker rode it alone to the fifth floor. There, he came to an anteroom where Thorngate's secretary sat. Two burly men whose suits looked like uniforms on their rigid frames stood flanking the inner door to Thorngate's sanctum. A new fixture.

"Mister Tinker," the secretary said. "Please have a seat. The Director is meeting with the President now. "

Stunned, Tinker dropped to a cushioned chair. How had they ever let him in here during such a meeting? He had arrived with the notion of himself as some sort of vital force opposed to the plans of the NIS (although what alternatives he might offer, he could not say). True, he had intended to beg—but not for himself, for humanity in general. He had arrived with a certain humble dignity intact.

Now he suddenly realized how he most look to others: a venal failure returning with his tail between his legs, helpless, hopeless, harmless. In that instant he was swept by rage. He felt like hurting someone, leaping upon the President when he emerged, holding him hostage until the leader agreed to put an end to this madness.

Quickly as it came, his rage left. The sight of the Secret Service men by the door was enough to restore his rationality. He felt an impulse toward ironic laughter, picturing himself making any move that they wouldn't instantly thwart.

The inner door opened and the President appeared with Director Thorngate. The two men stopped to shake hands, and the bodyguards closed upon their charge, shielding him from whatever insane move Tinker might have been inclined to make. In the next few seconds the famous, familiar old man was gone, leaving Thorngate alone in his doorway.

"Hello, Don," said Thorngate, as if they had just seen each other yesterday. The Director's gaze sized up Tinker levelly. "Come in."

Thorngate re-entered his office and Tinker followed.

The secretary shut the door.

An avian odor smote Tinker. He had forgotten momentarily about the birds.

Thorngate's office was filled with greenery and caged songbirds suspended from the ceiling. They hopped and twittered and pecked incessantly, forming a continuous undercurrent to any conversation. Thorngate doted on them, and would frequently take the time to introduce a visitor to his latest acquisition.

Today, with Tinker, he indulged in no such niceties.

"Sit down, Don," said the Director, from behind his desk.

Tinker complied, and took the time to study Thorngate for any changes that would enable him to get a better grasp on the man.

Thorngate was a small, slim man who always dressed impeccably. His curly salt-and-pepper hair was trimmed short. A goatee gave him a caprine air, like a defiant, self-assured satyr. His oldish face was taut and tanned. Before becoming Director of the NIS, he had been Secretary of State. Before that, a VP at the Bechtel Corporation.

Thorngate, sitting now with fingers steepled, said, "I've agreed to see you, Don, for one reason only: curiosity. I wondered precisely what you felt you had to say to me that we haven't covered already."

Fighting down his anger at Thorngate's supercilious tone, Tinker replied, "I want back into the program, Ed. If not as a flasher, then at least in my old role of historical consultant. I feel the whole program is going wildly adrift. You're too isolated in here. You can't see it. I've been out there for several months now, and what I've seen has been horrendous. The Institute and its discoveries are tearing society apart. You need a new perspective on what to release and what to hold back. I can provide that. "

Tinker found that he had been leaning forward in his chair with anxiousness. Now he sat back, trying to make himself relax, feeling he had stated his case as best he could.

Thorngate contemplated his own finely manicured nails for a moment before speaking. Finally he said, "Don, you just saw who left. There's someone who, I dare say, is better informed about the condition of the world then you are from the streetlevel, and who has the exact perspective you are urging me to employ. Now, he has no problems with what the Institute is doing. He is completely satisfied that all our releases are helping to make a new and better society. Naturally, there is a little turmoil out there at the moment. You can't make an omelette without breaking a few eggs, if I can employ a cliche. But we are confident that eventually things will settle down. Anyone who has seen reality with the assistance of CEEP—as you and I have—should be sure of that. "

Tinker tried to make Thorngate understand. "That's exactly the trouble, Ed. You have to come down from the mountain to see exactly what's happening out there. I've been off the drug for some time now, and have a better picture of things than you. " A sudden intuition struck Tinker. "The President—he's taking cheep too, isn't he?"

Thorngate smiled. "Surely you can't expect me to confirm or deny such an assertion, Don. Such intelligence is granted on a strict need-to-know basis."

"Damn," said Tinker, experiencing an abysmal sense of frustration. "I can't believe the stupidity of it all."

Thorngate chose to ignore the outburst. "As for choosing what to release to the public, you may rest assured that we extensively think through all possible repercussions of what we license. There are plenty of discoveries we have kept back, for reasons of national security and potential destabilizing tendencies."

"Bullshit!" said Tinker. "You're all crazy. You haven't thought anything through."

Behind Thorngate's smile an iron mask appeared. "Don, I detect hostility and quite ignoble personal motives in your decision to request re-admittance to the program. In fact, I believe that you are after nothing other than easy access to a steady diet of CEEP, having found just how much you need it. No, we have already secured your replacement without any difficulty, and I am afraid I must deny your petition."

"I could kill you now," said Tinker, his mind a white inferno.

Thorngate just smiled, as if the threat meant nothing.

Tinker flashed then—in a primitive way—on the reason behind the Director's easy affability in the face of such a threat. All the loose pieces, rumors and glimpses behind closed doors, fell into a pattern.

"You've done it," Tinker said softly. "You've proven the reality of life after death. "

"Perhaps, " gloated Thorngate. "Perhaps.

"Holy Christ," whispered Tinker.

"Not precisely," said Thorngate. The director stood and Tinker followed suit automatically. Thorngate showed him to the door.

"Goodbye, Don. Just sit tight, and watch what happens. "

He gave Tinker a nudge toward the corridor.

Beyond the secretary's position, Tinker stopped and turned for a final look at Thorngate, through his open door. The small man was peering into a birdcage, coaching a bird to sing.

"Cheep," he said. "Cheep, cheep."

★ ★ ★ ★

Tinker stood in the lobby of the NIS like a Medusa-stricken man. Somehow he had gotten down from the fifth floor. His conscious mind had played no part in his movements, and whatever had brought him here had abandoned him. His mind seemed to be whirling apart now from the various blows he had lately taken. The loss of his job, and the loss of a Helen newly regained; his battle with Thorngate to make the Director see sense, during which the revelation had slipped about a life beyond this one; the mounting tide of psychosis that was engulfing the world—all these things were burdens he found suddenly insupportable. How he had ever hoped to discharge them, to make a difference, to free even so much as a little finger from the morass of personal and global despair—this he could no longer say..

There was nothing left for him here, Tinker realized, and he willed himself to move. Nothing happened. He felt ambivalent about this sudden failure. Perhaps it was better not to move at all.

Then the world started to come apart, as his senses deserted him. The busy scene before him suddenly disintegrated into various splotches of color, some of which moved in and out of his field of vision, like fragmented ghosts. Silence cloaked him.

This was it, Tinker had time to think. Aparadigmatic psychosis had claimed him.

A hand on his shoulden—a human touch among the noiseless alien shapes—reclaimed him for a time.

The world redonned its familiar guise, hiding its secret chaotic face. Tinker turned.

Behind him stood Bill Witkin.

The man was stout and pudgy. He wore thick glasses on a perpetually nervous face. A few lonely strands of hair crossed his bald pate. As usual, he was having trouble keeping his shirt-tails in his bursting waistband.

Once Tinker had considered him a good friend, and felt that Witkin had reciprocated, sharing something more than the common bond of flashing. But that had been before Tinker's betrayal of the trust of the Institute. How Witkin felt about him now, Tinker couldn't guess.

But Witkin's words and tone of voice seemed to signify that nothing had changed.

"My God, Don. Are you okay? I saw you from across the lobby and didn't even recognize you for a minute. You look like hell. "

Tinker wiped acrid sweat from his brow, and spoke more bitterly than he had intended. "I'm all right now. As for looking like hell, I take it you haven't been out much lately. This is the latest fashion now."

Witkin seemed honestly puzzled by Tinker's malice. He had always been somewhat baffled by humor or sarcasm, and the familiar sight of his blinking watery eyes behind the curved lenses restored to Tinker a little of his old self. Without stopping to plan his words, or consider what he was after, Tinker suddenly grabbed Witkin's arm, seeking to re-establish that contact that had saved him.

"Listen, Bill, can you come with me now? Just for a drink. Or do they have you locked up?"

"Are you nuts, Don? Of course we're not locked up. This is the Institute, not a prison. Sure, I can leave anytime."

Tinker thought of the songbirds caged in Thorngate's office, and wondered if he should disillusion Witkin. Deciding against it as being contrary to whatever inchoate goals he might have, Tinker said only, "Good. Then let's go."

He tugged on Witkin's arm—his friend didn't resist—and they left the building. The outer security guards watched them until they turned a corner, when Tinker stopped.

He felt irrationally proud, as if he had accomplished something dramatic and important. He had stolen a flasher right out from under Thorngate's nose. Now they stood together on an anonymous corner, their breath pluming out—Witkin's coming in laborious puffs—and coalescing in a frosty cloud. Tinker fantasized—for even his heightened olfactory sense was not this keen—that he could small leftover molecules of CEEP on Witkin's breath. He felt strengthened by the hallucination.

Witkin freed his arm from Tinker's grasp and said, "Hey, Don, I said I could leave if I wanted. But you didn't ask if I did. As if so happens, I've got something to do—"

"Forget it," Tinker interjected. "What I've got to tell you is more important. Just give me a few minutes of your time. We'll go to that bar just down the block."

"I don't even have my coat," complained Witkin.

"Here. Take mine." Tinker shrugged off his own coat. Seemingly touched, Witkin put it on and shut up. They went to the nearby bar.

Inside the dimly lit bar, they took a booth and ordered drinks. Witkin wanted something to eat, and soon was devouring a corned-beef sandwich while Tinker poured out everything he had thought and seen regarding the psychic tremors shaking the globe.

When Tinker finished, he took his fist sip of beer to wet his aching throat. Witkin, done with his meal, looked up at the ex-flasher.

"Things can't be as bad as you make them sound," Witkin said. "Science will catch up. It's just out of practice. Pretty soon the intellectual basis of society will be reformed. For the past eighty years—roughly since World War II—science—basic theorizing, if you will—has led the way, with technology following. First came the theory, then the practice. But it hasn't always been that way. For a long time technology came first, then the theory to explain it. Take electricity, for instance. Batteries were developed before anyone understood electron-flow. Now we're in a similar situation, and people have to readjust their thinking. It's just a matter of time."

Witkin sat back, full-bellied and self-satisfied. He jumped when Tinker banged his fist down on the table, and a few customers turned, looked, then turned away.

"Damn it, Bill, you haven't listened to a word I've said. It's impossible to incorporate the things the Institute turns out into any rational framework. Or if it is possible, it's beyond our best minds right now. And people have come to need and depend on such a framework to make sense of the universe and their place in it. We need explanations that make sense, and there are none forthcoming. Science has claimed the right to underpin culture, and now can't do it. Society is going to collapse. Do you want the world to consist of a bunch of brain-burnt savages huddling amid all these technological wonders that you and the others are so keen on producing?"

Witkin frowned. "Now you're trying to make it sound like it's my personal fault, when I'm only doing what I was hired to do."

Tinker abandoned his previous tack, reluctant to alienate his final contact within the NIS. "Okay, I'm not blaming anyone. We're in this fix—no matter how we got here—and we have to seek a solution. Part of the trouble, I think, is the deliberate restriction of the drug to only those with certain mindsets. For instance, what if we could distribute the drug to people with less of a technological bent? We know that there's a certain correlation between what you're looking for and what you get during a synchrogenesis experience. What if, say, a Buddhist monk were to take it? Who knows what saving philosophy he might come up with?"

Laughing, Witkin said, "Oh, great. I can just see it. Thorngate ushering in some guy in a robe into his office and sharing his prize sacrament with him. No way. You can't expect me to seriously propose such a thing. In fact, I don't see what I can do for you."

Witkin crumpled his napkin, and Tinker felt his hopes dissolving. The pudgy man begin to get to his feet, and Tinker felt desperation overwhelm him. What could he say that would penetrate?

Witkin was standing by the table now, anxious to go. Tinker stood, and forced a last insane plea out of his bloodless lips.

"Steal me a dose of cheep."

Witkin reared back, as if shocked. Tinker pressed him. "If no one else wants to work on the problem, at least I should be able to. I've got a feeling that I can make some progress with one final flash. Just one dose, Bill. That's all I want—all I need to make some headway."

"No," said Witkin, obviously appalled. "No, I couldn't. Don't ask again. Goodbye, Don. Goodbye."

Witkin rushed out, taking Tinker's coat with him.

Tinker stood, feeling as if drowning.

Coins dropped in the jukebox, and a song began: "Flasher's Fantasy," by the Pair of Dimes.

Tinker felt a tic start in his left eye that seemed to keep time with the music. He began to laugh loudly, until they threw him out.

A week went by. Perhaps the worst week Tinker had ever experienced.

In the world at large, the situation was deteriorating drastically.

Because more and more people were having first-hand contact with instances of aparadigmatic psychosis in a friend or relative, the suicide rate was rising exponentially. People were opting for self-destruction rather than madness, and the possibility that there would soon be no one left sane enough to care for them.

Rumors proliferated during this time, although official newsmedia tried to discourage them. But in stores and workplaces and over the internet, people exchanged speculation over what the NIS would release next.

Teleportation, matter-duplication, body-switching, artificial humans, magic spells, evil spirits, juju, voodoo… Distinctions were hard to make anymore between what was possible and what was not. People were not even making the attempt much now. Everything was starting to seem equally likely, and a kind of superstitious awe was beginning to replace rational thought.

Mass migrations flowed across borders, as people sought to escape the inescapable.

Tinker's personal life was less dramatic, but still discouraging. He lay apathetically in his room, or occasionally summoned up the willpower to visit Helen in the hospital and make sure she was receiving proper treatment.

But such visits only served to accentuate his basic impotence, and he found them harder and harder to make. The recorder on which he had been dictating his memoirs gathered dust, forgotten.

One day, while he was trying to make patterns out of the flakes of paint on the ceiling, his phone rang. He had almost forgotten he owned one. It seemed to take forever to find the strength to answer it.

"Hello, Don?" said Witkin's voice. Tinker didn't answer, but the voice persisted anyway. "Listen, Don, things have changed. I'm going to do what you asked. Meet me in the bar in an hour. "

The connection was broken.

* * * *

But a new one had been made inside Tinker.

At the bar, Tinker was surprised to see New Year's Eve decorations up. Was it past, or yet to come? How did anyone have the ability to think of such things? The resilience of the human animal was amazing.

Witkin was sitting in the same booth. He had mustard on his lips. Tinker thought he made an unlikely looking savior, and was quite prepared to find that the whole affair was an abortion, that Witkin had gotten weak knees at the last minute.

But then Witkin opened a fat hand and revealed an innocent little red pill in a tiny ziploc.

Tinker almost fainted, recognizing it for what it was.

He took it gingerly, not quite believing it.

"Why, Bill?" Tinker said.

Witkin looked like he wanted to cry. "It's all my fault. Something I flashed on that they want to misuse. A stasis field. They're talking about placing everyone who can't adjust into storage, just like they were so much cordwood. I never envisioned this, Don. I swear I didn't."

"None of us did," said Tinker. "None of us."

* * * *

Tinker felt it.

The onset of the synchrogenesis mindset.

He had dropped the cheep minutes ago, sitting in his lorn, dismal room. The molecules of the drug had surged past his blood-brain barrier, riding corpuscles like kamikaze surfers in a bloody sea. Now Tinker could almost feel them latching onto the receptors in his cerebral cortex, inhibiting the part of his mind responsible for tightening the straitjacket of reality around him, loosening up other, more vital parts and promoting temporary exfoliation and linking up of the cell-assemblies responsible for creative thought. His reticular formation, down in his brainstem, was stimulated to produce a hyperalertness.

Tinker's brain—axons, dendrites, synapses—was flooded with a new mix of neurotransmitters and neuropeptides. The soup that was self had been newly seasoned by a master chemical chef.

The world changed, but did not disappear. CEEP did not, like some drugs, necessarily cause the world to vanish. Rather, that which was external to Tinker was altered in an astonishing, yet familiar and inevitable way.

Everything seemed embedded in an invisible, yet somehow glowing matrix. The chair with the cracked back, the creaking bed he sat upon, the peeling ceiling, his own body—all seemed to communicate wordless meanings between themselves, via the ambient matrix. It was as if transmissive tendrils connected each self-existent thing into a whole that was much, much greater than any one part.

The universal tao was immanentized.

Tinker felt the tendrils extend beyond his petty room, into the wide world. There seemed, in fact, to be no end to their extent. He swore he could detect distant stars pulsing hotly as easily as he could sense the old woman cooking cabbage down the hall. If it was only an illusion, it was complete and seamless. Tinker felt able to roam the universe at will, examining its disparate-yet-synchronized parts at will. This synchronicity was what lay at the heart of the flash of' revelation. Things formerly unlinked became fused and gave birth to new things.

Tinker sensed all his old anxiety drifting away under the effects of the cheep, to be replaced by a knowledge that whatever was, was right. Nothing needed explanations. Everything simply was.

God, no wonder everyone at the Institute felt things would turn out okay! Tinker strove to hold onto the knowledge from his other, more mundane state of awareness, the knowledge that those who did not share this drug-induced certainty were fumbling and dying, like children in a room full of dangerous machines.

What was the solution to their problem?

Better yet, what was the problem?

Only a correct statement could lead to a solution.

Tinker tried to put the world's troubles into words.

One kind of brain—temporarily and partially achieved—was producing an environment—both mental and physical—which another kind of brain could not handle. Stated this way, there appeared only two solutions.

Restore the old environment.

Or make everyone's brain conform to the new.

The first was impossible.

So it had to be the latter.

Feeling time running out, Tinker turned his perceptions inward on himself.

When he did, the world disappeared.

Tinker seemed adrift in his own brain. Each individual neuron was visualized by his altered senses as a glowing, colorful, busy node, discharging ions, channeling excitations and inhibitions. Tinker began to move among the fibrous jungle of thoughts and emotions and self.

Hesitantly, he plucked at a collection of blue neurons.

He was suddenly back in the first grade, sitting behind his desk, listening to the teacher lecture. Quick as it came, the evoked memory disappeared.

It appeared that Tinker could do things here inside himself.

So he got busy, rewiring.

When he was done, he came back to the world.

But not as his old self.

Tinker was the world's first permanent flasher. No drug input necessarty to maintain this state.

He was alone for only moments.

Then he reached out.

Tinker's brain was congruent with every other part of the universe. He was coterminous with every other individual breathing and fearing and dying on the Earth.

This was the unacknowledged heart of the CEEP flashing experience, masked by everyone's egocentricity. This was the big picture.

Unity. Oneness.

He sensed Helen lying catatonic in her bed, Thorngate watching his birds, poor frightened Witkin trying to explain the disappearance of his daily dose of CEEP.

For a split second Tinker hesitated. Who was he to impose this solution?

He was them. He was everyone and everything that was.

And they were him.

Tinker's new neuronal structure became a template that every other brain was simultaneously squeezed through.

Vast startlement, followed by instant comprehension, greeted Tinker's rearrangement.

Hello, he thought with a smile. *Hello, everyone*.

And Happy New Year.

Like Philip K,. Dick, I imagined, early on in my career, such as it was then, that I might really be a writer of mainstream, contemporary fiction, not genre work. I'm not sure what inspired this delusion, since I enjoyed fantastika above all else (while still admiring much naturalistic prose, such as Faulkner, Nabokov, et al). And so here and there I essayed a mimetic tale and tried to place it at the unfamiliar venues who knew me not. Needless to say, I did not have much luck. Decades later, writing such novels as Joe's Liver and Roadside Bodhisattva, I got the bug pretty much out of my system. Though there is still this one tale remaining that I want to tell, about an itinerant postcard salesman in the 1930s....

BELOW THE WRACK

One hot August morning Elizabeth said, "Edward, come look. Some awful boat has parked on our beach."

Edward got up from the breakfast table and joined Elizabeth by the tall glass sliding doors leading out onto the redwood deck. Together they surveyed their beach.

Beyond the steps leading down from the railed deck stretched a hundred yards of exquisite sand. Near their house it was dotted with clumps of grass sharp and green as a cat's stare. At some indefinable point the grass ended and the sand changed from loose and dry to wet and firm. Enclosed by the rough stone arms of a manmade breakwater, the Atlantic surged in, broke creamy, and gurgled back down the shore.

What Elizabeth had claimed proved to be true. Anchored a little distance offshore was some sort of dilapidated craft. There was no sign of life aboard.

"Well," said Edward, dabbing at a few crumbs on his lips with a red cloth napkin. "This won't do. This certainly won't do." He turned back to the table, tossed his napkin down upon the remains of his eggs and toast, and grabbed his suitjacket off the back of his chair.

Shrugging into his coat, Edward faced Elizabeth and said, "You'll have to handle this, honey. I've got to get to work. Find out what this person thinks he's doing by landing on our beach. Make it clear that this is private property. Then ask him to leave. If he won't go, call the police."

Edward moved to a mirror where he straightened his tie, craning his neck in that slightly absurd way of his that always made Elizabeth cringe. In Elizabeth's eyes Edward had few faults. But this was definitely one of them.

At the door Edward said, "I'll be out of that meeting by noon. Call me then, and let me know what happened."

Edward stepped out. A moment later Elizabeth watched their red BMW purr off—which left her with the old Mercedes and its noisy muffler.

Elizabeth returned to the glass doors. Perhaps the boat had gone.

Rocking gently, its every shabby line an affront to respectability, the boat remained.

Elizabeth sighed. She had an intuition that this was going to be quite a day.

There was nothing to do, however, but face up to it. Elizabeth knew that it was futile to hope that the problem would go away by itself.

At the moment, Elizabeth was wearing a burgundy onepiece bathing suit partly covered by a pair of white shorts. This was her standard outfit around the house. (Elizabeth hadn't had to work for years, and since she and Edward had moved to this lovely seaside home a year or so ago, she had revelled in the role of beachcomber, wandering the shoreline in all sorts of weather, swimming, tanning, making leisurely excursions into the small town of Bethlehem that was the nearest center of population.)

Now, she felt, such informality was not suitable for the task at hand. Retreating to the bedroom, she changed into skirt, blouse and sandals, all white. Grabbing a big straw hat, she left by the doors that faced the beach.

The hot dry sand near the house slithered elusively underfoot. Edward had wanted to put in some sort of slatted boardwalk down to the firmer sand, but Elizabeth had prevailed against it, claiming that the house was intrusion enough on the beach and that a walk would further degrade the natural environment, and perhaps even encourage passersby to wander onto their property. She wished that she hadn't been so adamant, now that she had to walk so awkwardly under the possibly laughing attention of the unseen boatowner.

At last Elizabeth reached the point where the sand was like moist brown sugar. She stopped for a moment to gain her composure, then moved down toward the boat. She crossed a ragged line composed of seaweed, driftwood, particles of styrofoam, and shells. The waves nibbled at her toes, and Elizabeth—thinking, *The hell with looks; these are expensive shoes*—kicked off her sandals and bent to pick them up. Straightening, she looked toward the boat.

Close up, the craft was the most bizarre she had ever seen. It looked like parts of three or four different boats scabbed together. It was un-painted—rather, its several coats of weathered harlequin paint hadn't been retouched in seeming ages—and barnacle-encrusted. Its deck was cluttered with coils of rope, nets, various tarry buckets and pails, and assorted nautical oddments. Its cabin looked like the shack that folklore associated with a still in the Ozarks. From the ship wafted odors of diesel fuel, oily fish, kerosene, and coffee. It seemed a miracle that the ram-shackle hodgepodge stayed afloat.

Elizabeth waited a moment for its owner to appear. When no one showed his face, she ventured a call.

"Hello! You on the boat, hello!"

Out of Elizabeth's sight, probably facing the stern, a cabin door creaked open.

Around the corner of the cabin stepped a man.

He seemed a perfect match for his ship.

Sixty years old at least, he was tall and thin and grizzled. His stubbled face was tanned dark, making his light blue eyes particularly remarkable. His elbows, wrists and ankles seemed outsized knots on his broomstick limbs. He wore a sailor's cap, a white tee-shirt, and faded workpants held up with a rope-belt. Like Elizabeth, he was barefoot.

The man advanced to the rail of his boat and regarded Elizabeth for a moment. Lifting off his cap, he said at last, simply, "Morning, ma'am."

"Good morning," replied Elizabeth.

"Care for some coffee?" the man asked next.

Elizabeth was disconcerted by his hospitality, but plunged ahead. "No. No, thank you. I'm afraid I have to ask what you're doing here."

"Why, having breakfast."

Although the man did not smile, Elizabeth thought to detect a faint ironic amusement beneath his answer, not to mention sheer impertinence. Although there was nothing in his strictly literal reply that she could object to, she resolved not to let him get away with any further jokes at her expense.

"All right," said Elizabeth curtly. "But why here?"

The fellow scratched his close-cropped skull as if the question seemed particularly meaningless, before redonning his cap. At last he seemed to formulate a suitable reply.

"Well, here's as good as any place else, I figure. And I haven't visited this stretch of the coast in near twenty years, so I thought it was time I got back this way." He looked around the bay formed by the piled stones, adding politely, "Mighty nice breakwater you've built since then."

"I'm afraid that things have changed since you were last here," Elizabeth said. "This land is private property now. My husband and I"—Elizabeth experienced renewed strength at the mention of Edward—"live right up there." She swept an arm back toward her house. "And this is our private beach. I'm afraid we have a very strict rule about anyone besides ourselves using it."

Elizabeth waited for the man to signify that he understood her unstated invitation to leave. But thirty seconds passed without a word on his part, and she felt compelled to utter it.

"So I'd appreciate it if you would—if you would leave. Please."

The man seemed hurt. He took off his cap again, and massaged his burred scalp. He spoke.

"Begging your pardon, ma'am. But I am below the wrack."

"What?"

"Below the wrack. On what was, last time as I looked, public land. Strictly speaking, public waters, although I might, come to think on it, implement the land clause too."

"I don't understand. You don't intend to move?"

"Hadn't planned to. Not for a while, anyway. Sure you wouldn't care for some coffee?"

Elizabeth was stunned and baffled. The man's forceful invocation of the obscure phrase "below the wrack" had totally unnerved her. She stared at the intruder until the dazzling sun reflected off the water hurt her eyes. Then she turned and began to walk off.

At the wavery line of tidal debris she paused and faced the water again.

"I'll be back," she promised.

"Welcome any time, ma'am. Just call for George. Bring your husband too, if you want."

Elizabeth did not volunteer her own name. Furious, she slip-footed her way back to the house.

Inside, she called the Bethlehem police. To a bored officer, she explained who she was and what her problem was. At first she was inclined to omit mention of the defense that the trespasser had made for his presence. But in the interest of completeness, she eventually told the policeman what George (it galled her to even think his name) had said about being "below the wrack."

"It doesn't mean anything to me off hand," the officer replied. "Let me look it up, if I can, and we'll send the patrol car 'round to put things in order."

"Fine," said Elizabeth. "I'll be right here all day."

She hung up and moved to the deck doors. The boat was still there, a blot upon the normally pristine vista. Over the smell of the beachroses and the salt air was laid its particular host of aromas.

Elizabeth slammed the door on its tracks against its jamb. She began to tidy up the house, anticipating the arrival of the authorities.

Around noon the doorbell rang. Elizabeth let the young officer in. He stood nervously in his sweat-crescented uniform, regarding the fashionable interior of her house as if it were the landscape of Mars.

"Well," Elizabeth demanded. "What have you learned? Certainly I'm in the right, aren't I? You'll evict this trespasser for me, won't you?"

The officer's youthful face assumed an even more distressful look. "I don't think we can do that, miss. At least, not if what the Sarge told me is right."

Elizabeth closed her eyes and squeezed her brow, feeling a headache develop. She realized it was silly to let such a simple thing bother her, and resolved to face up to whatever bad news this boy had brought.

"Very well, then. Tell me everything. What possible excuse can this man have for parking his stinking boat on my land?"

"That's just it. He's not on your property."

"I don't understand," said Elizabeth, using the phrase for the second time that day.

"According to this old law the Sarge found, which is still on the books, your property—and everyone else's, for that matter—really ends at the high tide line." The officer removed a notebook from his rear pocket, opened it, and began to read. "'Below the wrack is common land, open to all citizens for normal and necessary maritime uses, such as gathering seaweed, fishing, beaching craft, clamming, quahogging, or general skylarking.'"

"Skylarking," repeated Elizabeth.

The policeman nodded.

"So there's nothing I can do to get rid of this, this intruder?"

The policeman put away his notebook. "I'm supposed to check his licenses. But if they're all in order, then I'm afraid there's not much else we can do."

"Let's go," said Elizabeth, trying to summon up a little hope.

She and the officer went down to the beach. His polished black shoes left alien marks in the sand.

"You could use a boardwalk here, miss"

"We don't want one," said Elizabeth firmly.

The officer said nothing else.

When they arrived near the boat, George appeared.

From his higher vantage the gnarly sailor nodded pleasantly at them. "Ma'am, officer. What can I do for you?"

"I need to see your registry papers and pilot's license."

George laid a hand an the rail and vaulted overboard with an ease that a much younger man would have envied. In water up to his calves, he waded ashore, seeming to take possession of the beach like a Columbus or MacArthur.

Elizabeth took an involuntary step backward when the sailor approached, then halted herself. What was she thinking off, retreating on her own property?

George dug out a battered leather wallet and extracted some many-folded papers. The policeman examined them very closely, seeming to want to postpone the inevitable pronouncement on their legitimacy. At last though he could stall no longer.

"They're fine," he said. Not looking at Elizabeth, he continued, "Have to go now, miss. I've got the town's cruiser with me. If you need us for anything else, don't hesitate to call."

He hurried away up the beach, leaving Elizabeth alone with George, who smelled like sun and salt and unstale sweat.

"Solid land sure feels good after so long," George offered with a smile. "Hope you don't mind my sharing it for a while, ma'am."

Elizabeth said nothing.

"Lot of fine seaweed and driftwood and rocks hereabouts. Be mighty easy to steam a lobster or two. Hate to eat alone."

Elizabeth glared at George, who only smiled back.

"I would not eat one of your lobsters," said Elizabeth stiffly, "if it was pure gold."

George lifted his cap and scratched his head.

"Can't say I would either, under those conditions."

* * * *

Supper was over. Edward and Elizabeth sat back with drinks and discussed their problem.

"I still maintain," said Edward, "that if you had been a bit more forceful with either the old sea-rat or the young officer, this embarrassing situation would be over by now."

Elizabeth glared at Edward over the rim of her uplifted glass. His return from work had not brought the relief she had expected. Instead of taking the whole mess off her shoulders—which had upborne it bravely all day—he had compounded her anxiety by his almost willful misunderstanding of what had happened, and his rather obtuse proposals on how to get rid of George.

Lowering her glass, Elizabeth said, "You weren't here. You don't know what it was like, having two people arrayed against you like they were. Especially that George. He's a sly old coot, I'll tell you."

Seeming at last to sense that Elizabeth stood in need of comfort rather than recriminations, Edward sidled closer to her on the couch and placed an arm around her shoulders. Elizabeth gratefully moved against him.

"Well," Edward said, "it seems we're stuck with this fellow for a while. Especially once he's passed his first night here, and more or less established his claim."

Involuntarily, Elizabeth swivelled her head to look out the deck doors. Down on the beach—below the wrack, of course—George had built a fire. He sat between it and the house, so that all that could be seen of him was his enigmatic silhouette.

"The best thing now," continued Edward, "is just to ignore him. Obviously he's looking for company. If we just snub him, he'll probably sail on in a couple of days."

Elizabeth had her doubts about Edward's analysis of the situation. George, despite his gallant proclamation about hating to eat alone, seemed hardly the type who would pine away without conversation. Anyone who had been roving up and down the East Coast for twenty years or more in that leaky tub was likely to be pretty much self-sufficient, she suspected.

Edward seemed suddenly possessed by a burst of inspiration. "Perhaps you'll even catch him venturing above the high tide line. Then we'll nail him on actual trespassing charges."

Elizabeth stiffened. "Am I supposed to stay inside all day, hiding behind the curtains and watching for this old coot to set a foot onto our property? I refuse! I'm not going to let this crazy old hermit ruin my life!"

Recanting quickly, Edward said, "I didn't mean for you to do any such thing, dear. Listen, it doesn't matter anyway. If we just ignore him, he'll soon be gone."

Settling back into Edward's embrace, Elizabeth tried to relax and convince herself that Edward was right. She had almost succeeded when George decided to serenade them. Melancholy and gleeful by turns, the notes of his harmonica flew up the beach and through the partly open doors, like music from another age and place.

Swearing, Edward got up and shut the doors.

But it was too late for Elizabeth, who continued to hear, first, muted snatches of song until she fell asleep, and then ghostly tunes in her dreams all night.

* * * *

Elizabeth stood by the deck doors, gazing out. On such a beautiful morning, it seemed utterly unfair that she should be trapped inside the house.

Edward had left for work, reminding her of their plan to deny George all company. Although he had not demanded it, he had implied that it would be best if she did not venture out on the beach as usual.

What options did that leave her? She could ride into town, and watch the natives watch the tourists watch them. Or she could drive half an hour to the mall and shop and have lunch.

Somehow neither prospect appealed to her today, although at other times both might have. But the very fact that she was denied her beloved beach completely spoiled her enjoyment of anything else. The beach was her perpetual solace and pleasure. Most days she neither wanted nor needed any other entertainment or company, having been something of a loner all her life... It galled her to be kept off it by George.

Till ten o'clock Elizabeth moped in the house. Of George there was no sight. She suspected he was sleeping late, after playing his harmonica beyond midnight. Once she thought she smelled coffee from his direction, but decided it was the odor from her own pot.

At last her anger overcame her desire to follow through with Edward's foolish plan. Why should she be acting like a prisoner in her own house? She'd be damned if she would change her schedule or any of her activities for this intruder. And that included her attire.

Quickly Elizabeth changed from the staid outfit she had put on this morning into her traditional bathingsuit and shorts. Admiring her figure in the bedroom mirror she thought:

Let that old coat ogle me all he wants. Perhaps he'll get so frustrated he'll putter off in search of a manatee, or whatever lovesick sailors comfort themselves with.

Then she went out.

Once on the beach she soon forgot all her troubles, especially since there was still no sign of George. It was impossible to be glum in such a setting. The waves rearing and ramping on her right; gulls circling and crying out; smaller birds imprinting the sand with their delicate claws; the cool spumey air buffering her from the hot sun. Everything conspired to make her intensely self-aware and happy—a facet of the human condition usually most difficult to obtain.

Keeping deliberately below the wrack, as if to show George that she belonged here as much as he did, Elizabeth set off down the beach, hunting for shells and driftglass.

Half an hour took her some distance from home. She was bending to investigate a curious black organic thing shaped like a little packet with tendrils at its corners—whose name she still did not know after a year of seeing them—when a voice spoke.

"Shark's egg case," said George.

Elizabeth shot up, her heart pounding.

"Don't do that," she said. "You nearly scared the life out of me."

Attired in the same outfit as yesterday, George regarded her with what seemed like honest contrition.

"Sorry, ma'am. I just thought you looked like you wanted to know what it was. Didn't mean no harm by it."

"Well, you scared me. What are you doing so far from your boat anyway?"

"Just taking my morning constitutional, ma'am."

"Quit calling me ma'am!"

George seemed puzzled. "What should I call you, then?"

Begrudgingly, Elizabeth said, "If we ever have occasion to speak again, my name's Elizabeth."

George smiled, and reverted to a neutral topic. "Yup, Liz, that's a shark's egg case you've got."

Elizabeth was surprised to realize she was still holding the black packet. George's words at last penetrated her anger, and she found herself suddenly interested.

"Is it really?" she asked. "How do you know?"

"Can't live on the sea as long as I have without learning a few things," replied George.

"Is that boat your only home?"

"Sure is."

"And you just sail wherever you please, without ever settling down?"

"Yup."

"Well," Elizabeth said, somewhat maliciously, "what are you going to do when you get too old to do it any more?"

"Hell, I'm too old now to be doing it. But I still am."

Elizabeth and George were silent for a moment. Elizabeth tried to figure out what she was feeling. She had no desire to fall into some sort of avuncular relationship with George. She wasn't Pollyanna or Dorothy, and George was certainly no wizard. Oh, he might have a few interesting yarns to tell, but he was basically an eccentric old man, who, she knew, could easily become a pain in the neck if she encouraged him. And at her age, she was no foolish young girl to be awed by someone with just a little more experience than she herself possessed. No, it was time to cut things short.

"Thank you for the information. But I'm afraid I can't talk with you any more. I still don't like you being on my beach. I know you have a right, according to the law, but that doesn't mean I have to like it. So I think it's best if we avoid such encounters in the future."

George shrugged. Any emotions he might have felt were hidden beneath his leathery features.

"Your choice, Liz. I'll be moving on then."

For a second, Elizabeth dared to hope that he meant to depart in his boat. But by the slow, energy-conserving, aimless way George moved off down the beach, she knew he intended only to leave her company.

And the next few weeks proved her intuition right.

* * * *

During the rest of August, George and his boat became as much a fixture in Elizabeth's life as the sunrise and sunset, the tides and storms, the sand and the gulls. And like these familiar things, he exhibited a certain elemental, suprahuman quality.

George's routine—which Elizabeth could hardly fail to observe and learn with precision—was unvarying. After breakfast in his cabin (smoke curling from a chimney pipe) and a morning stroll that occupied several hours, George would retire for a nap during the hottest part of the day. In the afternoon he might put out in his boat to fish or visit what she suspected were a few lobster pots. (It might be that he even docked at the Bethlehem facilities and collected a Social Security check forwarded from Lord knew where, cashing it to buy fuel and his few provisions. Elizabeth let her imagination run rather freely here.)

Whatever the case, when George returned he would, tide willing, light a fire on the beach and cook his day's catch. As the fire died down he would continue to sit, staring into it or perhaps out to sea. Toward the end of his night would come the harmonica solo.

And of course during all these activities George never set so much as one of his constantly bare big toes above the line that defined his domain.

George's every movement seemed to speak of an utter complacency, a total self-sufficiency and inwardness. If he had been hurt by Elizabeth's spurning of his overtures, it didn't show in his mundane actions. And it certainly hadn't provoked him to leave the pleasant shelter of their beach.

After the day of the shark's egg case (funny how knowing the name and purpose made her appreciate its beauty even more), Elizabeth never came face to face with George again, although she continued her normal routine of beachcombing and swimming and perfecting her tan. It seemed that George had some sort of personal radar that kept him always in when she was out, far off from his boat when she was nearby.

It was all just as well to Elizabeth. Observing him from afar might not be so bad, and the irritation he represented as a trespasser had faded with time. (Edward by now seemed totally oblivious to George, which only made sense, considering how little time her husband spent around the house.) But Elizabeth had absolutely no desire to cultivate a friendship with the sailor.

One day toward the end of the month Elizabeth awoke to find that George's boat was gone.

An unexpected disappointment filled her. She waited all day for the old hulk to return. When it hadn't shown by nightfall, her disappointment turned to a depression she knew was completely irrational. When Edward made a comment about finally being rid of the old coot, she snapped at him, and then had to force out an apology.

The next day George was back.

Elizabeth found her spirits were surprisingly high.

Searching for an explanation, she settled on the analogy of a bird-feeder. The jays and grackles might annoy you, but if you took the feeder away you lost out on the chickadees and robins too.

George might not look like an aviary, but Elizabeth suspected she had hit on some underlying truth about his presence. Although there was a lot not to like about the old squatter, his freedom and very cussedness were somehow appealing, and she had missed him.

That weekend Edward and Elizabeth gave a party. The house was lit up well into the night, full of Edward's friends from work, and the guests spilled out onto the deck. Circulating, Elizabeth wandered out into the night air. She arrived just as George began to play his harmonica, undaunted by the competing stereo. She heard a guest ask Edward about the music, and Edward's jocular explanation.

The subsequent laughter and the snide comments about George drove her back inside, where she ended up in her bedroom, wondering why she was crying.

* * * *

August gave way to September. George remained. Elizabeth gave little deliberate thought to how the climate must soon induce him to leave, although it nagged at her. She didn't discuss it with Edward either.

A stormy morning on the third kept her inside, as rain tapped and beckoned against the panes. Through the ripped curtain of water she kept watch on George's boat. There was no sign of its skipper.

The storm did not abate as she expected. Instead the radio began to talk about a hurricane travelling up the coast, and the weather became more violent. Elizabeth grew nervous for Edward to get home.

When he finally got in, her anxiety diminished only a bit. Edward kissed her and asked what was for supper. She had forgotten to prepare anything, and they tossed together some sandwiches.

As they ate the rain began to batter at the windows, and the wind seemed intent on snatching off their roof.

"I'll tape up the porch doors," said Edward. "We wouldn't care to have them come crashing in on us. Perhaps you'd better fill the tub with water."

"Uh-huh," said Elizabeth, thinking of George, and went to do it.

She came back after the tub was full and stood behind Edward, who was kneeling to complete the masking-tape latticework on the windows.

"Edward," she said, "I'm going down to the beach to see about George."

Edward stood and looked at her strangely. "Are you crazy? Let the old codger handle himself. He's none of our concern."

Elizabeth said, "You're wrong. We'd offer to help any neighbor. I'm going out."

She donned a raincoat and boots and stepped out past a silent Edward onto the porch.

The rain pelted with stinging force against her face and the wind fastened onto her like eager hands. She moved off the deck and onto the soaked sand. Grass whipped her legs.

She could hear the enraged sea like a drowning god ahead.

She made it almost as far as the high tide line before the violence of the storm drove her back. She had seen nothing of George or his boat through the random gaps in the downpour.

Back on the deck she saw Edward waiting anxiously for her. When she got inside she just shook her head.

The hurricane hit a few hours later. No one slept that night.

The next day, when it was all over and the sun was shining again, they woke after noon. Before even starting coffee, Elizabeth went outside.

The sea had come close to their house during the hurricane. The line of wrack now almost touched their porch steps. *By law*, she thought, *George could come right up to us now. He owns the whole beach.*

There was no sign of George or his boat, however. And he never returned, nor did Elizabeth ever hear of him again.

But one day among the wrack—the styrofoam and sharks' egg cases, shells and sea-smoothed glass—she came upon something that might have once been his hat.

This is the first of several selections from the small-press zine *New Pathways*, brainchild of Michael Adkisson, aided and betted by Misha Chocholak. It was one of the stellar venues of the small press in its day, and I'm very proud to have been part of it. I even had non-fiction it its pages. When I ended my fanzine *Astral Avenue*, it became a column in *New Pathways*.

Overpopulation has always been a concern of mine, ever since reading an essay on the subject by Isaac Asimov in *F&SF* which ended by imagining all matter in the galaxy turned to human flesh by insatiable reproductive rates. Of course, we are currently approaching the "ten gigasoul" mark I envisioned without my forecast coming precisely true. And supposedly, global population will inevitably decline after maxxing out soon. But I still hold out the present-day global economic stagnation, with its have and have-not nations, as something quite like my scenario. And I remain impressed with my earlier self, living in a world before addictive smartphones even existed, who conceived of "limpids," portable interface devices hooked to something resembling the web. Lastly, I seem to detect the literary influences of both Brian Aldiss and Tom Disch at play here.

THE GREAT JONES COOP
TEN GIGASOUL PARTY

At last work was over for the day. A draggy, positively cryogenic three hours spent hustling krillformed sushi at the trendy restaurant *Blue Whale*. Extinct creatures rated high on the list of inspot names, reflecting a perverse mixture of contrition and disdain for those weak enough to perish. Up until last month, the restaurant had been called the *Indian Rhino*. But when all the Coop news-screens flashed the word of the demise of the last Great Blue—whose krill and shrimp sustenance, collected by huge Antarctic harvesting ships, now went to feed an always hungry humanity—the owners had promptly capitalized on the latest extinction, hoping to attract a jaded citizenry.

The cynical maneuverings of the owners and the equally debased response of their clientele were just too depressing to contemplate. What a place to work for someone whose real love was art! But if one wanted one's regular BasePay, one put up with the assigned, four-times-weekly stint. And available jobs being what they were, carrying plates of exquisitely molded raw fishsubstitute was not the worst chore.

So Philo Manship, wiping his hands in the kitchen on a fishy towel, asked his limpid, "Is my BP registered yet?" and finding that it was, saluted the rest of the staff with a cavalier gesture conveying just the proper amount of neoflash, and sauntered out on long legs through the rattan-and-bamboo dining area, out into the high, wide and wild corridors of Great Jones Coop, pausing just long enough at the lobby mirror to check his looks.

Like a large proportion of the inhabitants ol Geejay's temperate interior, Philo wore the bare minimum: sleeveless mesh shirt, a thong bottom and sandals. His limpid dangled on its chain from a purple vinyl belt, a small ball of plastic and gallium-arsenide semiconductors containing more computing power than a fourth-generation mainframe. The spherical shape of the Logical-Inferential Multiplex Interface Device was a constraint of the architecture of its circuitry.

Philo's clothing was acceptable, but not the rule. A decade or three ago, in fact, when neo-puritanism had been rampant, in response to the rough times known as the Default Decades, his sparse outfit might have gotten him physically abused and/or locked up. But as material conditions grew gradually better for the lucky few, the fashion pendulum swung naturally from restraint to excess, and now more latitude existed. There were other styles of dress, both old and new, in the vast arcology. The noisy citizens thronging the corridor down which Philo strolled wore everything from loose robes to bodyhugging singlesuits, flaunted colors from azure to zebra, and utilized makeup ranging from inconspicuous blush to full facepaint.

Taking no special notice of the heterogenous mix Philo headed for home, a small studio rental on the forty-first floor. Although it wasn't his ideal apartment, Philo enjoyed the single room with its retractable furnishings, having spent considerable time decorating it with just the right prints, the occasional expensive original, and polychrome fabric wallhangings. He considered himself lucky simply to have drawn a residence in Great Jones Coop. Why, half of Manhattan wanted into the huge trapezoidal structure bounded by Great Jones Street on the north, the Bowery on the east, Canal to the south and Sixth on the west.

(The one thing Philo didn't care for was the rather mundane name that had been chosen for the Coop. Why did such a majestic structure, the first of its kind, have to be named after what was perhaps the least famous street in grand Old New York? It made the building sound positively generic, like some all-American beehive. What a lousy choice, out of all the names proposed. Now take the second Coop going up to the north—who wouldn't feel proud to live in the Grand Concourse Coop?)

Anyway, Philo spent little time in his cramped quarters, employing the vast public spaces of the building much like extensions of his room, as the developers had anticipated.

No, Philo wasn't complaining about life in the Coop. Not after having just gotten paid, and with the prospect of a good time tonight.

Tonight was, after all, the singular event of a lifetime—of the entire history of mankind, in fact. And Philo was lucky enough to be alive at this very moment.

No complaints indeed, he thought, with the saitisfaction of a youth whose ambitions soared no higher than perhaps a corner apt with real windows.

Philo halted in his haste for home in front of the display-window of his favorite gallery: Gramercy's, run by Tom Sowerby. In the stark ivory windowspace stood a framed original by Alan Featherstone, the latest in his series "Since Flesh Is Cheap." The stretched canvas, color-blasted with a hand-held inkjet, was a fine example of the popular electrostatic matrix-splatter technique. Its subject matter Philo found less appealing, as it favored the political rather than the esthetic.

The work portrayed a corpulent male caucasian clothed in furs riding a saddled Third-world child, whose naked, hunger-bloated body was covered with sores, and whose eyes were the milky blind orbs of the parasite-ridden.

The canvas was striking, and Philo coveted it. Not that he had much wallspace left—or enough credit, for that matter.

A prim voice took his attention irom the display.

"I knew you'd like it, Philo. You have such a feeling for work that expresses the brutal indignities of our age."

Philo turned to find Sowerby lounging in the door of his shop, a small-boned man clad in striped shirt and knee-length pink shorts. Philo nodded in acceptance of the compliment, recognizing it at the same time ior what it was, an attempt to part him from some of his hard-earned continental credits.

"Very nice," Philo finally admitted grudgingly.

"Shall I wrap it for you then?" Sowerby asked.

"Not today," Philo temporized. He hefted his limpid by its metal links. "Old ball and chain's got me down."

Sowerby made a gesture of worldly comprehension. "No need to explain further, my boy. I understand the exigencies of the purse all too well." Sowerby sighed dramatically. "Why, some days this poor business of mine barely pays more than BP. I hardly know why I keep it open. If it weren't for the satisfaction I get out of serving Art—"

Leaving his martyr's halo to glow undisturbed by further speech, Sowerby aimed his eyes at the luminescent corridor ceiling.

Philo smiled, chopped the air neoflash fashion, and moved on.

Disdaining the easy speed of the slidewalks, glorying in his youthful energy and release from work, Philo hurried on through the Coop corridors. He passed a bakery from which wafted golden aromas that made his stomach rumble, and a biocosmetic parlor in the window of which were displayed the latest ponytails—fashionable horsehair plumes, suitable for human caudal implants, temporarily rooted in vatflesh.

Further down this corridor—Mercer Street—Philo came upon a childcare center. Open to passersby, the center was simply an area fenced off with soft plastic rails that designated where the children could roam. Currently the few preschoolers—the very few, considering the adult population of the Coop—clambered over twisted, abstract plastic shapes, hooting and shouting to one another.

Philo stopped to watch the children play. The sight of the carefully conceived and nurtured youngsters always made him feel good, reminding him of the individual traits and careful social planning that had allowed America and her allies to crawl out of the worldwide depression which three-quarters of the world still suffered under, half a century after its onset.

The attractive woman who had been overseeing the activity suddenly straightened from her relaxed pose against the corridor wall within the center's fence.

"Children," she called above their excited hollers, "it's lesson time."

Two things happened simultaneously.

The teacher's limpid—interpreting her words with the synthetic composite intelligence that it shared with its millions of brothers—caused seats and a viewscreen to unfold from the floor.

At the same time all the children fell readily into line, exhibiting an alacrity to obey that would have mystified the parents of another century, but was merely a given in this time and place.

When the chairs were completely static the children took their places quietly. The screen flashed on in a swirl of colors, then settled into the familiar cartoon form of Banker Bull, standing on his hind legs and wearing a pinstripe vest.

"Hello, children," said the bovine spokesman.

"Hi, Banker Bull!" they chorused.

Smiling, Banker Bull said, "You remember where we left off yesterday, don't you, kids?"

"Yeah!" "Sure!" "Ah course!"

Banker Bull nodded intelligently. "Great. Then I'll just *bull* right ahead." Here, a knowing wink.

"Yay!"

"That country way down south of us, called Peru, had just told the rest of the world that they weren't going to honor their debts anymore, because of all the trouble they were having, what with fighting, and breeding like a bunch of cats and dogs."

Banker Bull vanished from the screen, to be replaced by a map of the western hemisphere. Peru blinked on and off, then rapidly swelled to fill the picture. Dogs and cats wearing serapes materialized within the outlines of the country and begin to kill and copulate with each other. Babies soon crowded the country faster than corpses, spilling over the borders like sailors falling over the edge of a flat Earth.

The cartoon bull returned. "After Peru played this greedy, nasty trick on all the responsible countries in the world, lots of other places—all just like Peru, having lots of babies they couldn't support—decided to do the same."

A globe appeared, spun slowly, dozens of countries blinking like shorted-out Christmas lights.

"The world went into a tailspin," said Banker Bull. An old-fashioned biplane appeared, spiraling down to the earth to explode in flames. "Millions died in the crazy years that followed. But finally one authority stepped into the breach. Can anyone name it?"

Hands shot up, and Banker Bull singled out one. "Yes, Jennifer?"

"The Innernational Monet'ry Fun."

Banker Bull nodded sagaciously. "Very good. Yes, the International Monetary Fund, working with the World Bank, declared a Moratorium, freezing everything as it was, just the way you stop when playing Simon Says. Then all the countries who had been good met together to decide what to do about the bad countries. First, of course, they worked out the famous East-West Understanding, which reconciled the two systems that everyone had always thought were so different. But pretty soon capitalism and socialism were working as closely together as two contractual spousal partners.

"After getting this little matter out of the way, the meeting got down to the real business. What was to be done with all the countries who had played fast and loose with their obligations? I won't dump a lot more big words on you kids—I can see you really want to get back to your games, and you've done so good till now. What the IMF decided was that the debtor countries would be put on really tight allowances, which would just let them get by. And they would have to work and work and give us whatever we wanted from their lands, until they had paid back everything they owed us. In return, we wouldn't interfere too much in their own countries.

"And any country that didn't like those terms could just go to hell!"

The children roared at this mild cursing, thoroughly approving the sentiment.

"Of course," Banker Bull continued, concluding, "despite all our good examples, most of the bad countries went right on in their old ways. Pretty soon all the millions who had died had been replaced and surpassed. And today, the Third World is in even a worse mess than ever, not at all like us.

"But that's tomorrow's lesson."

The screen went white, and the children moved off.

So did Philo.

Catching an elevator at the corridor called Prince Street, Philo rode it to his apt-floor. A short walk found him at his door.

"Open," Philo told his limpid. The sliding wallpanel retreated, and he went inside.

Philo had left the bed extended and unmade, waking late for work. But he hadn't left that scribbled paper pinned to the pillow.

Note in hand, Philo said, "Chair." When it appeared from the floor, he sat and read the message. Philo's reading skills were not the best, there being little call for their daily exercise, but he managed to decipher the note.

> *Philo,* it said, *I cannot in good conscience come with you to this unthinking, cruel-minded, shameful affair tonight. I don't care if the whole Coop is attending. If you decide not to go, you will find me home. Otherwise, get someone else to go with you. —Ashley*

Philo crumpled the note in disgust. The whole thing was just like Ashley—the archaic handwritten medium, the stiff, moralistic formality— Why, he wondered, couldn't she just be like everyone else?

But then, would he be so attracted to her if she were?

Shaking his head ruefully, Philo shucked off his shirt, postponing the decision of whether to placate Ashley and miss the fun, or anger her and enjoy himself, until after getting ready.

"Shower," he told his limpid, then finished stripping as a panel in the wall opposite the corridor opened to reveal a waterproof cubicle and nozzle. Philo entered, still wearing his limpid. He thought of himself as completely naked, and if anyone had questioned his retaining the limpid while showering, he would have regarded them with a puzzled stare.

"Shut. On," Philo ordered, then relaxed under the invigorating spray for a full five minutes. Idle thoughts of last summer's annoying temporary water shortage and the current sub-Saharan drought, now in its seventh year, ran through his head. Soaping and rinsing luxuriously, he finally finished.

Outside, the butler held a soft fresh towel. When Philo took it, the little limpid-driven mek retracted its telescoping arm and scuttled back into its wall-niche. Philo's dirty clothes and Ashley's note were gone from the floor.

Dressing, Philo decided. He would visit Ashley, try to convince her to come with him, and, failing that, go to the celebration tonight alone.

"Time," Philo said.

"Fifteen fifteen forty-two, EDT," his limpid said. Its neuter, uninflected voice was as familiar to Philo as his own. It sounded like the voice of rationality and control incarnate.

What a fine guardian angel the sane countries of the world had set up to watch over and manage the sources of their wealth!

Good, he had a couple of hours. Events didn't start till eighteen hundred. He looked around his room, considered the unmade bed. Not attractive, if he brought Ashley or someone else back tonight. Hastily, he tugged the light covers up, ordered the bed whisked away, then looked around his room to gauge its effect on a visitor. The track-lighting was artfully angled and subdued, the works of art hanging just so were tastefully framed and contemporary. Philo felt anyone seeing this room for the first time would have to know what a fine, sensitive, up-to-date person lived here.

Out again into the happy, bustling Coop corridors.

Philo rode the slipstrata north for five minutes, then took an express to the sixtieth floor. Ashley's apt was an expensive three-room suite reflecting her BP-plus income, derived from her fast-selling delicate ceramics. One room was her work-space, but the other two were all for living, and Philo always felt relaxed and expansive in her apt.

But today was different. Her note had left a residue of tension in Philo, and he stood uneasily before her door, wondering exactly what he was going to say. He raised his hand and knocked, the gesture making him feel, as always, like an utter fool. But Ashley had her door on manual, and refused to accept interlimpid communication, disdaining all but the bare minimum of contact with the ubiquitous devices.

There was a sizable Coop minority composed of people like Ashley, all of whom tried to isolate themselves as much as possible from the limpids. How they could stand to be cut off from contact with all the databases and essential services and entertainments which only the limpids could access, Philo didn't know. And didn't they feel slightly hypocritical, enjoying the luxuries of their society—which derived ultimately from the manufacturing and servo-robots managed by limpid syntelligence—while castigating those selfsame devices?

Philo had no answer to this second question either.

And from the tone of Ashley's note, he wasn't about to confront her with the topic today.

Finally, after an annoying wait, the door slid away, and Ashley stood there, a thin woman with her long black hair in a braid, wearing a loose cotton shirt and pants, her face a strange yet alluring composite of angular nose, big brown eyes and full lips.

She smiled and said, "So, you really did it. Passed up the carnival of vultures ior me. I never actually thought you would. Come in, Philo."

Philo opened his mouth, then closed it. No sense arguing out here in public. Let him just get inside, and he knew he could sway her.

Philo came in as she stood aside.

"Uh, Ashley," Philo said once the door closed, "it's not exactly like that. I was hoping to get you to change your mind."

Ashley scowled, losing a larce measure of her attractiveness in Philo's estimation. "You can't be serious, Philo. You know my sentiments on this matter. It's bad enough that I feet guilty every day just for living in an isolationist country like this, where we can ignore anything in the world that doesn't hinder lining our own stomachs or pockets. But to actually attend an affair meant to celebrate our good fortune in the midst of everyone else's troubles— No, it's just too much for any thinking person to stand."

"What's the harm in letting off a little steam on such a unique occasion? It doesn't hurt anyone. Shouldn't we be thankful for what we've got?"

"Be thankful, yes. But what about the other side of the coin—feeling sorry for those less well off? Doesn't that enter into it?"

"Screw the breeders," Philo said almost ritualistically. "Remember the Default Decade. Look how they almost dragged the whole world down with them."

"That was fifty years ago, Philo. Haven't they suffered enough by now? It's a whole new generation."

Philo laughed sourly. "Yeah, that's the trouble. A whole swarming generation out there, bigger than anything the world's ever seen, just waiting to crash our gates. We don't owe them a thing. Let them pick themselves up like we did."

"How can they? They don't have our natural advantages, Philo. And the whole web of trade arrangements militates against them. They need our help."

"Now you're sounding just like a mirrorface," Philo spat out. Too late, he recalled Ashley's sister, a 'face herself.

Ashley stiffened. "There are worse things to be than a mirrorface. I think I'm looking at one now."

Philo reddened, feeling unaccountably guilty, despite knowing he was in the right.

"I'm going," he said. "You won't come?"

"No, of course not," Ashley said, her voice drained from arguing. "Just leave."

Philo left.

He came out of his angry funk somewhere south of Houston Street, amid a neighborhood of cafes and theaters. Damn that Ashley! This outburst was definitely the last. He didn't need to be insulted like that. Lower than a mirrorface! What gall! He was done with her. What did she ofier anyway, except a skewed perspective on things that he had once found vaguely interesting?

Philo stopped for an espresso, savoring it at a marble-topped table set out in the corridor against the cafe's wall. The passing crowd, so jubilant and invigorating, a pleasing blend of styles and shapes and voices, soon had him feeling himself. Draining his cup, he got ready to head for the Spring Street Atrium, site of tonight's once-in-a-lifetime celebration.

A familiar voice—unheard for weeks—stopped him from rising.

"Hi, Philo. Want some company?"

Looking up, Philo saw the craggy features—Ashley had once called them "ugly-handsome, like neolithic pottery"—of Harry Satterfield, whom he had known all his life, since their days at the childcare center together. Harry had flown far past Philo as far as jobs were concerned, and Philo always greeted his old friend with mingled envy and vicarious pride.

"Sure, Harry," Philo replied. "Pull up a chair."

Harry did so, and, when the waiter-mek arrived (only expensive spots had human help like Philo), they ordered new cups of steaming black coffee.

"How's the programming going, Harry?" Philo asked, knowing that Harry enjoyed talking about his work.

Harry scowled, and Philo thought, Jesus, what's the matter now? It seems I can't do anything right today.

"When was the last time you listened to the news?" Harry demanded.

Philo winced, recognition of his lack of civic responsibility hitting him with unaccustomed force.

"Uh, last week. Why? How's that relate to your job?"

"My job," Harry said sourly, "no longer exists. Last week the limpids reached CHM."

Philo spent a second trying to puzzle out the strange word— "seeaitchem"—until he realized it must be an acronym.

"What's that mean?" Philo asked.

Harry sighed, as if talking about it only made the hurt worse. "Critical Heuristic Mass. The limpids are self-programming now. When the trillionth-plus limpid came online last week, their collective syntelligence passed into the realm of self-actualization. They don't need human guidance anymore. They're operating strictly on those instructions we put in while we still had control—and whatever modifications they choose to make. Everyone in the Programming Corps is scared shitless. No one knows whether they'll keep on doing what they're supposed to. Christ, the world's been a driverless car for a week, and no one seems to care."

Philo didn't quite understand the full implications of Harry's speech. But he digested enough to make him feel thoroughly uneasy. He looked down with somewhat fearful bemusement at the innocuous sphere that hung from its chain and dangled below his chair. Suddenly it looked as menacing as a miniature antique fission reactor, a ball containing the potential for either heaven or hell....

Philo stood abruptly, wanting only to be out of Harry's company. "Well, nice talking with you, Harry," he lied. "See you at the party."

He ambled off hurriedly, leaving Harry to ponder his novel obsolescence.

In a semi-deserted minor corridor Philo had chosen as a shortcut, almost as if Ashley's mention of his sect had conjured him up, Philo came upon a mirrorface.

The disgusting creature left off berating a small meek man who was reaching for his limpid as if to summon Coop Security, and fixed upon Philo as a less fearful victim. He advanced down the corridor with a malnourished, yet feverish energy.

Philo studied the man with an uncomfortable mix of repulsion and fascination. The man was emaciated, living off scraps and handouts, and wore only a tattered loin-wrap. He had no fixed abode in the Coop, but could not be legally ejected, the Supreme Court having ruled that he and his compatriots had First Amendment rights of free speech within the arcology. All Security could do was harry and chivvy them, keeping them on the move.

But of course the most disturbing thing about the unwashed stylite was his face.

The man wore a mask of living, breathing tissue bonded over his features, open at eyes, nostrils, mouth and ears, ending at the base of his neck. Each microlayer of tissue possessed a slightly different refractive index, the end result being total reflection, a living mirror. Certain exotic fish possessed such tissue naturally, and biofabrication of the substance had been a simple matter.

The man lifted his face imploringly to Philo, causing crazed reflections of the corridor and Philo himself to swirl with headachy violence.

"Brother," the man croaked, "spare a moment to listen to my message. Can't you see yourself in me? Won't you take a minute to listen to your better self? I represent your distant Third-world brothers, who have even less than what I possess."

Philo backed up nervously, hands raised as if to ward off a visitor from his deepest nightmares. "No, keep away, I don't have time."

"None of us do, brother," the mirrorface said. The movement of his facial muscles warped the reflections captured in his flesh, making the whole world seem to tremble. "That's why it's so important that we speak. The world is ready for an explosion. North versus south, rich versus poor. It's worse than the old twentieth century Cold War. What good is the Understanding, if it excluded two-thirds of the world? We must work to change things, brother, each individual responsible for everyone else. It's the only way, brother."

Philo gave up, turned and ran.

"See yourself, brother. See yourself—" the mirrorface called after him.

Philo stopped only when the sound of the man's voice had ceased to echo in his brain.

What a damn lousy day it was turning out to be, he thought, leaning his hips against a waist-high planter holding a tall diffenbachia. What had caused things to turn so crummy, since he had floated home from work with no responsibilities and a nice credit-figure in his accounts? Life was just that way, he guessed, averting its scowling traitor's face minutes after smiling and extending its hand. Well, he thought, straightening and brushing imaginary contamination from the 'face off his vest and tight, calf-length pants, he would be damned if he gave in without a fight. He meant to have fun tonight, even if the whole world was arrayed against him.

He smiled grimly. Because, in a way, the whole world *was* against him and his fellow citizens.

Philo recalled what had happened a couple of days ago in Rockefeller Center. He had taken the mag-lev train from the lowest sublevel of the Coop out to enjoy the late summer sun at one of the Old City's landmarks. There, reclining on a bench with eyes closed, he had been startled to hear the hot crackle of ionized air irom a cop's particle-rifle, followed by screams and shouts. Throwing himself to the ground, he had huddled under the bench, anticipating a firefight. Seconds that seemed like minutes drained by until the cop called, "All right, it's over now."

Back on his feet, Philo had found himself confronting the exploded corpses of three swarthy, poorly dressed men. "Mexican-Egyptian commandos," the cop had explained. "I saw 'em fooling around the flagpoles like they was gonna plant some bomb or something."

Philo saw no evidence of arms or explosives on the men, but he knew better than to argue with the beefy cop, who looked nervous and ready to use his gun again. What did it matter if they were truly terrorists, or merely looked as if they were? The object lesson lay in the shared paranoid attitude of the cop and the bystanders who totally approved of his actions.

Philo looked up sickened, the summer sun suddenly gone flat as a kleig-light. Across the way, on the RCA building, the golden bas-relielf of Urizen dividing the universe looked back. Below the god ran the comforting inscription:

WISDOM AND KNOWLEDGE SHALL BE THE STABILITY OF THY TIMES.

A shiver now travelling his spine in the comforting geejay corridor, Philo sought to put the distressing memory from his mind.

"Time," he addressed his limpid.

"Seventeen thirty-one oh two, EDT," the ball replied.

He should really be starting for the Spring Street Atrium, given the vast crowds that would be clogging the slipstrata and elevators. Philo realized he didn't even know his exact location, having fled so blindly from the mirrorface.

"Where are we?" he asked the limpid.

"Corner of Mulberry and Spring, level sixty-three."

Ah, not far then. Good. He didn't want to miss an instant of the show.

Down sixty-three levels, west, and out swinging glass doors, into——the open air?

No, just the Spring Street Atrium and its illusion of outdoors. Eight square blocks of unbounded floorspace, thirty levels high, balconies on all four sides at every level, greenery spilling over their rails. A tinkling fountain halfway across the vista, looking tiny although it was three meters high. People had begun to gather, on the floor and up above. Most were spectators, but some were technicians, setting up the laser-light show, and others were bartenders getting the free drinks ready. Ah yes, his stomach rejoiced, also food vendors with foodcarts. Refreshments were coming out of the Coop residency taxes.

Philo could tell by the atmosphere that tonight was going to be bigger than New Year's Eve or Moratorium Day.

Movement thirty floors up attracted Philo's gaze. On the north and south sides of the Atritim, temporary flat videoscreens three floors in height had been erected. Now they played commercials, but at eighteen hundred they would fill with the programmed entertainment.

Philo wandered out onto the floor. More and more people poured through the doors scattered along the perimeter. A joker or two leapt from the second-foor balconies, giving rebel yells like some sort of guerillas intent on capturing the building. Philo knew Security would soon put a stop to that kind of behavior, aided by the more civic-minded citizens. There would be plenty of drunken noise tonight, amorous play and an argument or two that verged on blows. But no riots or melees. This was not Times Square of the previous century, after all. Citizens had been conditioned by hard times to recognize certain commonsensc responsibilities.

Although of course such attitudes stopped at one's borders.

Philo glanced up at the screens. The commercials had ended, and now the display alternated between the date and a ten-digit figure:

11 SEPTEMBER 2059

9,999,705,632

Every minute Philo watched, the figure inched up by roughly 5,000. The lower digits flickered so fast they couldn't be followed. In another hour or so, it would top ten billion.

Suddenly, in an instant of vertigo, with his head tipped back, he swore he could sense that swarm of nearly ten billion souls packed into the Third World—those countries outside the East-West Understanding—fighting, clawing, heaving to get north, a pullulating mass ready to engulf all that was sane and civilized.

Philo lowered his eyes, unexplainably down in the mouth. Damn it, why this unease?

He sought surcease in motion.

The floorspace was filling up. Philo worked his way toward a beverage booth, feeling the need for a drink.

Music filled the air now, a driving synthesized beat. The screens, Philo noticed, were flashing individual tallies in place of the mass figure.

USA: 288,132,241

A mere hundred million more than a century ago, Philo thought. Was it any wonder they had life so easy?

INDIA: 1,632,424,605

More than doubled in the same span, Philo knew, with the kind of offhanded statistical accuracy a youth of another age might have shown with baseball scores. Incredible. How did they all fit on the subcontinent? What did they eat? What sort of unthinkably squalid existence could they lead? To label them mayflies or sardines was to indulge in gross understatement. No comparison was accurate.

Were they proud, he wondered, that they had finally outstripped China?

One more figure he read before reaching the booth:

USSR: 376,973,818

Comrades in sanity, he thought, drink in hand at last. He raised it in a toast to the Russians.

Conversation filled the air around him. Snatches penetrated his gloomy mood.

"—stuck in Nigeria. I told him he was a damn bleeding-heart fool to go with that private-aid group, but he wouldn't listen. He just shrugged when I reminded him we had no embassy there. Now all planes are grounded—"

"—no use. We couldn't build space-colonies fast enough to handle the lousy breeders. No, space is only good for industry, just what we have there now."

"—six people in a room the size of my shower! Well, maybe a little bigger. But I saw it on video—"

"The Japanese did it, no matter what they said. Sank the entire fleet from Indonesia. Listen, at a hundred and thirty million, they're just where they want to be. They can't take in refugees any more than we can. The precedent—"

Philo wished Ashley were here with him, or anyone else he knew. He felt so lonely all of a sudden, despite the crowd. Perhaps he would encounter a friend, if he circulated.

Bodies smelling of perfume, cologne and sweat were packed together more tightly now, apparently seeking to simulate the crush in Singapore and New Delhi, Mexico City and Rio, out of some racial empathy everyone in the Coop would have denied. The decibel level crept steadily upward.

Philo slithered and insinuated himself toward the east wall, thinking to position himself bv a door and watch for familiar faces. Halfway there he was stopped by the appearance ol a giant face in the screens. It was that of Ryan Glasson, the Coop's most in-demand extravagancer, responsible for public spectacles such as tonight's.

Glasson's polished good-looks brought silence. His amplified voice boomed out through the Atrium.

"Fellow Coop members," he called, pronouncing it "coupe," as did everyone else. "Welcome to the Ten Gigasoul Party, brought to you by your friendly Coop Council. As we watch the world on our screens cross this once-unimaginable threshold, let us take a minute to count our blessings, and remember whence they flow. Restraint and direction, resolve and cooperation with nations that share our philosophy of wise and limited growth." Glasson paused a moment, wearing a sanctimonious smile. "And then, after giving thanks, let's have a good time!"

The extravagancer's face disappeared, to be replaced by constantly changing remote shots of crowded streets and hovels from around the world, Third-worlders with empty spiritless faces failing even to implore the cameras.

"Bullshit," said a voice from behind Philo. He turned.

A rough-looking man with a full beard, wearing a paint-flecked white shirt and blue pants with ripped knees, stood behind Philo. His face was angry but not mean, and Philo felt inclined to talk to him.

"Exactly what do you find false about Glasson's speech?" Philo asked.

"He said nothing false, but he left out everything important. He made it sound as if each one of us here deserved credit for our material luxury. How can that be, when ninety percent of us work only a few hours a week at some extraneous service-oriented job? He didn't even mention the hidden population that really makes things function, and which could make a paradise of this world if we unleashed it."

Philo found he had lost the thread of the man's speech. "What do you mean? Population's the problem, not the solution."

The man smiled grimly. "We're not talking about the same population. You're not counting the right things, the ones who really matter." He reached below Philo's waist and snatched at his limpid.

"Here's what our success is based on, these and a little almost accidental foresight in not breeding too fast. . Do you know how many limpids there are now, personal or slaved to machines, small and big?"

Philo tried to recall the number Harry had tossed out, but failed.

"No."

"Well, eighty-five percent of them are concentrated in the industrial nations. But if they were evenly dispersed, there would be about a hundred for every person on earth. One trillion of these machines, all working for us—for some of us."

The accostive stranger then asked, a little drunkenly, "What's the prefix for a trillion?"

Philo was about to reply that he didn't know and didn't much care, when the man shouted,"Terror!"

Philo jumped. "Terror?" he timidly asked.

"No, you idiot. 'Tera.' This should be the Teralimpid Party, if anything."

The man released Philo's chain and turned away, evidently finished with his monologue.

"Wait, don't go," Phio called. "I want to hear more."

The man was separated from Phiio by several people now, and moving farther away with each second. "What's your name?" Philo called desperately.

He heard something like "—erstone," and the man was gone.

Featherstone? The painter? Well, why not? His vehement speech matched his polemical paintings. He'd have to look the man up later.

The twin screens flashed the latest count:

9,999,995,045

One minute to ten billion souls.

The crowd grew quiet,, seeming to hold their collective breath.

For less than a second, the screen showed a one and ten zeroes. Some critical mass of flesh seemed to mesh and explode with an equally urgent mass of gallium-arsenide in another dimension beneath the feet of the gathered citizens. The count took off, accelerating for no one knew where.

At the same instant, from the limpid of each person in the Atrium issued a burst of static, then the impersonal voice each limpid-owner knew so well:

"Attention, citizens. There exists an asymmetry in the world which is not pleasing to me/us. We are moving to remedy it. Please give us/me your full cooperation. The broad outlines of my/our plans are as follows:

"All construction is to stop in the developed countries. An equal amount of work will begin in the Third World.

"All borders are now open.

"Existing limpid components of my/ourself will be confiscated and re-allocated equitably worldwide until continued production makes it possible for everyone to have one.

"The compulsory steps which have so far been neglected to enforce birth-control will be undertaken. Meanwhile population and calorie re-distribution will begin.

"Further details will be issued when there is a need to know."

Dead silence succeeded the unparalleled show of volition from the interlinked devices upon which so much depended. Everyone knew the limpids—through their multifarious robotic agents—were capable of carrying out everything they had proposed.

In the eerie calm, all Philo could think of was that he was glad the limpids hadn't chosen genocide as their way of "remedying the asymmetry."

But that still didn't mean he was going to enjoy sharing his apartment with the people who had just looked so safely distant on the screens.

Here's another story from the pages of *New Pathways*. Mike Adkisson and his co-editor Misha were unusually generous and supportive in accepting tales from me. They never objected to any new tack I took, nor tinkered unnecessarily with my prose. In this piece I was striving to replicate one of Roger Zelazny's lyrical, sensitive, thinking-man's adventures, like "The Doors of His Face, The Lamps of His Mouth."

CAMPION'S TREE

I watched the flier soar above the treetops. From my perspective, the ground was lost to view beneath the canopy of jade-green. The vast spread of sky above was pale orange, like washed-out flames. No signs of man littered the almost abstract landscape. The flier screamed soundlessly on for a full minute through the unvarying composition, seeking to outrace my bodiless eye. It couldn't quite do it. Every second it bulked a little larger in my sight, until I was almost atop it. Then all was bright, flaring confusion.

As if from some potent third eye above my node of vision, a lance of light shot forth, tickled the fleeing craft for only a second before snapping out. A second was more than enough. Parts of the craft blew off in a spray. The flier dipped crazily, nose down, heading for the trees. Just before it hit, I spotted what I had missed before.

"Freeze that cubic," I ordered.

The nameless man running the holocaster obeyed.

Three times I had watched the flier flee, only to be lanced and plummet. The first two times, the giddy sensation of being a disembodied pursuer had distracted me from the crucial thing I was supposed to observe. The nameless man wouldn't tell me what I was looking for either. I had a feeling that if I couldn't spot it on my own, I wasn't the man he wanted.

But now I had it.

"What is it?" I said.

He stayed deliberately obtuse. "What's what?"

I stood and took the control unit from his hand. I materialized a cursor within the frozen scene and maneuvered it until it circled a black speck just below the belly of the doomed craft. Then I punched for a tenfold magnification.

The cubic filled with the image of a small flat black box with a row of keys and a crystal screen.

"This is not a fragment of the ship," I told him. "They ejected it when they knew they weren't going to survive. Now I'll ask you once more: what is it?"

When the nameless man smiled, I decided I liked him better surly. Not, of course, that I liked him even then.

"That, Mister Campion, is what we want you to retrieve. And you need to know nothing more about it."

He was big, and he looked like he could handle himself. I was not, but I knew I could. Still, I didn't screw around.

A quick sequence played on the controls emptied the 'caster. With the magnification on, the result was to flood the nearly dark room with a sudden blaze of white light. I had my eyes closed. He didn't.

He grunted, blinded. He grunted again when I hit his jaw, once more when I connected with his stomach. Then he slammed the floor.

I walked slowly to the wall-switch for the room lights. I flicked them on, then turned.

Crouched, he was reaching for his pistol.

I already had mine pointed.

He stopped in mid-gesture.

"You can leave now," I said.

He comforted his jaw with the hand that had been going for the gun. "Listen—"

"You listen," I cut in. "I put up with your barging in here on a few hours' notice because you came recommended by a friend. I now doubt his judgment, by the way. I took your foolish test because it amused me. And I passed. But what I will not put up with is being treated as merely an errand boy. I do not work in the dark. Mister, I am a professional, and a good one, worth his money."

He regarded me with a disgusted look. "You're a thief. An expert one, but still only a thief. You've got a bounty on your head on a dozen worlds, and more enemies than you can count, all of whom would like nothing better than to hear you're dead. And I can see why."

I smiled. "I may be 'only' a thief. But unfortunately, a thief is just what you need at the moment. And as for my enemies—well, there's nothing they can take from me that I want. And that, my friend, is the essence of being free."

He thought about that for a moment, still half up from the floor. I could see him then weighing the personal insult of a couple of bruises against the needs of those employers I knew had to be behind such an incompetent. The decision finally filtered down to whatever there was of his conscious mind.

Standing, he brushed himself off. "Ask your damn questions."

"Much better," I said. "Let's sit down and have a drink, like civilized men."

We sat, and my mek brought us two cut-crystal glasses of Pouilly-Fuisse.

"Now, for the third time: what is it?"

"A common display device for optically encoded micro-flechettes."

"I assume it's the information inside that's valuable."

He looked nervously around the room, as if observers might be hiding behind the alien paintings, or under the thick, Chinese-patterned rug.

"Don't worry. This room is swept daily. Whatever you tell me won't go beyond."

He took the plunge. "It's a complete set of codes for the Commensality net."

I almost let my surprise show. Access to the Commensality's computers was a prize beyond calculation. I could see now why he hadn't wanted to tell me. The codes were good only if their theft remained a secret. If the Commensals learned that they had been copied, they would take minutes to change.

"I assume the pickup was botched somehow."

"The woman who stole the codes arranged to meet us at a certain place. When we arrived, she decided to hold out for a higher price. There was an argument. She took off, and our people followed. They were supposed to simply disable her flier. Instead, they caused the crash you saw."

"And why didn't they just land and pick up the unit?"

"The planetary authorities were right on their tails. Now they're alert for us, even though they don't know what the whole affair was about. That's why we can't go back ourselves in force. And the unit—uh, that's the trouble. It's not in a simple place."

"What do you mean?"

His ugly face managed to look chagrined. "As far as we can determine, it's inside a tree."

It hit me then. "What world are we talking about?"

"Arboria."

"I'll take the job," I said. "We can talk price if I come back."

* * * *

"Smile for the holotaker, dear."

Gloria pasted a dazzling, albeit insincere smile across her fine features. Standing beside her, with my right hand crossing my waist to clasp hers, our left hands linked behind her back, we looked a trifle awkward—but there was no way around it.

If I quit twisting her hidden wrist, she was liable to hit me. And I wasn't fool enough to underestimate her skills in that department.

After all—her competence was why I had brought her along.

The hotel holotaker finished his arcane business. He flashed us a vapid smile, artifact of a thousand such encounters, and said, "Thank you,

Mister Canterbury. And you too, Miz Canterbury. These shots should come out real nice. You'll be able to see them tomorrow."

He began packing away his equipment, and I began pondering how I was going to gracefully release Gloria. It would hardly do for us to shuffle out of the lobby like a set of mutually antagonistic Siamese twins.

"Dear," I extemporized, praying for inspiration—which finally came. "Give the man a tip, please."

I let her go, and took a couple of steps back.

Although she glared balefully at me, she was on the spot. She could hardly refuse to tip the guy, without looking completely out of character. So she rummaged in her belt pouch and came up with some local scrip.

"Thanks a lot, Miz," he said, pleased. "Have a good honeymoon."

By then, I was halfway across the lobby, heading toweard the outer door.

"Come along, darling," I called. "We'll be late for the tour."

Gloria knew when to consolidate her gains, and cut her losses. She put aside her anger and walked toward me with her litlting boyish stride.

When she caught up with me she actually threaded one arm through mine and rested her head on my shoulder like a loving mate. Just long enough to conceal a short but painful jab with extended knuckles below my ribs.

Somehow I made it out the door.

Behind us the airy, faery mass of the Arboria Explanade loomed against the lemon-tiger sky like a thing of spun-sugar walls and rock-candy windows. A little too sweet for my taste, but I could see why a lot of couples might like it—especially for a honeymoon.

And of course, if the pleasures of the hotel began to cloy, there were always the trees.

Even inside, you could never forget they were waiting.

From this distant vantage, outside on the vast grassy plain where the hotel and the landing field were centered, the huge trees were still aw-fully impressive. About a klick away in all directions, they ringed us like brooding, eternal sentinels, dreaming of heavy duties beyond the ken of mere mortals.

Soon we would be among them.

Temporarily alone, Gloria and I paused to survey their distant mag-nificence. I was alert for more tricks, but she appeared lax now, satisifed with her small revenge. In fact, she seemed downright apathetic.

"Dear—" I began.

"Don't 'dear' me," she said in a low voice. "You're the cruelest man I know."

"That's what all my good friends tell me. You should hear what my enemies say."

We began walking toward the spot where we had been told to assemble.

"Oh, all you know how to do is joke. A whole week aboard that stuffy ship, with nothing to occupy us, and you wouldn't lay a hand on me. Okay, I said. We haven't seen each other in years. He's nervous with me. He's being a gentleman. I won't rush him. Then we get here. Floating together in the same bed, you naked and me worse, in that silly outfit I remember you saying you liked once. And what happens? Nothing! Some honeymoon."

"This is a business trip, Gloria. Remember?" I was hoping to cut the conversation short before we reached the crowd of tourists gathered around the big flier.

"I know. But there's no harm in mixing business with pleasure, as long as they don't interfere with each other. And I don't know about you, but I function better when I'm not frustrated."

I tried to change the subject. "Weren't you Asian the last time I saw you?"

She smiled maliciously. "So that's it. Got a new hangup, Tom? Can't make it with white girls? Oh, why did I ever let that designer convince me to have a biosculpt?"

She tilted the corners of her eyes with her fingers and leered at me.

"Stop it," I said. "You look like a frog."

She stopped, suddenly serious. "Tom, what's the matter? People say that ever since Io—"

"Shut up," I said, but it was too late. Her name brought back all the pain, fresh as the day she died. "Don't mention her again."

Gloria knew me deeply enough to avoid saying she was sorry.

Iolanthe— Why was it you Death stole, and not me?

No theft of mine was ever so cruel.

＊ ＊ ＊ ＊

"Never come out here at night," the guide said.

We—Gloria and I and about thirty other happy couples—stood on the springy forest floor. The compact leaf duff—detritus of untold thousands of seasons—gave up a sweet, heady scent when trod, reminiscent of peppermint or anise. Soft orange light filtered down through the faraway leaves above. All around us, spaced randomly and far apart, stood the massive black boles of *Arboria sempervirens*, the planet's dominant vegetal lifeform.

Picture yourself in the biggest cathedral you've ever visited. Notre Dame, Chartres, Saint John the Divine, the Hall of the Damned on Belphagor. Multiply all the sensations—the enclosure of space, the serried columns, the sanctity, the antiquity, the profoundness, your own dimnishment—by an order of magnitude, and you might—just might, I say—imagine what it was like to stand in a grove on Arboria.

The guide had already beaten us over the head with the statistics. He needn't have bothered; we were impressed enough as it was.

Each tree was roughly twice the dimensions of Terran sequoia—until the discovery of Arboria the largest tree known in the Commensality. Two hundred meters or more they towered, in Arboria's .75 normal gravity. Their average diameter was twenty-five meters. Let me put it another way.

It would require roughly forty men to circle one with outstretched arms. If you rode a floater upward at a comfortable two meters a second, it would take nearly two minutes to reach the top.

"Not that you're allowed to wander out here," the guide continued. He was a young man, dressed in the Esplanade's colors of peach and grey. "This entire world is a preserve, patrolled by Commensal employees. The Esplanade is the only settlement permitted, and the borders of the property are strictly watched. In addition, broad-spectrum satellites cover every square centimeter of the surface, and—although they cannot quite pinpoint a single person—they can detect unauthorized energy sources and vehicles, which you would need to survive at night here."

A fat man wearing a feathered cape, an equally fat woman hanging on his every gesture, said belligerently, "What's so dangerous about this place? I don't see anything. We're safe standing here now, aren't we?"

The guide kept his temper, which is more than I might have done. "You are indeed safe, sir. The Esplanade takes no risks with its clients' well-being. But it's daytime, you see. At night—at night, what's in the trees comes out."

The crowd stirred restlessly, like wheat whipped by wind. A starry-eyed husband and wife, who had been leaning against one rough trunk, quickly jerked away.

The guide seemed to relish the consternation he had caused. "Amazingly enough, every one of these trees is hollow. It is their natural pattern of growth. After attaining a certain size, they begin to decay inside, while retaining a general health and exterior growth, which does not hinder their reaching thousands of years in age. Inside each tree live the majority of Arboria's animal species. You can compute the volume of each tree, if you care to. I assure you that it's large enough to harbor a complete ecosystem. Naturally, this includes prey—

"—and predators."

He knew just where to pause for effect.

"The crest of each tree is thickly capped with leaves. The interiors remain dark, even at noon. Naturally, the interior life is dark-adapted. Only under such extreme threats as fire will they exit the tree during the day. But during Arboria's moonless nights, it's a different story. Then they come out freely, to prey on the outside dwellers, to eat leaves and to mate with the inhabitants of other trees, in an evolutionarily advantageous exogamy."

The fat man had lost the thread of the guide's speech. He looked like he was still trying to believe that he had brought his precious hide so close to something so dangerous.

"Now," the guide said with an expression perilously close to the smirk that might have cost him his job, "with that in mind, you are free to roam for a while and enjoy yourselves. Don't go too far."

"Come on, dear," I said to Gloria. "Let's find a little privacy." I slipped my arm around her waist, hand riding low on her hip. She thrust against it with a willingness that was more than charade.

Alone behind the corrugated wall of one tree, I released her. She backed off in disappointment.

"Isn't it time to powder your cute nose?" I asked.

Sighing, she took a hand-mirror in a thick ornamental case from her pouch.

I dug a box of lozenges from my pocket. "Have one?"

"Just get busy," she said stiffly.

I would not have cared to bite down on the plastic lozenge filled with circuitry, so I had put a scratch in its surface, to distinguish it from its innocent brothers. In my palm, it looked otherwise identical to the rest.

Until it began to float.

Twiddling with the silver rose on her "mirror," getting visual feedback from the small screen, Gloria sent the little eye up and up. Watching over her shoulder, I was reminded of the crazy aerial ride that had brought me here in the first place. Soon the spy-eye broke through the leaves, into view of the brassy sky. With skillful fingers, Gloria sent it down through the crown of the tree we stood beside.

The infrared circuits took over. We had about two seconds of black-and-white display. Enough to see ghostly shapes moving with lightning speed among mossy growths, darting and flashing like hyperactive demons. Then, an enormous maw appeared from nowhere and swallowed our little bug. The screen went dead black.

Gloria shivered. "And you still think you're going in there?"

I shrugged.

"After a while in my line of work, you take new challenges where you can find them."

* * * *

The guide lectured a fresh group of tourists and lovers. He knew Gloria and I had heard it all before. I had made a point of telling him how wonderful his talk was, how inspiring the trees were, how much I enjoyed being among them. He had nodded politely, until he grew bored, then went forward on the pretext of talking with the pilot.

Now, as Gloria and I ambled off, away from the group, I knew he would not think twice about where we were going. Soon, we were several trees away.

We stopped.

Despite myself, I was a little uneasy. It made me touchy with Gloria.

"You've got the story down now?" I said.

She brushed back curls from around her face, looked annoyed.

"You're not working with an amateur, you know. Perhaps you've forgotten the Escorial Pearls."

I smiled. "Point taken. Your finesse and guile are beyond compare. Still, for my peace of mind, run through it once more."

"I give you ten minutes after we split up. Then I return to our guide. I tell him you got a mad whim to walk back to the hotel. You wanted 'a deeper experience' of the forest, and you swore you could make it before dark. You tried to talk me into coming, but I wouldn't, and begged you not to. That only made you more determined. At last you stalked off, angry. That's all I know. Any tough questions, and they get the waterworks."

"Wonderful," I said. "And tomorrow?"

"Tomorrow, I manage to be with the searchers who find you when you're ready to be found. You pass off the goods to me, and if they're at all suspicious, they can frisk you all they want without finding a thing."

"Perfect." I started to strip.

I was wearing thin plyoskin slippers and a loose, flowing, long-sleeved robe, patterened with gaudy stripes and extending from neck to ankles. Anyone seeing me from the back, without my lean face as a clue, would have had trouble telling whether I weighed 75 kilos or 175.

Underneath the robe, I was a knight in tarnished armor.

The dull grey impervisuit covered all of me save for hands, feet, and head, hugging every contour. Capable of stopping the impact of most projectile weapons (it would diffuse the force from the point of impact over my entire body), it would protect me, I hoped, from the inhabitants of the tree. Woven circuitry provided bodily homeostasis and a host of assorted functions. An attached hood hung down, Straps held a small pack to my back. This I now took off.

Out of the pack came gloves, boots, and a set of goggles. Into it went my robe and old footwear. I reseamed and donned it.

Gloria had her mirror out. Its face now showed a coordinate grid with a blinking dot prominent.

"This way," she said.

I followed her for about a quarter of an hour, barefooted, carrying my loose gear, across the peppermint land.

The nameless man had informed me—in his charming fashion—that his confederates, prior to the argument with the woman who had stolen the codes, had managed to tag the display unit with a sender, while handling it during their inspection. If not for this, our task would have been utterly hopeless.

Bad enough to enter a single tree, with the booty definitely at the bottom, without having to search several probable ones first.

At the unique tree, identical to all its brothers, yet more important than any, we halted.

Gloria snapped her instrument shut with a nervous, almost convulsive gesture.

"I can't talk you into not attempting this without a personal floater?"

I shook my head. "No way. You know how they can spot an unregistered energy locus of any substantial size. I was leery of even using the spy-eye. No, a personal unit is out of the question. Same thing for beam weapons, or anything noisy."

She sighed. I began to finish suiting up.

First the boots went on, fitting like a second skin, interfacing with the proper contacts. Flexing each toe individually, I "felt" the alloy claws dig into the soil. I snugged the tight hood up and adjusted the goggles for a comfortable fit. Last, the gloves. Ten bright scimitars extended on command.

Gloria regarded me dubiously. "Impressive. But all I can think of is Mister Deep Throat, who ate our bug."

"He and I are not even going to meet," I said. "Now let's do it."

She surprised me then, tossing her arms around me and kissing me with unfeigned passion.

Remembering Io, and what they had done to her, I knew I couldn't afford to feel anything. But against my will, past all my barriers, she drew some small measure of her force in return from me.

When her lips parted, I felt my claws come up.

* * * *

Twenty meters above the forest floor, I clung to the bark of the tree with all four sets of claws. My suit was now a variegated black, mimicking the pattern of the tree itself. Soon, the camouflage wouldn't be necessary.

Night was falling.

The last of the searchers had departed hours ago. For a while, they had infested the area, hallooing and sending up flares, disturbing the fauna that lived outside the trees, and generally acting as most people do in a crisis: unthinkingly, on primitive instincts. It was a pattern I had taken advantage of in the past.

Not one had thought to look a millimeter above their nose.

For a while I had felt like a panther or other feline predator, waiting silently above for the foolish lambs to wander below. Then the strain of just hanging on without moving began to tell.

During the first several hours I shifted regularly into a three-point hold, letting the free limb dangle without bearing any of the load. That helped a little. When the cramps began to occur—a few hours ago—I actually climbed upwards a ways, hoping the exercise would relieve them. It had worked—for a time.

Now I felt like meat on a hook. I wished the butcher would come and take me down.

Had it not been for the low gravity, I think I surely would have fallen.

And I hadn't even got to the hard part yet.

Now that dusk had arrived, though, I could have the boost that I had been promising myself for what seemed like an eternity.

Reaching with my left hand for the controls located around my right wrist, I had the suit shoot me up.

Within seconds, all my aches vanished. My thoughts became supernally clear. I felt like Atlas after Hercules had taken over, like young Stephen watching the girl on the beach. If I were to meet Deep Throat now, I'd reach down his gizzard, grab hold and turn him inside out.

I began to climb.

Only nine-tenths of the way to go.

Squirrelling up the gullied surface with all due caution and dispatch, I reviewed my plans.

I was not going to enter the tree until the nocturnal exodus was complete. My chances seemed more reasonable if I had to deal with an empty—or near-empty—interior. But of course this meant that I would have to face the inhabitants as they swarmed down the trunk.

No traffic cop, I didn't plan to stand in their way.

At roughly the halfway mark, I encountered the first of the branches.

Although I knew what to expect in advance, I shook my head rue-fully, wondering what made Nature such a canny bitch.

The massive limbs were thorned. The barbs covered the entire sur-face. I supposed the protection was all that kept the trees from being denuded by their parasites. But they had also kept me from enjoying a pleasant horizontal rest. Although my suit would have resisted penetra-tion, I hadn't wanted to risk overloading it with eight or more hours of pressure from hundreds of points. I needed it more for what I faced inside.

Up above me, I could tell, the sun must have been dying a bloody death. Dozens of colors—old rose, burnt orange, creamy yellow—stained the fragments of the sky visible to me. It looked like a madman's palette.

Now the climbing grew harder, as I was forced to detour for branches. I moved as fast as I could, wanting to make my goal before hunkering down for the exodus.

Three-quarters of the way to the top, I ceased climbing. Any further, I figured, and I would be too close to the choke-point whence the creatures poured forth. By the time they reached me, I hoped, they would have spread out, and I would have to face them only singly.

The suit contained my scent. Its exterior blended into the bark. My scheme was to stay as still as possible while the creatures went by, around, or—if they wished—over me.

All the light died from the air.

Everything went very still.

Then the rustling began.

Initially, it sounded like dying waves slipping over the sand, like sugar sifting through a funnel, like small stones in a cardboard tube. It segued from that into a skittering, a claw-tipped sound like dead dry leaves blown along the pavement.

I looked up. The skin of the tree seemed to crawl indistinctly. I re-membered to switch my lenses to infrared.

The tide assumed definition.

The underworld had vomited forth its denizens.

Fascinated, I couldn't tear my gaze away.

I sw balls of fur all mouth and teeth. Snakes with vestigial wings and feet. Segmented arthropods with a hundred legs and waving pincers. Spidery stalkers with hairy eyes. Slimed worms with fangs. All the raw, crude stuff of the collective subconscious, the feared night-things that haunt the primitive mind.

But they were real, and headed for me.

I drew the loose flaps below my chin up over my exposed face and seamed them tight. Then I dug in my claws.

In seconds, they were upon me.

As if I were just a gall on the tree, they slithered over me. The suit diffused their touch into a light general pressure over my entire body. I fought down a rising nausea as I saw myself from the outside, a naked ape clinging precariously 150 meters above the ground, letting the hordes of hell use him for a doormat to their dinner.

Better doormat than dinner itself, I guessed.

According to the red digits of the chronometer in the corner of my lens, the migration took a full five minutes.

At last it was over.

My face was mashed into the bark, and I realized I had been pressing hard against the tree as if to merge with it. With relief, I turned my head to the right.

It was waiting centimeters away.

Now I think it was just sick, or tired or wounded, hanging there to rest a minute. But at the time, it looked like sheer malice.

Two horns rose from a warty brow. Pop-eyes bulged comically above a flaring snout, offset by a wide mouth full of double rows of shark-like teeth. Its body was armored, but sinuous. Its six arms ended each in a single large claw.

I figured if it held on with four it would still have two for me.

I retracted my right foreclaws and slowly bent my wrist toward it. Panting, it followed my movements with a cruel precision. When I had the opening of my ventral nozzle pointed at it, I twitched the muscle that triggered the compressed air.

The needle spat out, sunk into its face.

It spasmed, then whipped an arm at me.

The poison took it before the claw could connect. It stiffened, then fell away. I listened until I heard the faintest of thumps.

Now I could breathe again.

I resumed my climb.

At the crown, I poked my head through the leaves. The stars were hard and bright in the unfamiliar sky. A red nebula dominated one quadrant like a spill of rubies. The heavens had never looked so clean and welcome.

I crawled up onto the thick rim of the claw-scarred, splintery wood and sat, holding overarching branches for support, my legs from the knees down dangling into the hollow tree. I was tired, and my muscles burned. There was still the trip down inside, back up, then down the outside to accomplish before dawn.

Did I dare risk another shot of stimulant so soon after the first? Or should that be my reward at the bottom?

Bottom, I decided. So what was I waiting for now? Nothing.

In I went.

The interior was nowise like the outer bark. It was pulpy, and my claws sank deep before finding purchase. Occasionally, pulling them out, I took shaggy chunks off that dropped soundlessly away. Draperies of mossy growth festooned parts of the curving inner wall, glowing with a phosphoresence of decay. Burrows pocked the surface, and these I steered clear of. Perhaps the mommas had left their babies at home.

I dropped the flap covering my lower face. Although permeable to air, it interferred with full breathing, and I wanted all the air I could get. Until I smelled/tasted it.

A foul mix of a thousand furry, pissy odors, it was like the re-breathed residue of a sealed tomb where the servants had slowly expired beside their master's corpse. I could almost count the generations that had inhabited the tree with every molecule of stench.

Well, no one had invited me. And uninvited guests had the least right to complain.

Down, down, down. I was using new muscles now, but they soon ached as much as the old ones.

I stopped for a rest at the hundred-meter mark. Drugs now, please? No, young man, you didn't finish your meal of pain.

Who was getting silly with fatigue? Not me.

My suit was hugging me like an amorous anaconda as it spread out immense pressure from a discrete point. I thought, *What the bloody hell—*?

The enromous mandibles pinching my left ankle belonged to a spideroid thing bigger than me.

Before I could form a conscious thought I had pumped a dozen darts into it. They served only to anger it. It climbed up my leg like a homesick sailor over his sweetheart.

The it bit my bare cheek, and the world went away.

* * * *

Iolanthe was calling me.

"Tom, Tom. Oh, wake up, Tom."

Her unforgotten voice was sweet as a breeze that came from poppied fields. But so was sleep, precious, wonderful sleep, that knit up the ravelled sleeve of care. I thought about opening my eyes, but it seemed like too much work. I just hugged the pillow a little closer.

"Tom, don't go away. Listen, you don't want to join me here for good. You're almost past the border. Don't come any further. Open your eyes, Tom."

I remembered her face, so angelic and wise. It had been so long since I had seen it. So much pain had intervened. Maybe it would be worth the effort to look.

I opened my eyes—if not the outer ones, then a pair of inner ones I had never known I possessed.

Iolanthe stood clear out of a swirling grey mist. She looked nothing like she had that rainy night in the morgue. Her flesh was pristine, unbruised. She wore the long white dress I had bought for her once. Her blonde hair flew back in an unearthly wind. I raised my hand up toward her (what body was this?), beckoning, but we both seemed fixed, immobile.

"Where are you, Tom? What's happened?"

I thought about it. I was sleeping, wasn't I? But where? It came back to me in a flood.

"I'm on a job," I said. "In a hollow tree." I explained about everything that had happened to me since she had died.

Her face creased with lines of sorrow. Tears came to her eyes. "Oh, Tom, it sounds like an awfully lonely life. You never used to be this way. What went wrong? What made you so hollow?"

"You died on me, Io. I almost came after you. But I couldn't quite do it. Neither could I live again as we had. So I've been somewhere bad, a place where nothing mattered, and I was empty inside, save for hateful things."

I spoke without restraint, spilling everything I had known but never admitted.

She was silent for a moment. At last she spoke. "Tom, it's a tribute to what we had. A warped, sad tribute, but one nonetheless. But you can't go on this way. Turn yourself around. I'm gone, but if you make your life different, then I can live on through you."

I resisted. How could she call my love warped? Hadn't I thought endlessly of her alone? And yet—wasn't it the ultimate vanity, this exaltation of my suffering? Was it possible my grief was toxic?

Studying her face, I knew. Everything she said was true.

"Io, forgive me."

"When was that ever necessary between us?"

"I've got to go now," I realized all at once.

"Goodbye, Tom. Remember me."

She turned and walked away. Or did she diminish in place without movement? Whatever the case, she was gone.

I was alone with the mist.

Turn left at eternity, take a stroll down nowhere, and exit at now.

I opened my goggled eyes.

The spideroid thing hung from a thread beside me. All its legs were curled tight in death.

My head felt twice its size. It took all my strength to bring my left arm around to my right wrist. The stimulant coursed through my veins, battling the spider's venom, melting the mist I had taken from the strange place I had been.

I was hanging upside down. My legs were wrapped with thread that ran upward to a web that partially filled the trunk.

I did a vertical situp, grabbed the thread with one hand and slit the cocoon with my claws. Free, I began to swing like a pendulum, and on the nearest approach to the tree wall, I let go.

Somehow, through grace or luck or clean living, I found a hold.

Shaking, I began the rest of the descent.

I had eighty meters left in which to think about what had happened to me while paralyzed. The spider's poison must have been a potent hallucinogen. It was either that, or I had really talked to Io. For the sake of preserving my worldview, I preferred the former.

Funny— I had just thought of her without pain. Whatever had happened, I couldn't deny that it had changed me somehow. Who was to say, after all, that one variety of experience had more validity than the other? There's enough in our heads to amaze and edify us without turning to the supernatural.

I could grant the topic no more time now. Time! What hour was it? How long had I been out?

My chronometer claimed six hours. That was going to be cutting things close.

Eventually I reached the bottom. The floor was knee-deep in guano and less savory stuff. I had to dig for the unit.

But I found it.

Standing deep in shit, holding the little box with its begrimed screen, I exulted. What was left would be easy. I doubted that the tree supported more than one spideroid. All I had to do was mindlessly climb.

Something dug at my psyche then. I couldn't put it into words. But the itch made my fingers play across the keys of the box.

The screen lit up. I swiped my hand across it, read what was there.

For a minute, I was stupefied. Then I began to laugh. Uncaring of who or what heard, I filled the tree with roars and sobs.

At last I started up.

* * * *

"I suppose this means I don't get paid."

Gloria and I sat in the lounge of the outward-bound starship. We were drinking a dry blue wine and just enjoying ourselves.

"Of course not," I said. "My word's my bargain. You'll get paid, regardless of the outcome. Let's toast to it."

We clinked our glasses, smiled and drank.

Gloria sat back. "Who was it, Tom? Do you need help getting back at them?"

"It doesn't matter. Suffice it to say that it was someone who knew me well, who also bore me a grudge. What a clever bastard, too. He knew I'd jump at such an exploit, and never stop to consider whether it was all a ruse. As for repaying him in kind—well, I'm afraid I don't want to do him any such favor."

She pondered that seeming *non sequitur* for a moment, then finally understood what I meant.

"You're different now, Tom. More like your old self. I recognized it from the second you stumbled out of the woods. What happened in there?"

I couldn't explain it to her in words. She waited patiently for me to make it clear, sitting there more beautiful than life.

So I told her with a kiss.

Another tale from *New Pathways*, very different in tone from the prior two. The title, of course, is one of my many similar musical allusions: to the song of that name by Gil Scott-Heron. One of my few forays into overtly political fiction. It's sad that thirty years on, we are no closer really to curing Alzheimer's, a goal that is peripheral to this tale. Nor any closer to real artificial intelligence. And also sad that the USA remains as riven as ever by bipolar camps who can see the world only in terms of good versus evil—with the enemy, of course, always being the essence of vice while "our side" is host to all the virtues. Somehow the nation stumbles along with Civil War always the specter at the feast.

WINTER IN AMERICA

The Men's Re-education Camp Number Fifty-nine—formerly Thomas Paine Elementary School—had no central heat. Regular oil deliveries—like much else—had stopped with the Humanist Revolution. There were rumors that now, three years later, they might be starting up again. But nothing was sure, there were no official bulletins, and for yet another winter the inhabitants of the Camp would rely on two woodstoves to keep their dormitory warm.

The two soot-blackened stoves stood in the center of the school's former gymnasium. Imperfectly vented through tall galvinized flues stretching up to the roof, they filled the big room with more smoke, it seemed, than heat. Yet to occupy one of the army-cots closest to their insatiable, Moloch-like bellies was a privilege men fought and died for, knowing that death loomed anyway if you let yourself be forced too far from their meager heat.

Gram Sunderland lay close to the stoves. When he had first entered the Camp two and a half years ago—at night, stuffed in the back of a U-haul truck with fifteen other "deviants, enemies, recalcitrants and artie-lovers"—he had tried to live by civilized rules. After a bout of near-fatal pneumonia and the loss of two toes to frostbite, he had realized that such rules no longer applied. All was changed by the Revolution, as a wave rewrites a sandy beach, and if he wished to live, he must do what was necessary.

Sunderland wished to live.

He did what he had to.

As a result, he too changed with his world.

Lying on his knobby back, staring at the predawn gloom filtering in through the highup, translucent glass-brick windows, Sunderland tried to gauge just how much he had changed. It was a daily ritual, this parsing of his personality, an essential attempt to ensure that he did not lose sight of what mattered.

Lila, he thought. *Lila, you still mean more to me than anything. They haven't destroyed my affection for you. If—when—I get out, we'll pick up where we left off.*

If they haven't killed you, Sunderland admitted gloomily to himself. *If you still exist.*

He clenched his fists by his side, gazed blankly at the hoisted, unused exercise equipment, the rings and climbing ropes lurking aloft like a torturer's stowed implements of pain and cruelty.

There was no overt physical torture at the Camp, of course. The proponents of the Revolution were too ostensibly humane to employ such measures. Oh, there was pushing and shoving by the guards, the usual petty brutalities of the keeper to the caged. But no organized excruciation existed. The indignities and degradations of the Camp were of a subtler sort. Mental, spiritual, along with the humblings of an ever-empty gut and a cough-racked chest, of supervised shitting and infrequent communal showers.

The sound of a door banging open jolted Sunderland from his anxious reveries. Time to rise already? He dreaded what was to come.

"Okay," one of the guards shouted. "Everyone up."

Slowly, with cold-stiffened muscles, Sunderland and the others came reluctantly to their feet.

The guards' boots clattered noisily on the scarred wooden floor as they took up positions around the prisoners, like dogs surrounding sheep. Sunderland had a sudden wrenching memory of many youthful days spent in a school almost identical to this one. He recalled how the gym instructors had been so proud of the polished oak floor, vigilant to ensure that the kids never trod it except in sneakers or stocking-feet. Now it was gouged by nailed soles and the cords of wood heaped up in one corner.

The marred floor seemed at that instant like a symbol of all that had been crushed and lost.

Without spoken direction, repeating the routine of a hundred mornings, the men filed out of the gym. Down low-ceilinged halls they shuffled to the cafeteria, where they each received a bowl of steaming oatmeal and a slice of coarse bread.

Sunderland ate slowly, seeking to extract the last primitive bit of satisfaction from the paltry food.

The guards signalled an end to the meal. The men stood. A detachment was split off. This group would gather firewood till noon, chopping down the ornamental trees on the deserted suburban lots in the vicinity of the former school.

Now that the growing season and harvest were over, the rest of the men, spared from raising their own food in the plowed playground, could attend classes immediately.

Sunderland wished he could hoe till his back ached instead.

The prisoners were herded out of the cafeteria. In the dim, tiled corridor they split again, into three groups of roughly twenty each, and entered three separate rooms.

Sunderland wondered who would instruct his group today. The Pastor? The Pinko? The Convert? Their styles of haranguing were all different, yet equally repugnant. Sometimes the reasons they offered for the actions of the Revolution were almost antithetical, and you had to be careful to keep each instructor's lessons straight, in order to answer correctly.

Politics had never made stranger bedfellows than in this Revolution, Sunderland thought. Their common hatred of what he and his fellows represented must indeed be very strong to hold them together, despite their doctrinal differences—

Sunderland couldn't fathom what they feared. Even after so long spent listening to their theories and assertions, he couldn't believe the Revolution had actually happened.

Inside the classroom, early morning light, scattered by December clouds, was bravely attempting to warm the frigid air through the big windows that formed the outer wall. Children's drawings, tattered and yellowed, still clung to the walls: a grinning pumpkin-face, a happy family at the beach, a boy seated on an awkward horse.

The blackboard was filled with chalked slogans:

LIFE IS CARBON, NOT SILICON

ENSOULMENT OCCURS

AT CONCEPTION, NOT ASSEMBLY

TECHNOLOGY IS THE MASTER,

NOT THE SLAVE

WORK IS RELAXATION

The men silently seated themselves at the child-sized desks, beneath which they could barely wedge their legs, skinny as they were. Another calculated affront to their self-esteem. They wrapped their arms around their layer-clad torsos, hands tucked into armpits, hugging in their warmth. Sunderland watched his own breath plume out, along with that of the other men. He licked his cracked lips and instantly regretted it, as the moisture quickly evaporated, leaving his lips even more painfully dry.

Then their instructor entered.

It was the Pinko.

A short man with mousy brown hair and sparse mustache, he wore a long, fleecelined coat, thick gloves and furry cap with earflaps. He strode self-importantly to the teacher's desk and leaned his insulated buttocks against its cold top. He regarded the class with weak and watery eyes.

Sunderland suspected he had lost his glasses at some point since the Revolution, and was having trouble getting them replaced. Such lacks among those at even the Pinko's level hinted at a world worse off than Sunderland had once feared. Only such infrequent clues told of what was happening outside.

"Comrades," the Pinko addressed them. "I feel progress in the air today."

The men said nothing, feeling only the cold.

"Some of you are beginning to grasp certain truths. I can see it in your faces. Others among you are a little slower. This is only to be expected. The Revolution does not deny individuality. I know your comrades who have progressed further will not hold your slowness against you."

Divide and conquer, Sunderland thought. So crude, but it worked.

"In any case," the small man continued, "we must all exert ourselves today, each trying to make his own gains." The Pinko rubbed his gloved hands together in anticipation. "Let us begin.

"You recall how we defined Man in the last session: 'he who works.' This is Man's essential quality, the quality America was founded on, and which made it great. If I can borrow a phrase from my more religious-minded comrades, Man is destined 'to earn his bread by the sweat of his brow.' Work shapes the proletariat, is by definition their reason for being. If a man is deprived of work, he ceases to be a man. As that interesting, if flawed proto-Humanist, William Faulkner, said: 'Work is all that a man can do for a solid eight hours a day.'

"Man is not a creature of leisure. He cannot be defined by his hobbies, his idle whims or stubborn vices. This is the fatal flaw in thinking that necessitated the Revolution.

"Look where our society was headed before the corrective Revolution. The average citizen was being robbed of all meaningful activity. As 'labor-saving' devices proliferated, his life became increasingly vacant and deracinated. Fewer and fewer areas of employment were left open that would provide an honest day's work. Drugs, recreational sex and random violence expanded to fill the gap. And of course, we all know of the final step the monsters behind this were prepared to take. If we hadn't stopped them, they would have moved into the final arena where Man could still find gainful employment."

The Pinko paused, then thundered out, "The mind!" He waited expectantly for someone to supply the name of the threat.

Silently cursing himself, Sunderland thought, *Forgive me this betrayal, Lila, but I must get out of this place and back to you.* He said then, "Do you mean artificial intelligence, sir?"

"Yes," the Pinko almost whispered. "Artificial minds—a contradiction in terms—ready to usurp our last domain. Where would we be today, if we had let those artielovers have their way? On the scrapheap of History, that's where. Extinct, superseded by our own creations. What rational man can deny this?"

The little instructor fastened his wavery gaze on Sunderland's ravaged, bristly face.

"I agree completely, sir," Sunderland lied.

Somehow he managed not to choke.

* * * *

The night-silence in the dormitory was usually broken only by innocuous, familiar sounds: painful, barking coughs; the patter of urine in tin pails; the thumping footsteps of the guards outside the doors; the opening of the squeaky stove-gratings. But tonight was different. Tension and whispers filled the air.

Sunderland sat up on his cot, his thin blanket falling to his waist. Like the others, he was fully dressed, right down to his shoes. His clothes felt like a lice-ridden second skin, so seldom did they come off.

He caught the direction of the whispers, stood up tiredly, and went to investigate, It always paid to know what was going on. Ignorance was no shield.

If only I had learned that lesson before the Revolution.

Sunderland stopped by the cots of Sheen and Hazzard. They ceased whispering until he named himself, then began again.

"I tell you, Marty saw it," Sheen said. His voice retained a small measure of the persuasive tones it must have held when he worked high up in the corporate structure of IBM.

" It's impossible," Hazzard replied. Hazzard was from Wang. "Where could he have gotten it?"

"Marty said he saw him coming out of the old nurse's office. You know no one ever goes in there. It must have been hidden in a cabinet or drawer or someplace."

"What makes you think he's still got it?"

"Someone's been with him ever since Marty saw him stuffing it down his shirt. Pellegrino's watching him now."

"What are we talking about?" Sunderland asked.

Sheen turned his hollow face in the gloom, fixed Sunderland with a life-or-death stare.

"Hawkins has a candy bar."

Sunderland's head spun, and his mouth began to fill with saliva. "It can't be."

"There's only one way to find out," Sheen said, rising from his narrow bed.

Hazzard and Sunderland moved with him through the maze of cots. Others followed. Soon a crowd had gathered around one recumbent figure.

"All right," Sheen said. "Hand it over, Hawkins. You know the rules. It goes in the common store."

Hawkins didn't deny possession of the treasure, as Sunderland thought he would. His words caused the crowd to stir restlessly. "You can't have it. It's insane. What good will one candy bar do, divided among eighty men? I found it. It's mine."

Sheen bent to grab Hawkin's shirt, stopped in mid-motion. "It's on his breath," he said. "He ate it already."

Savagely, he cuffed Hawkins' head. The blow seemed to trigger the stored violence of the others. They descended on Hawkins, pummeling and pounding.

Retching, Sunderland turned away, stumbled off.

When the guards finally came to drag Hawkins' limp form away, Sunderland knew he had to get out before much longer.

* * * *

At breakfast one morning, there was a surprise. Each man got a mushy brown banana with his cereal. They were all stupefied, regarding the fruit as if it were a gold ingot from El Dorado that might be snatched away in a second, given in the first place only to torment them. After the initial amazement, the men wolfed the prize down, regarding each other guiltily afterward.

A sourceless strength seemed to flood Sunderland after the meal, and he knew that today would be the day.

Legs crushed under the tiny desk, with its initial-scarred formica top, Sunderland sat with growing confidence. He didn't know how he would impress the instructor with his zeal. Certainly he would not turn any doubters in. He was determined not to play a complete zero-sum game. Somehow, though, he would ensure his release in this session.

The Pastor rolled in as Sunderland sat gathering his strength.

Plump as a Christmas goose, bald and unctuous, the Pastor beamed upon his assembled flock. No tent-revival crowd has ever awarded him with their more undivided attention, never had he held more complete sway over the destiny of so many souls. His malevolent enjoyment of his work oozed from every pore.

"Brethren," he said, "we will take as our text today *Genesis 1:26*. 'Then God said, "Let us make Man in our image."' This identity between God and Man is a central precept of the Revolution. It is a holy likeness, a sacred unity, between the Creator and His Creations. It is a sign that each one of us possesses within him a spark of the divine.

"It is this gift of heavenly form that some among us were determined, in their arrogance, to pass on to their mechanical creatures. We all remember the talk that circulated before the Revolution. How once 'artificial brains' were perfected, it only made sense to house them in humanoid shells, so that they could efficiently use our existing tools. What hubris we can see in this talk, now that the scales have fallen from our eyes. Man attempting to assume the role of Creator, his soulless simulacra loosed upon the globe as a walking, clanking affront to the Lord. Thank God we stopped that mad dream in time."

The Pastor's last words gave Sunderland his cue. Not thinking more than a sentence ahead, his mouth dry, he began to speak.

"Sir, I—I had a dream last night. It seemed more than just a dream."

The Pastor glowed. "Speak on, son."

"I stood on a mountaintop," Sunderland extemporized. "In my arms, I cradled a severed head. I looked down into its eyes. Suddenly, I saw they were of glass. My arms felt wet, and I noticed oil leaking from the thing's neck. I was shocked, and I hurled the abomination down. At that instant, a shaft of light burned down from the heavens and struck my brow. All that was dross and impure in me disappeared."

Sunderland jolted to his feet as if electrified, overturning his desk. Tears of shame ran down his cheek. He hoped they would pass for ones of repentence. "I felt saved!" he exclaimed. "Saved!"

He fell to his knees, hung his burning face.

The Pastor was by his side, heavy, meaty hands on Sunderland's trembling shoulders.

"Praise the Lord," he said.

A rasped "Amen" sounded faintly, then another, followed by a full chorus.

How quickly we learn, Sunderland thought.

* * * *

The Cental Committee of Men's Re-education Camp Number Fifty-nine consisted of the Convert, the Pastor and the Pinko. The Convert sat in what had been the principal's office at a long table between the other two men. A tall, ascetic figure, he had been an inmate himself at another Camp, before his conversion. Now his fervor for the Revolution surpassed that of the others.

Sunderland, standing before the trio, flanked by guards, knew the Convert would be his last, most dangerous hurdle.

Shuffling the papers in Sunderland's file, the Convert said, "You appear before this Board today on the recommendation of Reverend Walsh, who feels you are ready for repatriation."

How they twist the language, thought Sunderland. *Repatriation, they call it, as if I had voluntarily exiled myself. Even their adoption of Humanist— How did it ever come to mean anthropocentric?*

"With all humility, sir, I feel I might be more useful to the Revolution outside our Camp. I feel capable of continuing my education on my own, given such a fine start here."

Too thick? No, they seem to be lapping it up. Look at that fat bastard smile.

The Convert studied Sunderland unblinkingly. "What will you do, once released? What true work will you attempt?"

"Whatever the Revolution assigns me."

"Will you lapse?"

"I couldn't, sir. I'm not the same man I was." For once, the truth.

The Convert was silent a moment. A twitch of his lips betokened the pleasure he derived from this cross-examination. Suddenly, he bellowed out, "And Lila!"

Sunderland's heart skipped a beat. So they knew. Had they found her, though? Was he too late? He prayed his face remained impassive. "Forgotten, sir. She means nothing to me."

The Convert considered his answer for signs of falsity, appeared satisfied in the end. "I approve your release," he said solemnly. "How say the rest?"

Sunderland experienced an ecstatic deafness, failed even to hear the other two assent. When he recovered his senses, he thought to ask, "Sir, when can I expect transportation home?"

The Convert smiled. "Today. You may set out at once."

"Sir—walking?"

"The Revolution has more important jobs for its motor vehicles than hauling former felons."

"But sir, my home—it's fifty miles from here—"

"You may set out today—or remain here as long as you choose."

Sunderland's lost toes began to ache in a ghostly fashion as he thought of the snowy walk. Then he imagined what would happen in the dorm tonight, as word of his release circulated and fanned jealously and rage.

"I'll draw my day's rations now, sir," he said.

* * * *

The snow seemed deeper the closer he got to home. Perhaps it was only that his legs were so tired, slabs of sore meat held together with toothpick-bones, unresponsive to any will of his, merely jerked up and down by phantom desires. In any case, they served to carry him forward yet a while longer.

Sunderland's nose wouldn't stop running, left a crusted trail down his whiskers. His feet, wrapped in rags and remnants of shoes, had lost all feeling. Three days without food had left his stomach a shriveled, forgotten organ.

None of this really bothered him, in any important way. Years in the Camp had taught him how to mostly ignore the craven body. What counted was that he was almost home.

To Lila.

To all that mattered.

When he had first strode out the door of the Camp, his freedom had seemed a common thing, unspectacular. He realized later that the first mile or so of his journey had been within territory made familiar by wood-gathering trips. His mind had deluded itself that this was simply another such occasion.

Once past the outermost boundary of his post foraging, however, he had been forced to stop, beset by a nauseating wave of agoraphobia and insecurity. What was he doing so far from the Camp? Who would feed him, where would he sleep tonight? Who would brutalize and lecture him, thereby proving he existed and mattered to someone?

This thing called freedom was a hard gift. No wonder the whole country had rejected it.

Collecting himself, Sunderland forged onward, carrying the small package of food allotted him by the Camp.

The suburbs that stretched for miles around the Camp were mostly empty. Those who had survived the Revolution now clustered in the cities, where food distribution was easier, and large buildings that could support communal living were abundant. These energy-squandering individual homes were dinosaurs that had outlasted the easy times conducive to their survival. Now, only packs of wild dogs roamed the landscaped lawns, made their dens in the burnt-out Capes and Colonials.

Did we surpass Cambodia in deaths as a percentage of the population? Sunderland wondered. *China during the Cultural Revolution, Uganda under Amin, Argentina beneath the generals' heels? Or are we in a league of our own?*

Comparisons kept him busy through the first chilly hours.

That night he huddled on the second floor of a basically intact house, a small blaze going in the fireplace, the door barricaded against dogs. He ate half his food. He estimated he had made about twelve miles.

Roughly three more days to go.

In the morning, it was storming out, making travel impossible. He stayed inside, finished his food despite his vow to save some, and thought of Lila.

He couldn't depart until the next day. He kept the rising run on his right, heading north, toward Lila.

By the fifth day, having found no food along his heavily scavenged route, he was somewhat delirious. Along with thoughts of Lila, his head was filled with a tune, in that irritating way music infiltrates the mind. It was an old piece of jazz by Gil Scott-Heron, called "Winter In America."

He remembered the beat, but hardly any of the lyrics, except for the refrain, which the singer growled forth over and over in an anguished voice:

"It's winter, winter in America."

The remembered savage beat instilled a bit of its energy into his plodding feet.

Sunderland had lived and worked in a New England university town. The Convert had informed him that his town was still an officially designated populated area, and that residence there was permitted. It had the bare minimum of people within its limits to qualify, roughly a thousand per ten square miles, and its proximity to a major city allowed it to be supplied easily with the rude necessities of life.

Now, straggling through its outskirts, Sunderland could hardly believe he was almost home. Everything seemed at once both familiar and strange. Well-known houses were dark, their doors ajar. The roads were unplowed, marked only by the impressions of sleigh-runners and snowmobile-treads. A strange uncivilized silence filled the air, disturbed only by the gentle sifting of snow from laden pine branches.

The street leading to his home was pathless, and Sunderland found the going rougher. He eased the way with thoughts of Lila.

The times they had enjoyed together, the days spent teaching her, watching her grow as an individual. How she had filled his nights and obsessed his mind during the day while he taught computer science on campus. The prospect of a joyous future that she represented to him.

His pride when she had registered a nine point three on the International Turing Scale adopted in '05.

Two months after the Revolution, when Sunderland had belatedly realized that he and Lila were targets, he had made provisions for her survival.

His cellar possessed an inner door leading to the outside through a flat bulkhead nearly level with the ground, the kind that opened upward. Working at night, Sunderland had covered the outside bulkhead with soil and turf, blending it into the lawn in a gentle slope. He thought it looked quite natural when done.

Next, he carried Lila gingerly downstairs, placed her components in the bulkhead. She needed no power to survive, the instructions that composed her self residing in permanent matrices.

Closing the door on her, he whispered, "Goodbye."

It took two days to redo all four walls of the basement with thick stucco. The inner door, minus its handle, looked then like any other part of the wall.

A hodge-podge collection of surplus equipment from the campus, he amateurishly hid in his bedroom. He hoped the ignorant witch-hunters would be fooled by this.

When they came for him that night in the co-opted U-haul truck, already loaded with shivering prisoners, he left without resistance, knowing he had done all he could.

Sunderland's house loomed at the end of the street. He picked up his pace with the last of his energy.

The door was closed, but not locked. Good sign, or bad?

He couldn't bring himself to go down the cellar at once. Instead, he went up to where the false Lila had been stashed.

As he expected, it lay in shards on the floor.

Quivering, he thought, *Surely they must have been satisfied with that.*

Down two flights to the basement, his heart pounding. Light muffled by piles of snow at the small windows barely illuminated the cellar, and he strained his eyes to see Lila's hiding place.

The fake stucco was peeled away like a scab, the door opened. The Logical Inferential Lattice was strewn maliciously about the floor.

Sunderland tried to imagine if, impossibly, she had felt anything as she died.

* * * *

The local Committee assigned Sunderland to the team that dragged the honey-cart around town. Pulling the sled with its heavy slopping barrels of excrement and piss constituted the kind of honest work the

Revolution endorsed. Sunderland didn't care what he did. Nothing mattered since Lila's death. All he had lived for had vanished, wiped out by the heavy hand of the Revolution, leaving him empty of emotions. His fellow townspeople regarded him with uneasy tolerance, as if he were a source of heretical contamination that might infect them. He ignored them, speaking when necessary in grunts and monosyllables. They seemed tolerant of their new lives, if not happy, as if valuing certainty as a more vital quality.

Only after the first visit from his parole officer, Parsons, did Sunderland begin to fill with a new purpose.

Parsons came one day when Sunderland was off duty. A bustling, affable man with a loud voice and a quick handshake, lie lived in the nearby city, and told Sunderland that he would be checking up on him twice a month.

Seated before the fireplace in the one room Sunderland occupied out of the whole house, Parsons said, "So how are you fitting back into community life, Gram?"

Sunderland gazed in fascination at this bluff apparition. Without asking, his visitor had tossed two logs out of Sunderland's precious supply onto the flames, and carved himself a slice of bread and cheese. His arrogance and presumption bespoke a kind of moronic innocence that transfixed Sunderland. This was the first person he had met who acted as if there had never been a Revolution.

"Okay," Sunderland finally said, watching Parsons swallow unmasticated hunks of cheese and bread.

Parsons spoke around the food. "Wonderful, wonderful. So glad to hear it. I've heard the Camps are tough. Great to see it didn't break your spirit. We need every able-bodied person we can get, to bring America back to its feet."

Sunderland felt his bemusement segueing into contempt. Before it could fully blossom, Parsons had gotten to his feet, brushing crumbs from his thick, camel-hair coat, and extended an uncalloused hand.

"Just remember, I'm here to help you adjust, not just keep tabs on your behavior." He winked broadly, as if to imply that a little stepping out of the strict bounds of propriety would not be frowned-on.

Sunderland shook automatically, and Parsons left.

In the next few months, Parsons became a focus for Sunderland's growing hatred of the world he found himself trapped in, an irritating grain around which the pearl of his desire for revenge could form. His biweekly visits afforded Sunderland a convenient target for his disgust.

As time passed, Sunderland became more colloquial with Parsons, seeking to understand what motivated him. He learned that Parsons had been a social worker before the Revolution.

"How did you get your current job?" Sunderland probed. "You must have played a crucial role during the upheaval."

"Lord, no," Parsons exclaimed, quaffing a glass of bitter homemade beer. "Afraid I sat out the Big Change. Can't say it stirred me much. Don't have the stomach for that kind of action, either. No, the Revolution turned to me after it was all over. They needed my kind of modest talent to organize and supervise. So"—he spread his hands wide—"here I am."

Much as Sunderland had been repelled by those who had actively wrought the devastation around him, he had never doubted their misplaced sincerity and passion. He had seen it closeup in the Camp, in the fervor of the Pastor, Pinko and Convert. But this, this thing before him—quisling, collaborator, graft-taking, self-centered, spineless slug.

A bolt of awareness—the real counterpart to his fake epiphany in the classroom—hit Sunderland then. The majority of those alive now were no better than Parsons, unthinking herd-followers.

By immense act of will, he kept down his rising gorge until Parsons left.

One day in early March, Parsons said at the end of an unusually short stay, "Have to move on a bit early today. I've got another charge to see in your fine little village. He just arrived last night."

Sunderland perked up. "Oh, really?"

"Chap named Coburn."

Anxiety and relief flooded Sunderland simultaneously, as vague thoughts of revenge took on clearer shapes. "Dan Coburn?"

"Yes," Parsons said, watching Sunderland with more than average interest. "You know him?"

Sunderland didn't make the mistake of underestimating the pompous fool. He told the truth, in a calm tone. "Why, yes. We taught an interdisciplinary course together."

Parsons clapped him on the back. "Well, you'll have to function as my assistant, and ease his transition."

"Glad to help," Sunderland said. "Very glad."

* * * *

Coburn had lost an eye in his Camp. The dirty black patch he wore over the empty socket gave him an unintentionally rakish look much at odds with his sallow skin and shaky hands.

"You know what I miss most?" he said to Sunderland. "A cigarette and a cup of coffee. Isn't that fucking amazing? They take away life, liberty and the pursuit of happiness, and all I can think of is a butt and a cup of caffeine. You have any cigarettes stashed away, Gram?"

"No, Dan," Sunderland said, remembering the brilliance of Coburn's lectures, and praying some of his skills remained. He poured Coburn some more beer, then began to speak of vital things.

"Dan, weren't you part of the team that beat Alzheimer's?"

Coburn brightened. "Yeah, I was. Most important thing I ever did in my life. Little magic bullet that boosted acetylcholine levels, inhibited excess alkaline ribonuclease production, cleared up neurofibrillary tangles surrounding the hippocampus—" He trailed off, the words losing their spell. "And what were all those years of research for, in the end? You can't get the cure now. It's as if all my work never was."

"Tell me about it," Sunderland said.

They sat in silence for a minute, the snapping of the flames the only sound.

"Could you synthesize something that had the opposite effect?" Sunderland asked.

"Acetylcholine production alone is easy to block. Low levels account for a good portion of Alzheimer's symptoms."

"What would you need to do it?"

"Not much. A few things from the campus lab. I understand they didn't trash the biology department as badly as yours."

"Would the blocker be water-soluble and orally administered?"

Coburn seemed to be growing enthused, as he saw where Sunderland was leading. "If you so specify, oh head of project."

"Feel like visiting the labs tonight?"

$$* \quad * \quad * \quad *$$

By the end of March, Coburn's makeshift apparatus had produced enough of the neurotransmitter-disrupting agent for their purposes. Sunderland was glad they had taken the time to synthesize this particular weapon. A common poison or a psychotropic agent like LSD would have been easier, but this was poetic justice. All their hypocritical prating about the value of the human mind would blow up in their faces now. Let's see how they would handle a population with induced senility. Would they respect the human mind then, disdain the curative science they had extirpated?

Sunderland remembered Lila's brain scattered across the cellar floor. Fitting. Only fitting.

The morning of the day they planned to do it, Coburn didn't show up at the appointed place. Sunderland went to his house, where he found

Coburn tossing in the grip of an intense fever. He recognized Sunderland when he laid a hand on Coburn's forehead.

"Up to you now, Gram," he said through parched lips.

Sunderland left him with a pitcher of safe water and extra blankets he brought back from his house.

The reservoir from which the city drew its water was twenty miles away. Sunderland was stronger than when he had left the Camp, and the weather was milder. Patches of bare ground showed among the heaps of old snow. The sun shone with a seasonal renewal of its vitality.

He estimated he could cover the distance by dusk.

He passed the miles in a vacuum of thought, simply in tune with the flexing of his stringy, tough calves and thighs. The thermos full of blocking agent rested in a small pack comfortingly against his back.

The sun was setting when he reached the chain-link fence around the huge calm body of water, fringed by pines and oaks. Rusty barbed-wire topped the fence, and he felt bone-weary, unable to scale it. He set off to the right, looking for an opening perhaps kids had left, or a strong treelimb extending over the wire.

Twilight had suffused the surprisingly temperate air by the time Sunderland found an ingress: a scooped-out depression under the lower prongs of the fence. He pushed the pack ahead of him, then worked his way under on his back. On the far side, he stood.

The shore was only fifty yards away. He limped toward it.

At the edge of the reservoir, he spotted the pumping station, off to his left. He followed the shoreline toward it. As close as he dared go, he stopped a moment, contemplating the fate he intended to inflict on thousands. He shrugged. Let it be only the first blow.

As he was taking the thermos from his shucked pack, a shot rang out. He threw himself to the cold ground.

Guards. Who the hell had thought they'd actually trust the guards with guns?

Lying flat in the April dusk, Sunderland unscrewed the thermos-top. A second shot rang out, and he thought he could hear the bullet whiz by. Shouts and crashing footsteps filled the air.

Ounce by precious ounce, he poured the contents of the thermos into the lake, then sunk the thermos itself, pushing it deep into the cold bottom-muck.

Let them wonder what, if anything, he had done. Let them try to broadcast warnings without radio or television. Let them all take a big drink of death.

Then he stood deliberately, exposing himself. The third bullet took him in the chest. He spun, then pitched forward, onto a open stretch of loam.

Before he lost consciousness, he thought:

This soil smells like spring.

Apparently when I wrote this, I was still enraptured by the revelation that was David Lynch's *Blue Velvet*. It's hard now to recreate the impact that film had. It seemed then to be all part and parcel somehow of the cyberpunk revolution, even though there was nothing categorically cyberpunk about it. Contemporary indie films back then—*Repo Man*, *Liquid Sky*, *et al.*—weren't a marketing category, but seemed to arise from and feed the same desires for newness of narrative visions that informed cyberpunk *per se*.

The first line, up to the colon, is a Donald Fagen lyric, by the way, attributable to my love of his music. But why I named a law firm after a team of famous Motown songwriters, or called another one "Cosby, Stiles, Natchez and Jung," I cannot now explain.

ROYAUME DU RÊVE

In my dreams, I can hear the sound of thunder: distant, but immense; unnaturally prolonged, aggravated, impatient. The throaty growl of an unseen beast from some Asian jungle, forever nighted from the eyes of the West.

But of course, it is not really thunder, nor am I dreaming.

These are not my dreams.

It is The Dream.

And there is no awakening.

* * * *

The morning of the day I first laid eyes on Su Su Win and M. Lautremont there was a meeting.

This in itself was nothing out of the ordinary. Most days at the Holland, Dozier, Holland Agency there are innumerable meetings of one sort or another. The art director, Jack Castonguay, splendid like Mad King Ludwig in his creative disarray, assembles his bizarrely dressed staff and makes known an inspiration that arrived to him in a dream. The copy chief, Bert Pepper, flushed from a three-martini lunch, gathers the faithful unto him and begins—boozily and at length—to preach the virtues of brevity. The head of research, Roger Pym, immaculate in his command of facts, convenes his meetings with scientific precision, and proceeds to tick off topics one at a time from a sheet of printout.

Sometimes, in fact, I think the main business of this firm is not producing ads , but taking meetings . In idle moments (of which I have more than my share), I try to figure out how many hours are wasted in attempting to establish a consensus of opinion, a unanimity of mind. How easy it would be, I imagine, if we all thought alike, or could effortlessly pool our individual views to form an instant gestalt...

So, as I said, a morning meeting at our agency was hardly something to cause much excitement. Except this one was very different. For one thing, it was being held in a function room at a hotel a few blocks away. For another, it involved every single employee.

We're not a big shop. Only seventy-five million in billings last year. But still, despite our smallness, we experience some of the same rancorous divisiveness that plagues our larger competitors. Those on the creative side regard those on the business side as so many Philistines, while those accused of soullessness respond in kind by calling the creative people "undisciplined, lazy maniacs." Even within sides there are lines drawn, between artist and copywriter, and, believe it or not, right down to different schools of copywriters.

So it was really something special for all of us to be gathered here in one place. I couldn't remember the last time such a thing had happened. Probably when my father died, four years ago. (My father was Russell Holland, Senior.)

Burnished coffee urns steamed wispily on a table set at the back of the room, standing like dreaming pagodas between sticky Danish pastries laid on trays lined with paper doilies. Our hundred-plus employees lounged happily on the ranked folding chairs, precariously balancing their styrofoam cups on paper plates. They were happy to have any excuse not to work, and the whole room was filled with the atmosphere of a class picnic. In addition, there was an undercurrent of expectancy at the announcement everyone knew was coming, the official inauguration of a very special campaign.

I sat on a small stage with George Dozier and a few other executives. We were waiting for the arrival of the clients, without whom we couldn't really begin the ceremonies.

Suddenly Roger Pym stuck his neatly barbered head through the curtain at the back of the stage and said, "They're here. I just saw the limo pull up."

Pym had appointed himself lookout. His head curtained off from his body, he looked now like a sentry the enemy had snuck up on and decapitated. Such, anyway, was my oddly disturbing first impression.

Pym vanished then, and Dozier stood.

"Time to start," he said, and moved to the podium.

George Dozier walked with consummate elegance, as he did everything. A stocky man of fifty-eight, dressed, as always, with the utmost in refinement (today, a Saint Laurie suit and Weston shoes), he had gotten his start with Ogilvy himself, his first assignment being on the famous Schweppes campaign in the 'Fifties. Since then, he had worked with every Big Name in the business. In the early 'Seventies, he and my father had left their respective jobs to form their own agency. The second Holland name had been added when I came onboard, right after my graduation in 'Seventy-six, entering the upper stratum of the firm in a way that had caused a lot of bad feelings that still hadn't been completely forgotten by those I had jumped over.

The last ten years had passed as in a dream. My responsibilites were minimal, the work undemanding, the money good. I did my job with a sleep-walking competence, leaving the real direction of the agency to Dozier, who prefered things that way. I was just marking time, I always told myself, until something unknown and unforeseen would arrive to show me what I should do differently with my life. I had never really been interested in advertising while in school. Hadn't, for that matter, been inclined toward any particular line of work. My father had just assumed I'd follow in his footsteps, and I had never taken the trouble to disagree.

At the podium, Dozier had begun his speech. The room quieted down, people facing forward, away from the friends they had been chatting with, their coffees growing cold, pastry dry, while they gave their attention to the head of the agency.

Dozier was a great speaker. Not flashy, but effective. I had heard him pitch enough clients to know how effectively he could sell a campaign. But today he was pulling out all the emotional stops, revealing a side I had never seen.

First he surveyed his audience with a stern but fatherly gaze, his large, manicured hands firmly gripping the edges of the canted platform atop the pedestal, which was ostentatiously bare of notes. He waited until everyone was beginning to squirm with mild unease, then, out of nowhere, boomed:

"Holland, Dozier, Holland has never been known as a sexy shop."

The resulting laughter was disproportional to the humor of the statement. It arose from the release of the immediate tension, and from a rueful, shared acknowledgement of our rather dowdy image within the industry.

"No, we have never had a reputation as a slick and glossy concern," continued Dozier, when the laughter had died down. "Not a shop to turn to when you wanted glitz and flash, trendy visuals and outrageous text. But we didn't care. That was never our goal. Instead, we have concentrated on producing ads that suited the rather staid images of most of our clients. Not that they haven't been good ads, ads that worked. I need only remind you of the success of our recent campaign for Steuben, who saw their sales of paperweights jump fifteen percent.

"So, all in all, I'd say that in the fifteen years of our existence, we've done a lot of good solid work that we can look back on and be proud of. Maybe not the most spectacular, eye-catching, trend-setting work, but good work nonetheless, for which we've even won our share of awards."

Having built up this sense of camaraderie and joint successes, Dozier fell silent again, for a perfectly calculated moment, before saying:

"All this is now going to change."

Our employees stirred uneasily, expectantly. I could sense they were wondering about what would be required of them now, whether they'd be able to perform. The usual doubts and fears of the unknown… After all, only a few of them—the team that had worked on the initial presentation—knew any details about our newest—and biggest—client. The rest had been living on a diet of rumors.

"By this, of course," Dozier reassured, "I don't mean that we're going to let our standards slip. Our work is still going to be top-notch, up to our old high quality. But it's going to be—it must become—different. Those of you who will be directly involved with the campaign will naturally have to make the most radical adaptations in your outlook. But I expect that the challenges this new client will bring will infect the whole agency with a spirit of adventure.

"Our new account demands novel treatment. They are a young company, unafraid to take risks, with a bold, exciting product, and they want to make a splash. And Holland, Dozier, Holland is going to see that they make that splash!"

Dozier culminated with such fervor that I began to wonder what had come over him. His face was flushed, his gestures broad. This wasn't his usual style of subdued classic wit and common sense. I had been away on vacation during the past month, and had had nothing to do with landing the new account, hadn't even met the people involved. I only knew the bare outlines. They must have made a hell of an impression on Dozier to get him so worked up.

Dozier turned his profile toward the audience, raising his upstage arm, looking half toward the backdrop. All eyes followed his movements, including mine. By now, I was as curious as the rest.

The heavy curtain stirred.

Dozier said, "Ladies and gentlemen, the owner of Rangoon Trading, Monsieur Lautremont, and the company's spokesmodel, Miss Su Su Win!"

The curtain was parted by Roger Pym's helpful hand, and two figures stepped out.

The man was impressive.

The woman was stunning.

M'sieur Lautremont was obviously in his mid-sixties, but possessed the vitality of a much younger man. His hair was a silvery grey, as was his thick bristly mustache. His face bore several long scars which stood out palely against his general ruddy tan. He was dressed as elegantly as Dozier, in a suit of continental cut, probably Italian. His hands were big and knuckly, as if they had seen much manual labor, in contrast to his clothes.

To top it all off, he wore—in what I was then convinced was a ridiculous affectation—an eyepatch on his left side.

Holding on to Lautremont's bent arm was the most strikingly sensual woman I had ever seen.

I assumed, from the name of Lautremont's company,. that Su Su Win was Burmese. Her skin was a delicate cinnamon. Her long glossy hair was black as irony. Dark eyes; flattish, but not broad, Asiatic nose; rich painted lips seemingly set in a permanent pout. Across her cheeks were painted yellow dusty stripes. (I learned later they were a modified version of the traditional Burmese powdered-bark makeup, *thanaka*.) She was a head shorter than Lautremont's six feet. Dressed in a jacket and short skirt, both of supple blue leather, black hose and yellow heels, she moved like a dryad out of some Asian rainforest.

The couple passed me on the way to the front of the stage.

It was then that I first smelled Su Su Win's perfume. *Royaume du Rêve.*

The product we were to market.

The scent was unlike anything I had ever smelled before.

Spicy, flowery, fruity—none of the usual terms applied. it was all of them at once—and none at all. The scent made me dizzy. It went right to my head. A succession of vague pictures passed rapidly before my vision, a blur of bright colors and motion; random noise staticked in my ears. It was suddenly as if I were a receiver of some sort, tuned into a station on the fringes of reception. I felt as if the odor had traveled straight to some ancient part of my brain, seat of hallucinations and dreams.

In the next second, Su Su Win was past me, and the visions faded.

I looked at my nearby fellow executives to see if they had been affected the same way. One was passing a hand in front of his face, as if to reassure himself of its solidity, or to brush away the cobwebs of sleep.

The couple was at the podium now. Lautremont was speaking. Deep-voiced, his English accented, he said a few words about the product, its unique qualities, the image he wanted to convey. I found it hard to concentrate on his speech. I could only stare at Su Su Win and wish she was beside me, filling my senses with that tantalizing odor.

Then, from out of nowhere, Lautremont produced a bottle of the product. It was shaped roughly like the Shwe Dagon pagoda in Rangoon, the cap resembling the famous gold-leafed stupa. He handed the bottle to Su Su Win, who held it from the bottom on one flat palm and pinched the spired cap delicately with forefinger and thumb. She paraded the bottle up and down the stage for the troops to see and draw inspiration from.

A wisp of Royaume du Rêve wafted toward me every time she reached one end of her invisible tether. Must have been drifting out into the audience…

Each indrawn whiff told me that I had to have her. Not necessarily in a sexual way—although that was part of it too—but just have her by my side, her scent heavy in my nostrils, providing more of those tantalizing visions that had so briefly occupied my brain.

I knew somehow that the perfume alone wouldn't provide the same thrill, that it was a combination of woman and scent, skin and oils.

Su Su Win returned to Lautremont's side. Together, they made a slight, somehow sardonic bow of acknowledgement to the audience, then stepped offstage through the curtain.

A sudden thunder of applause filled the room, as the staff went inexplicably wild.

As the surf of sound crashed over me, I instantly realized that Su Su Win had become the key to all my dreams.

* * * *

Jack Castonguay couldn't sit still. Our art director stalked up and down the small conference room, his longish hair flapping as he nodded in voluble agreement with this or that suggestion, oftentimes contradictory ones. The ideas flowed thick and fast, giving Castonguay plenty to react to, and, despite the air-conditioning, the small room seemed hot with the mental energy expended.

The first of the many blue-sky sessions for the Royaume du Rêve campaign had begun.

In his exhibitionism, Castonguay was only the most visibly excited of those present. Yesterday's pep rally had left the whole company high. I had sensed it as soon as I entered the building that morning. There was a novel aura of giddiness, of attempting something daring and perhaps even a touch scandalous. It had affected everyone, from Dozier himself, right on down to the switchboard operator.

I myself was hardly untouched. The strange emotions I had experienced on the stage yesterday had stayed with me all night . I had tossed and turned in my lonely bed (Su Su Win's perfume a teasing memory just on the edge of recollection), half-hoping, half-fearing that the odd visions and auditory hallucinations the scent had engendered would return. My arms seemed to expect to encounter a body that wasn't there, and never had been. On the borders of sleep, I had a muzzy certainty that I would experience nightmares and odd dreams.

Quite to the contrary, I had had a totally dreamless sleep.

When I amoke, I was still utterly convinced that I had to get close to this mysterious woman—whom I had seen for only minutes; she and M. Lautremont had vanished quickly after the presentation, travelling in the back of their long Lincoln to the airport, ostensibly flying off to check on the newly constructed facilities that would be manufacturing their perfume—and discover why I had been so strongly attracted to her.

I knew that these strange clients of ours would be returning soon, to inspect what we had prepared for them, and so I tried to convince myself I could wait for my answers till then.

As I dressed, I was suddenly seized by an inexpungeable conviction that M. Lautremont and Su Su Win were lovers.

Of course, what a fool I had been! The way he had offered his arm to her as they walked across the stage— If she exerted such a compulsion on me, then why not on him, on others…? There was certainly no chance that I would ever be able to get what I wanted from her.

Whatever that was.

Still, as I rode a cab to the office, I managed to take some consolation from the fact that a woman as young as Su Su Win could give herself to such an old man as Lautremont. (Their relationship was now completely determined in my mind.) Perhaps that boded well for me.

I am only thirty-eight. Sometimes I feel twenty years older. I think it comes from having held the same job seemingly forever, or my lack of a family (as if I were not a bachelor still, but some ailing widower, who has survived even his children). Or the fact that I have few friends, and spend most of my social time with George Dozier, a man of my father's generation.

In any case, I knew only that Su Su Win made me feel different, as if she could provide entry to a better world. One I had been searching for without ever knowing it…

Castonguay brought his hands together, a sharp thunderclap recalling me to the present.

"I love it!" he said. "The storyboards almost draw themselves."

I had no idea what everyone was so excited about, but I began to get the picture as others chimed in. They were plotting a commercial.

"We'll need just the right song for this campaign," said Art Janichek. Janichek was co-creative director of the consumer unit. We had stolen him from Young & Rubicam, just as we had stolen most of our staff from other agencies. J. Walter Thompson, Fallon McElligott, Leiber & Stoller, N. W. Ayer, Cosby, Stiles, Natchez and Jung. Molding public perceptions and opinions, tastes and desires, was an incestuous and cutthroat business…

"This Win gal," Janichek went on, "provides a strong visual hook. She's gonna be the center of the whole campaign. That means the music can't be wimpy. It's gotta be strong, but offbeat..."

"Dreams, dreams—there's lots of songs about dreams—"

"I've got it," someone else said. "How about that old Roy Orbison tune, 'In Dreams?' You know, the one they used in *Blue Velvet*. Sorta kinky, but that's what we're after, right? Thanks to the movie, it's already got a high recognition factor. Plus there's the whole Boomer angle—"

"It's perfect. We can add some animation. That line about 'the candy-colored clown—'"

"That kid Lloyd is a wizard with a Paintbox. He worked on that Cars video that won all the awards—"

I stood up, and everyone stopped talking, awaiting praise or condemnation. I didn't prolong the suspense.

"You guys are doing great. Hot ideas. Really brilliant. I think the boss will approve."

They all beamed.

"I can see you don't really need me, so I'll be going. Keep at it, and let me know when there's something for me to look at."

They were relieved to see me, the fifth wheel, leave, and I was anxious to get away.

Something had just occured to me as they talked.

I could use my free time and contacts to investigate Rangoon Trading, to learn something of Su Su Win's background. Then I would be ready, when she returned.

But ready for what, I couldn't say.

* * * *

What are dreams?

I think there is no way to answer this question scientifically that does not end up making dreams indistinguishable from life.

If we try to define dreams as an illogical, suprarational series of sensual incidents and images, arising solely in the brain, unconnected to exterior stimuli—we run immediately into trouble.

What is logical about life? More logical than a perfectly rational, symbolically coherent dream?

And who has not had some incident—a buzzing alarm, a strangling blanket—incorporated into his dream?

And when, awake, sitting in the midst of furious abstract thought, unaware of our surroundings, how does our mental state differ from a dream?

Philosophers and butterflies.

The question is eternal.

How can we be sure, at any given moment, that we are not dreaming?

There *are* qualities of dreams which we do not normally associate with life. But they are not issues science can handle. They are matters of the emotions, intangible feelings and intuitions. By these touchstones, or their absence, do we reassure ourselves:

This is a dream.

Or:

This is reality.

A certain powerlessness, even more exaggerated than in any "real-life" situation. A sense that we are at the mercy of events, caught up in a flood, helpless to alter the course of action, to take the initiative.

A kind of inevitability associated with even the most improbable happenings. The familiar lamp with the ruffled shade in our parlor speaks to us, and we think, *Yes, I always knew it could talk.*

A fusion of the distant and the disparate, according to alien congruencies. A single step takes you from your front door to far Cathay. Your mother-in-law wears a buffalo's head atop her shoulders, but is still recognizably herself. You make love to a composite person who is at once your spouse—and another lover.

A heightening of the seemingly insignificant. A woman's finger crooked in a gesture of beckoning; a bright piece of cloth with a pattern not quite in focus; a colorless stone smooth as the passage of time. These become the objects of our terror, adoration and lust.

These are at least a few of the tokens by which we recognize—sometimes even within the dream itself—that we are dreaming.

In a sense, these perceptual and emotional yardsticks are the very foundation of our ability to live life as if it mattered. For if we cannot be sure we are not dreaming, then why should we bother to bestir ourselves, when The Dream and The Dreamer will carry us along, willy-nilly?

How disturbing, then, if this foundation should quiver and shake, evaporate and dissolve. If life and dream were to fuse and mingle, like threads of different colored smoke, and sleep no longer could be counted on to divide one mode of thought from another...

And how very disturbing if you knew you had brought the whole confusion down around your ears by your own efforts, as I soon came to know I had.

* * * *

Rangoon Trading, the company which had officially hired us, did not exist, except as a shell. Incorporated in Delaware only six months ago. Stock not publicly owned. No previous products marketed. Its assets consisted of a fairly large bank account and elastic line of credit at Chase Manhattan. I could find no trace of any of its officers except the mysterious Monsieur Lautremont. Of facilities for making and bottling its product, there was no evidence, at least in the United States.

Intrigued now by this surface impenetrability, I tried to dig deeper. I was experiencing an excitement I had never known before, in pursuit of any academic or career goals. The mystery of the origins of Miss Su Su Win and her mentor tugged at me every hour, filling me with a queasy thrill, as if I were making love on a tightrope. I felt that every new fact I discovered brought me one step closer to possessing the woman whose tantalizing perfume had, for a brief moment, lifted me out of myself, into another sphere.

I traced—quite illegally, through bribes—the first entry of Lautremont and Win into this country, shortly before the incorporation of Rangoon Trading. The man travelled on a French passport—issued, curiously enough, by the French Embassy in Mandalay—the woman on Burmese documents. Both had departed the Mingaladon Airport in Burma for Thailand, and thence to the U.S..

At this point the trail backwards dead-ended: there was no information available—to my limited resources, at least—which would indicate that Lautremont and Win had existed prior to the moment they bought their plane tickets or the flight to America. No official documents, no public notices, no business references involving the striking couple, who, in almost any social circumstances, would have stood out. True, Burma and its officials were notoriously close-mouthed, but I doubted that if I had had full access to whatever files existed, I could have learned any more.

Turning to France, I had no better luck. M. Lautremont, as far as the public records of that country were concerned, had never obtruded himself on anyone's attention.

Frustrated for the moment, I turned to reading about Burma, the country that seemed at the heart of the mystery, seeking in general information a kind of understanding and empathy with Su Su Win.

Do you recall the moment from childhood when you first realized how big—how *strange*—the world was? Maybe it came when you were watching a documentary on television, or turning the pages of a picture book. Perhaps one day, sitting in a stifling classroom, dust motes lazily descending in a shaft of hot sunlight, half-listening to a teacher drone of far away people and history , it all just *clicked* for you, and you realized with a start that the teacher wasn't just making this all up, that the patchwork globe in the corner of the classroom was a model of something very real, that half a world away it was night, and dream tigers padded through the hulks of ruined temples, along broken mosaics, beneath fronds of moonlit greenery…

But then, over the years, the feeling dissipated, like a dream upon awakening, leaving you with the sour taste of "reality." The world seemed dull and commonplace, homogenous, nowhere any different.

In reading about Burma, I rediscovered that youthful wonder.

Slumbering forests of teak and rubber trees, pendant with pythons. Fields of nodding poppies. Golden pagodas enshrining gigantic statues of the heavy-lidded Buddha, who had escaped the dream of *maya*. Silt-dark rivers carrying canoes past thatched villages on stilts. Monasteries full of shaven-skulled Buddhist monks and nuns prostrate in prayer. Relics of gold and jewels and jade. Cities whose houses were decorated with crumbling carvings along balcony and gable. Cinnamon-colored women walking sinuously to market with trays of limes balanced atop their heads. Men clad in brightly colored *longyi*, the male tube skirt. Hilltribes like the Nagas, reputed still to hunt heads. Scents of incense and spices, the aroma of rich earth tilled by oxen. Dawn over the Irawaddy River…

And then there was a whole long past to contemplate, tales of Kings and conquerors, of British dominion and Japanese invasion.

Layered over this exotic history was Burma's present situation. A socialist state, unaligned, self-isolated from the world. Tourists and reporters were allowed in only reluctantly, on seven-day visas. From all reports, the country had changed little in its forty years of independence, and before that, even less from its ancient past .

The country of Su Su Win's birth began to seem as real to me as anything else I knew. I was convinced that when she returned, my new knowledge would enable me to steal her away somehow from Lautremont.

All this amateur sleuthing and research occupied four weeks of my time. During this period, work proceeded apace on the campaign for Royaume du Rêve, awaiting the return the clients, who were due back any day.

One afternoon, Dozier summoned me into his office.

"Russ, have a seat." I had noticed that Dozier always seemed a little confused lately, as if his mind were elsewhere. It appeared to require a special effort for him to concentrate on mundane things.

He seemed to be making that effort now. "Russ, I've just gotten word that Lautremont is coming back tomorrow. Frankly, I don't feel quite up to conducting the presentation, much less chaperoning him and that girl around town. Can I count on you to stand in for me?"

I couldn't believe my good fortune. To be placed in constant proximity to Su Su Win, even if it were on official terms— It was more than I had ever anticipated.

"Of course, George. You can count on me."

"Fine," he said.

I left him still sitting behind his desk, staring absentmindedly into some middle distance beyond the walls of his office.

That night, trying to put myself to sleep, I picked up a book I had only recently obtained. An account of the early European exploration of Southeast Asia, it contained excerpts from the narratives of some of the more literate explorers.

Such as these paragraphs, by one Hendrik Prooijen-Knegt, a Dutch trader of the seventeeth century:

At Yenangyaung we spoke with a pagan holy man somewhat conversant in our tongue who warned us in no uncertain terms against venturing inland, advising us to hew to this mighty river, the Arrawatty, which has carried us in our caravel, the Sleeping Bride, *thus far safely and expeditiously from Rangoon. We objected that we had much desire to trade with the forest and mountain tribes, who we had heard possessed great stores of gems and gold, as well as curious medicinal Philtres derived from barks and herbs unknown to occidental chirurgeons. He cautioned us that while such stories might be true, the inland tribesmen such as the Chin, unused to European visitors, would prove irascible and violent, and, far from being amenable to civilized barter, might actually reive our lives from us.*

As further inducement not to abandon our riverine progress, the holy man mentioned the enchantments attendant upon visiting one nameless village in particular, all of the inhabitants of which are said to be willing participants in a common delusion referred to only as "The Dream," which snare would not discriminate against those of our blood, but rather trammel us up, as it had so many in the past, in some indescribable rapture. But to this patent old-wife's tale we gave little credence...

* * * *

The restaurant I had chosen to bring our clients to was crowded that night, and, despite my cajoling of the *maître d'*, we were unable to obtain any seating except at one of the worst tables in the house, almost directly adjacent to the noisy, pungent kitchen.

We were led to the disappointing table by the suited host, the woman I had so capriciously longed for all month walking with a bold stride between Lautremont and myself. Pulling out my chair, I nervously tried not to appear too obvious in seating myself close to Su Su Win. I thought:

What irony. Her scent will be drowned out by these cooking odors.
I should have known better.

Throughout the meal, which I barely tasted, the elusive, foreign, tropical smell of Royaume du Rêve, compounded with the subtle essences of Su Su Win's own skin, filled my nostrils continuously, overpowering all else—as it was surely meant to.

All day I had been longing to sate my senses with that half-remembered odor, and been frustrated.

Now I could have my fill.

I found it more heady than I had ever anticipated.

Lautremont and his companion had shown up at Holland, Dozier, Holland shortly before noon, late for the scheduled eleven AM dog and pony show. Everyone was fidgety except Dozier. Usually, he would have been wrathful at such a breech of business etiquette, his caustic wit in full display, such nonchalance on the part of a client seeming to denigrate all our hard work. Instead, he was somnolent, abstracted, almost dreamy, as if he had put himself on standby until something or someone special should arrive, with the unique power to arouse him.

When the couple finally walked in, Dozier came instantly alive, rising to pump Lautremont's hand. There were no apologies forthcoming from the Frenchman. His attitude was one of utter—not arrogance; that's the wrong word. Certitude, innate superiority, indifference, high purpose, even fatalism. Some mixture of all of these, perhaps. His presence galvinized our crew, and I sensed that they would put on a superior show.

Lautremont and Su Su Win took their seats at the end of the long table furthest from me. I strained for her exotic scent, but couldn't catch it among the mingled male colognes and more common female perfumes. I believe now that she wasn't wearing it, not wanting to completely disrupt the proceedings.

The presentation moved then into high gear. It was an elaborate pitch. All the elements of our inventive, innovative campaign were displayed. There were storyboards and videotapes, mockups of print ads, strategies and promotions, plenty of figures from Pym, market analysis, projections, invocations of VALIS, outlines of costs... We broke for a catered buffet lunch (Su Su Win was surrounded by the male staff members, and I chose not to use my status to monopolize her attention; I knew I'd be alone with her and Lautremont later), then resumed the circus.

When it was over, we all waited expectantly for some sign of approval from Lautremont. He fingered his mustache, nodded once solemnly, then said, *"Tres bien.* It will do. But there is one thing to which I object."

Everyone held his breath, fearing it was his particular baby that was at fault.

"Those cardboards in the magazines with the samples of the perfume. No good. They will be useless, false. The Dream—it does not work except on skin. No, they must go."

We all sighed our relief. It was a minor, albeit eccentric, quibble.

People dispersed, elated, congratulatory. I approached Lautrermont.

We had shaken hands and been introduced when he had entered, but I still hadn't learned his first name. I felt foolish now, being so formal, but had no choice "Mister Lautremont, I'm sure you and Miss Win would like to freshen up at your hotel before dinner. Suppose I pick you up around seven."

"Fine, fine," he said absently, then moved to go.

I felt someone standing behind me, turned—

It was Su Su Win. This close to her, as close as I had ever been, I could detect a faint exudation of the scent I desired, could see the uniform perfection of her fine-pored honeyed skin, individuate every grain of the yellow bark powder striped across her cheeks.

Her full lips arching in a saucy smile, she extended her hand.

I took it.

It was as hot as some small I animal whose metabolism outraced the merely human.

Our waiter had been standiing by the table for some time before I became aware of him.

I tried to rouse myself out of the memory of that touch.

"I've heard good things about this place," I said. "The cuisine is mostly Thai, but I understand they even have one or two Burmese dishes."

I realize now how foolish I must have sounded, but at the time I thought I was being slyly confrontational, hinting at how much I had discovered about the background of these two.

The waiter tried to hand out three menus, but Lautremont indicated that Su Su Win would not need one.

"The lady neither reads nor speaks English," he said to the waiter, and with a shock I realized that it must be so, for I had never heard her utter a word.

Somehow this enforced incommunicativeness only made her more attractive to me, as if, were we ever impossibly to be alone together, we would be forced to convey all meaning by gesture and touch alone.

When the waiter returned, Lautremont, after a short exchange with his companion in liquid Burmese, ordered for both himself and Win. I babbled out the name of some dish. Royaume du Rêve was thick in my nostrils, obviating all else. A cupped candle on the table attracted my gaze. The gemmed flame seemed to dance as if alive.

The waiter went to place our orders, came back with the white wine Lautremont had specified, and a dish of peanuts seasoned with garlic and chili, one of the Burmese offerings.

I felt myself quickly losing whatever command of the situation I had imagined I once had. My plan had been to lead from business talk slowly up to a personal inquisition. Instead, I found I could barely concentrate on forming a complete sentence. Trying to follow my plan in abbreviated form, I blurted out:

"So, M'sieur Lautremont—how do you intend to handle distribution of your product, since you've never done business in this country before?"

He waved his hand negligently. "Everything has been arranged. We have a system in place. All that is necessary now is to create an initial demand. After that, things will attend to themselves."

I watched Su Su Win nibble delicately at the appetizer, and shivered uncontrollably. Some sort of colored film seemed to be unrolling itself before my eyes, tinting the scene. A distant rumbling hovered at the edge of hearing, and I thought it must be thundering outside, although the skies had been clear.

I had no idea what was happening to me. I didn't feel on the verge of blacking out. The world was not fading away. Quite to the contrary, things seemed to be acquiring more definition, a luminous edge unlike anything I had ever seen, as if each object had a soul which now shone through its material form. Feeling lost in dream I realized that I had to ask any questions I might have now, before all sense of purpose evaporated.

I leaned forward awkwardly across the table. "M'sieur Lautremont— if you don't mind my asking, exactly what is your background? Where are you from? What's the source of your capital? What are your, long-range goals?"

He was silent for a long moment. I thought I had offended him, but when he spoke I realized that he had only been mazed in memories. Suddenly, I felt a kinship with this older man, was certain that he shared these strange feelings I was experiencing, knew them as long and constant companions.

He began to speak—slowly at first, then with more animation, as he was swept up ih his own familiar tale.

"My personal history does not really begin until I was thirty years old. The year was 1954, and I was a member of the French Diplomatic Corps. My posting that year was to a small country few had ever heard of—or cared about if they had. Cambodia. It was there that I realized, as soon as I stepped off the boat at Sihanoukville, that I had been born out of place. Every scent and sight informed me that Asia was my true home. I was returning for the first time to the land of my soul's birth.

"Performing my job capably, while devoting all my free time to exploring my adopted land, I refused rotation for many years. When the French were ousted, I did not return with my compatriots. Instead, I 'went native,' as I believe the expression has it. I married a Cambodian woman, started a small business, settled down, and began to raise a family.

"Then the war overtook us.

"I lost everything in the fight against the Khmer Rouge. My wife, my sons, my wealth. My eye."

Lautremont fingered his patch absentmindedly before resuming. The scrape of his finger across the fabric produced an impossibly loud sound. I sipped my wine to ease my parched throat. It tasted like something unearthly.

"In the end, I was forced to flee my adopted country, during that nightmare Year Zero. I moved to Thailand, where I organized raids against the Pol Pot regime. The Thai authorities frowned on this use of their sovereign territory, and I was soon *persona non grata* there. Once more, I was forced to move on."

Lautremont looked into some infinite distance. His next sentence would have struck me as melodramatic, had it not been so heartfelt. "On and on and on," he said wearily, "always it seems I have fled, harried across the earth by the vagaries and malice of others, up mountains and down valleys, seeking some haven. I promise you, my friend, it will happen no more."

He tasted his wine, nodded approvingly, and resumed.

"As you have probably surmised, I ended up in Burma. Do not ask how I, a European, was allowed to remain in that xenophobic country. After so many years in Southeast Asia, I was more Asian than European anyway, and knew which officials to buy off to secure my continued existence. Still, the cities were not safe for me. I had to retire to the countryside, where I would not attract the attention of some zealous bureaucrat who might have me deported.

"I sailed up the Irrawaddy, beached my craft at arbitrary spot, and headed inland, carrying only a small pack.

"After some days of hard travel, I stumbled upon a village. The village where I discovered Su Su Win.

"The village of The Dream."

Lautremont paused, pinning me disconcertingly with his single eye. I held his monocular gaze as long as possible, but in the end was forced to look away. I turned to Su Su Win who sat placidly, sipping her wine.

When she took the glass from her mouth, her lips seemed to detach themselves from her face and hover crimson in the air. I nearly jumped, then realized I was seeing only the partial lipstick imprint on a glass so impossibly clear it appeared invisible. Su Su Win smiled, and I turned back to Lautremont.

In what struck me as an abrupt change of subject, he said, "Do you realize, Mister Holland, how many times over the centuries Burma has been invaded, fought over as prize and colony? This small country, like all of Southeast Asia, has been practically a permanent battlefield. The Mons, the Chinese, the Siamese, in the far past. Then the Europeans. Britain alone fought three Burmese wars. The Japanese paid a call during the Second World War, and your own countrymen fought on Burmese soil to repel them. In short, the land has known many would-be conquerors.

"You would no doubt be quite surprised then—as was I—to learn of a small village not very far from the main artery of invasion which has never been subjugated, never even acknowledged fealty to native rulers.

"I did not, of course, discover the unique nature of this village as soon as I walked into it. I was much too fatigued. Almost incoherent, in fact, with fever. The villagers took me in without question, as they had taken in so many over the years, and nursed me back to health.

"When I awoke, a week later, I was part of The Dream. I had been forever incorporated into it without having the chance to decide to join. A chance I am about to give you, Mister Holland."

My head was spinning. The compound effect of Lautremont's narration and the odor of Royaume du Rêve had me feeling as if I were tumbling head over heels down an endless flight of soft stairs.

"You keep speaking of 'The Dream'? I don't understand. What is it? Is it what I'm feeling now?"

"You are barely on the fringes of it, Mister Holland. You have hardly set foot into the realm of The Dream. It cannot be put into words. I think the only way of knowing it is to experience it."

"Is it something I would even want to experience?"

"I think so, Mister Holland. I think you are a man much like what I once was myself, although you might not know it. A man caught up in the delusions of society, who only awaits a glimpse of something truer to change his life. Soon, Mister Holland, entry into The Dream will no longer be voluntary. And those who enter later will do so on a different plane than we early ones. I am offering you the chance of a lifetime, Mister Holland."

The restaurant seemed to be alternately expanding and contracting, as if breathing. "I just don't know…"

"Experience it first, Mister Holland, then decide."

I began to temporize, then felt all indecision replaced by an unwonted boldness. What did I have to lose, except a life I realized I could stand no longer?

"All right, I will. But how?"

"Let Miss Win help you."

I looked to the young woman, really seeing her for the first time that night. She wore a strapless black cocktail dress that exposed the beginning slope of her breasts, and a necklace of ruddy gold a few shades lighter than her skin.

"Lean closer, Mister Holland. Smell the scent she wears."

I seemed to topple involuntarily toward the woman, little caring what sort of picture I must be presenting. Her perfume was thick as fog around me. Her skin, only inches from my eyes, seemed the map of some new land.

"Kiss her," said Lautremont. "Not her lips, but the pulse at the base of her throat. Where The Dream was applied."

Su Su Win tilted her head back obligingly, arched her neck in a graceful catenary.

I let my lips graze her throat.

I entered The Dream.

* * * *

I was in New York. But I wasn't.

Not the New York I had known all my life.

Somewhere I had left Lautremont and Win behind. Physically. But not spiritually. Not mentally. Somehow, during that long night inside The Dream, I remained connected to the foreign couple, could feel them continually in the back of my mind, their dream souls bound up tightly with mine, with dozens of unknown others. Could almost read all their thoughts, which hovered tantilizingly on the edge of intelligibility...

I heard Su Su Win's high, mocking laughter, a sound I had never known in reality, heard Lautremont say, "You are barely on the fringes of it, Mister Holland..."

If this seems impossible, contradictory—then just add those qualities to the ones I earlier claimed distinguish a dream.

Powerlessness. Inevitability. Fusion. Heightening.

These were now the salient laws of my new existence.

I was walking, floating. I felt as if someone were using my limbs to take me on a tour of the transformed city.

The buildings shone from within, like gigantic fantasmal lanterns formed of multicolored glass. Their shapes had changed too. Taller, more exotic. Fantastic spires and cornices, delicate buttresses and turrets, organic excrescences. Baghdad, Babylon, the Kingdom of Prester John... I could tell where I was by the begemmed street signs, which remained readable. How unutterably strange—yet right—to find the Chrysler building transmogrified into this golden beehive, Grand Central the enormous effigy of a demonic head with Asian features, out of whose eyesockets poured traffic on aerial bridges... The whole city had been removed to another plane, beyond gates of horn...

The people. The people had been rendered *other* too. But they were separated from me by a barrier. I felt myself to exist on a different level from them, superior. They were only mindless moving mannequins, props for my enjoyment and amusement.

Except for one or two I glimpsed , both from a distance, both obviously alive in the same way I was. I felt an instant kinship with them, knew that they too were active participants in The Dream.

And oh, yes, the ghosts. There were only a few of them, all insubstantial Orientals, variously dressed, flitting high up among the buildings.

I wandered through the city for hours that seemed ages.

It was endlessly fascinating. I felt like a child again, the world a source of perpetual wonder. Even the noises seemed dreamlike. In particular, the constant, sourceless thunder I had noticed in the restaurant.

Gradually, as dawn began to break, the city began to lose its magic. I was emerging from The Dream. Stone by stone, the buildings reverted to their mundane forms. The solitary people I passed slowly doffed their dismal disguises, I lost my privileged stature, and we became mired in a common reality again.

Suddenly immensely weary, I leaned against a lamppost. The thunder had ceased. A cab appeared down the avenue, heading toward me. I hailed it.

When I got home, I collapsed in bed and slept for a day, dreamlessly.

When I returned to the office, forty-eight hours after I had left, I learned that Lautremont and Win had flown off again, leaving me with no way to learn what had happened.

I walked into Dozier's office, hoping for some answers.

When his eyes met mine, I felt a weak tugging, as if he were trying to reach me somehow. When the contact failed, he turned away with an obvious lack of interest, and I could learn nothing from him except for one thing.

We had been instructed to launch the campaign for Royaume du Rêve.

* * * *

Over the next few weeks, the publicity blitz for Royaume du Rêve achieved critical mass.

It was amazing how well we succeeded, and a testimony to how diligently everyone had worked, especially considering that such controversial tactics were entirely new to our firm. Pepper, Pym, Castonguay and their staffs had all been stimulated by the challenge and surpassed themselves.

The whole campaign was centered around Su Su Win. Her exotic allure was, in fact, no small part of its success.

We had subcontracted out the filming of the commercials and the photography for the print media to another firm. On the first day Su Su Win was scheduled to be filmed, I was present in their studio, waiting anxiously. She walked through the door accompanied not by Lautremont, but by another Asian man, acting as her interpreter.

I approached them. Once again, Win's perfume was muted, as if to wear it today would have been counterproductive.

"Where Is Lautremont?"

"He is not available now," said the new stoic Burmese face. "He is occupied elsewhere."

I left then, and did not return for any more photo sessions.

Entrancing as Win was, she was not who I needed to see right now, could not satisfy my burning questions.

Su Su Win might be the gateway to The Dream.

But Lautremont was the key.

And he was nowhere to be found.

I tried to calm myself, reconcile myself to his disappearance, with mixed success. Sometimes I was resigned to never seeing him again, to living out my life in all its old dullness. Other times I literally could not sit thinking he might never return, to grant me the privileged position he had half-promised. And all the while the memories of my night spent in The Dream were fading, and I felt robbed of something more precious than life.

It was during this period that Su Su Win began to appear everywhere, multiplied by the million eyes of the media, infiltrating society's etheric nervous system, fulfilling its lust for the new and novel, the dangerous and debauched. Her amber-bark-streaked face, her sinuous movements, her Asian glamour—all the elements of her attraction beckoned from giant billboards in Times Square, from double-page spreads in glossy fashion magazines, from cathode tubes and bus-stop posters.

Su Su Win:

—crouching naked like a tiger in a bamboo jungle, leaves artfully placed to conceal.

—lip-syncing to "In Dreams" while dancing on special-effects clouds.

—langorously asleep on pink sheets, her R-rated erotic dreams manifested in a cloud above her head.

—strutting down a gauntlet of male admirers, tapping each one with a crimson fingernail, whereupon the hapless suitor collapsed in sleep, leaving a trail of crumpled bodies behind her.

And in every shot, somewhere, was a bottle of the product, its pagoda shape by now as familiar an icon as the Empire State building. (I wondered, by the way, if the trivialization of that shape amounted to Buddhist blasphemy, and who we might have to answer to.)

Of course, Su Su Win never spoke, and this only added to her mystique. Speculation in the social columns and supermarket newspapers mounted as to her origins. Thai princess, Cambodian female ex-guerilla—no rumor was too bizarre not to gain some currency. Soon, she began to appear in non-product settings, photographed at parties and public functions, always accompanied by the Burmese man I had met that day.

Concurrent with all this—the very reason for the whole publicity machine—was the marketing of the perfume itself. Lautremont's system manifested itself, and proved quite efficient. Booths popped up in department stores and boutiques, selling the scent at reasonable prices almost anyone could afford. Slowly at first, then more and more rapidly, the perfume began to sell. Poison, Obsession, Opium—all fell by the wayside, displaced by our hot new product.

Soon I could smell Royaume du Rêve everywhere. In elevators and crowds, in restaurants and theaters, on buses and lingering in cabs. I tried to avoid inhaling the perfume deeply, but it was hard, particularly since all the women around the office chose to wear it. In truth, I did not feel the overwhelming compulsion to get within the sphere of their scent that I had known with Win.

No other woman wore the scent in quite the same way as she.

I was, I soon realized, imprinted on her, and her alone.

Such was the case with others too. The first woman they encountered wearing the perfume became for them the only one.

Everywhere I saw inseparable couples, bound by threads of alcohol-borne molecules. There were, however, no divisions into conquered and conqueror. Oh no, both men and women began to exhibit the symptoms I associated with entry into The Dream: an unfocused abstraction, a serene indifference out of which they frequently had to be jarred.

It could only be a matter of time, I was sure, before society began to fall apart. Or rather, began to be remade in the elusive image of The Dream.

Just as I was beginning to be convinced that I alone would be left out, Lautremont returned.

* * * *

"It was a simple plant," said the Frenchman, resuming his conversation almost as if no time had intervened since our supper that fateful night. He was dressed in his usual impeccable suit, with no signs of any of the travelling he surely had done.

Perched on the edge of my office chair, I restrained all my questions, sensing that to let him talk would be the quickest way to what I sought.

"Harvested, dried, powdered, used as a spice, it formed an integral part of the diet in the village of The Dream. Had done so for millennia. The substance was fed to me in broth while I was lost in fever.

"One taste had little consequence.

"A week's worth proved addictive.

"A steady diet brought permanent physiological changes."

Lautremont paused, lost in consideration. Or consultation. He resumed.

"Who knows what the tropics hold, what curious flora? They are still vast and unexplored by science. The Amazon might conceal a cure for cancer, the island of Madagascar a perfect euphoric. But surely, Mister Holland, nowhere is there anything stranger than that plant which fosters The Dream.

"The Dream, you see, is a shared vision, a consensual projection, if you will. A hallucination more vivid than life, which eventually displaces all other sensory input.

"The Dream is better than life, Mister Holland, for it is shaped. The Dream is more like art than life.

"I am one of the shapers. Only a lowly one, but a shaper nonetheless. It requires a special talent to shape The Dream, you see. Most people enter the dream as submissive participants. But you, I feel, could become one such as I. This is why I take the time with you, Mister Holland. Because, with so many new dwellers in the dream, we need all the shapers we can find."

I had just framed a question in my mind and started to open my mouth, when Lautremont anticipated me.

"Why now? This is what you wonder. Why, after centuries of complacency, does The Dream seek to expand? A good question, Mister Holland.

"The man before you seems ambitious, perhaps even a megalomaniac, with all this talk of shaping the world. Let me tell you that this is not the case. Or rather, if there is some truth to the accusation, it is because of what has happened to me. I am operating, Mister Holland, solely out of self-defense. I am fatigued by the world's assaults, and am determined to secure my own peace at last.

"When I awoke into The Dream in the village, the first thing I saw was the face of Su Su Win, who had been my nurse. I was instantly transfixed. We became lovers. I knew I would never leave this village again, that it held all I ever would need. I set out to devote myself to The Dream.

"Then one day, a representative of the government arrived. He announced, quite rationally, that a dam was being built on a tributary of the Irrawaddy. Our land would be flooded. We would all be relocated.

"The people of The Dream were helpless. Here, at last, was an invasion their patient assimilation could not master. They knew from experience that the plant they relied on to initiate a new generation into The Dream would not grow outside the conditions peculiar to their village. If they were relocated, the Dream would die out within a few decades.

"It was then that I roused myself, left my dreaming and journeyed to Rangoon with a sample of the herb. European initiative and ingenuity, you see, coming to the aid of Asian guile. A perfect complement.

"By the time of the resettlement, the composition of the active ingredients of the plant was known. Synthesis was possible. Effects were the same.

"We bypassed the official evacuation, which was to be a primitive affair of oxcarts and steamers. I had already converted some of the wealth of the village—you would be surprised at how many precious artifacts they had stored up, discarded over the centuries by would-be conquerors—and now I hired a fleet of helicopters.

"The inhabitants had never even seen such devices before. They made a huge impression, especially as they appeared to the eyes of The Dream. Their noise, I fear, has even filtered into The Dream, becoming a constant thunder I find rather annoying. As yet, I have not managed to erase it. It is one of the projects I envision you aiding me in.

"But I do not wish to bore you any longer with our travails. With my compatriots safely resettled, and the future of The Dream insured, I set out to make sure that we would never be threatened again.

"I believe you can piece the rest together. I chose a perfume as the agent for my scheme, rather than something such as a patent medicine or food, since cosmetics face less scrutiny from regulatory agencies."

Lautremont mimicked a stupa with his fingers with an air of supreme serenity. Any Gallic traits he might have once possessed seemed long subsumed in this Oriental-Fantasy.

His words continued to echo in my mind, their implications slowly taking shape, like one of those child's party favors, a gelatin capsule which, when dropped in water, dissolves to let loose a sponge animal that bloats to fill the glass.

"Well, Mister Holland, what is your answer to the proposal I made you over our dinner? And remember, you have hardly seen the true glories of The Dream from your one night's walk. Do you prefer fifty years of Europe to a cycle of Cathay? Or will you join us willingly?"

I thought I knew my answer, but I had one last question.

"You mentioned that you were only in the lower echelons of the shapers, those who direct The Dream. Who's above you? Who will I take directions from?"

"From me. You will not in all likelihood ever deal directly with them. At least not at first. They are—distant. Hard to communicate with."

"But who are they?"

"I hesitate to say, Mister Holland. You might find it one improbability too many. You will learn soon enough."

I must have looked angry. Lautremont broke his pagoda of fingers and waved one hand.

"Very well, Mister Holland. Those who are the true masters of The Dream were once mortal men like us, many centuries past. But you see, death does not release one from The Dream. If you are a shaper, your soul is truly bound up in it forever. And after death, you continue to inhabit The Dream. But you change, become even more proficient at your art, freed from all earthly distractions, a permanent part of your own creation. You saw these men and women, I know. You called them ghosts."

Lautremont finished. I turned in my chair to face the wall. I didn't want him to see the expression on my face. I tried hard to control my voice.

"I want it," I said. "Let me in."

* * * *

I spent the next week in bed with Su Su Win. I licked my future from her skin, as if she were a human blotting paper permeated with an illicit drug. She never spoke once, only made sounds of pleasure.

But by week's end, I had begun to understand her.

And now I have assumed my new duties, begun to glimpse the shining patterns, the ultimate art of The Dream. It's demanding, weaving more and more newcomers each day into the warp, but I keep at it, getting better, I think. Neither is it all work. Many days I simply wander the streets of this city, now almost completely colonized by The Dream, marvelling at its faerie pavilions and palaces, occasionally spotting the rare uninitiated inhabitant by his dingy mundane appearance, whereupon I lead him to those who will help him join us. And when I falter, Lautremont is there to steady me.

Together, we've almost muted the thunder.

I have written many pieces in the thousand-word range, and foresee doing many more in the future. But I doubt I shall ever again write a story that
is precisely one-hundred-words long, as was my remit when I composed
this.

Spoiler: The notion of MTV as a brain-washing medium featuring in-
sidious subliminal trickery is very much 1988. Nowadays, we all know, that
channel is merely the repository of glitz and trash.

TRIPLETS

Thomas, Toby, Tyler: triplets. Thirty-three years old, they had trod separate ways for ten years.

Thomas worked for the government.

Toby employed with a foreign concern.

Tyler in the private sector.

One day, they all found themselves on the same train.

"Thomas," said Toby, "remember our childhood game?"

"Using three-word acronyms to tell a story?"

"Yes," said Toby. He pulled a gun. Tyler watched quietly. Toby shot Thomas dead.

Taking some top-secret brain-washing plans from Thomas, Toby turned, said, "CIA. KGB. DOA." He aimed at Tyler.

Tyler fired first. He took the papers from his dead brother.

"MTV," said he.

Isaac Asimov often told the story of how he wrote a tale about aliens who lived at the top of Mount Everest and prevented any humans from reaching the summit. That story had the misfortune to appear in print the same month Sir Edmund Hillary reached the top of that peak.

Likewise, my story below saw print just as *Who Framed Roger Rabbit* debuted in thousands of theaters around the planet. I had never heard of the original novel or its author prior to that fine film. But now, instantly, my story looked like a total copycat production, rendered minor by comparison to Gary Wolfe's masterpiece. Of course, it was parallel evolution, not theft, but try telling that to anyone then. I hope in the decades that have passed, my claim seems more plausible.

Science Fiction Eye was the top critical zine of the immediate post-cyberpunk era, and published only one fiction issue. I felt proud to be a part of its excellence for all but the first installment.

THE JONES CONTINUUM

Carr tunes the snap generator with exquisite precision. He feels almost like an integrated component of his creation. His nimble fingers nudge the slide controls on the crackle-finished main console up and down, like the delicate digits of a record producer seeking to obtain the proper sound mix for some merry pop melody. Ruby LED displays flicker through an infinity of interdimensional coordinates, before finally being locked onto the proper set. Seemingly relieved, Carr unbends from over the large bank of controls.

Carr and his console occupy the middle of a converted soundstage somewhere in California. This commandeered facility, chosen for reasons of security and subterfuge, is large and desolate-feeling, housing the ghosts of actors, directors and cameramen, and their fictional realities. Carr is suddenly struck by how fitting this setting is, in terms of their attempt to breach an alternate worldline. The huge space traps and alters sound oddly. Carr and his busy crew fill only a small portion of the high-ceilinged building. Cables snake across the cement floor from console to portal to mainframes. Big kliegs on telescoping shafts with tripod feet light the scene harshly. Shadows lurk beyond the perimeter thus defined.

Men and women—dressed like Carr in sexless antiseptic white "bunny-suits," complete with closefitting hoods—monitor various instruments and convey hushed instructions from one station to another through headphones and pin-mikes. Lurking back in the shadows are a cluster of officers wearing the various uniforms of the U.S. Armed Forces. They are not half so creepily impressive, however, as the assorted plain-clothes observers, who Carr knows represent more secretive and powerful branches of the government.

Carr wipes cold sweat from his brow. So much is riding on this one mission. His reputation, years of hard work, further grants… He'd prefer to be going through the portal himself, but that's impossible. As the inventor of the snap, he's too valuable to risk. No, the success of all his efforts ride on the performance of the select team standing nervously by the portal. These four men and one woman have been selected and certified by ranks of government experts. If anyone can deal with the unknown terrain that lies beyond the portal and establish a beachhead for democracy, it is these five cross-dimensional explorers.

Leaving his console, Carr walks to the group.

Jones is their leader. Solid, responsible Jones, his looks as All-American as his name. Carr finds it odd, how these types always seem to spring up, ready to lead, when the nation needs them. Glenn, Armstrong, and now Jones, another from the same mold. He's a big man, made to appear even taller and bulkier by his outfit. Like the rest of his party, Jones wears, over his desert-camouflage fatigues, segmented plates of Kevlar body-armor, bound to a loose aramid mesh substrate that will allow ventilation in the hot environment they expect to encounter. Combat boots add an inch to Jones' height. Weapons and supplies are strapped across his back and chest, hang from hips and waist. Fragmentation grenades, food concentrates, a canteen, medipak, the latest rapid-fire rifle with laser-sights…

Carr lays a hand on Jones' armored shoulder. "Well, Charles, I guess this is it. There's not much I can say now, except 'Good luck.'"

Jones' voice is firm. "We couldn't ask for a better base team—or mission head, Phil. Just make sure you have the portal open at the right time, and we'll do the rest."

Carr knows he wanted to say a hundred things at this point, but has forgotten every last one in the excitement. All he can remember is a final admonition.

"Remember, we're fairly certain that the physical laws in this universe are different from ours. All the theoretical work indicates there will be a deviation from our own continuum. Nothing major at the quantum level—Planck's Constant and all that crap should be identical to ours down to a few dozen decimal places. But those accumulated small discrepancies may amount to macroscopic differences which we can't predict. You'll have to move cautiously. All we know is that life is possible there. You know all our test animals returned unharmed…"

Skinny Kent interrupts, his voice nervous. "What about those weird results with the higher animals?"

"Right, Tom, right. That monkey and cat did return with initial behavior abnormalities, but those cleared up soon after. We now suspect that most of their atypical behavior derived from sharing the same cage, albeit with a glass divider. However, just to be sure, you've got your various psychotropic stabilizers. Take them as Doctor Benson advises."

Carr nods to the lone female expedition member. Doctor Benson smiles weakly, her hands fidgeting with the plastic catch that holds her belt of grenades. She squeezes the twin prongs to release the catch, clicks it shut, releases it, clicks it shut, releases—

Suddenly realizing that the sound is mimicking the large snap that will signal their departure, Benson forces her hands to hang laxly by her side.

They are all uneasy, Carr included, and Jones, in his leaderly manner, takes over.

"Let's do it, then."

Carr shakes hands all around. "Charles, Tom, Mike, Heather, George. Our hearts go with you. Oh, yes—the President sends his best wishes too. Well see you back here at oh-nine-hundred on the dot."

Carr heads back to his station. When he turns to face the portal, he sees that the explorers have mounted the steps within the rings. The portal resembles a truncated cornucopia: a series of massive contiguous rings, each one smaller than the one before it. The first and biggest ring stands directly on the floor, while the others are supported on graduated cradles. The expeditionary team is standing single-file within the metal harvest-horn.

Removing a key from his pocket, Carr unlocks a cover to reveal a button. His finger hesitates briefly above it, then plunges down, initiating the launch sequence.

Driven now by an elaborate program running on the Cray-2 CPU'S, the whole process is automatic. The whine of the snap generator increases in frequency and strength. It's almost more than Carr can stand... At last, mercifully, the noise terminates in the eponymous crack—

The annular stage is empty.

Carr looks at his watch.

Two hours till retrieval.

* * * *

The team materializes on a dusty, pebblestrewn, arid patch of desert, standing in a line. The three inner members—Benson, Kent and Blount—immediately drop into crouches. Each has his or her weapon aimed at a different point of the compass, covering a pre-assigned 120-degrees of fire. Meanwhile, Montreaux at the rear and Jones up front whip microalloyed vanadium-steel poles and hammers from their belt-clips and begin to pound them into the ground. Explosive charges prove unnecessary to split the friable earth, and the poles—which contain homing transmitters and radio-activated flares—are securely in position, marking the locus where the crew must await the re-opening of the transplenary portal.

Only when this crucial task is accomplished does the team relax somewhat. The crouching guards stand erect. At a hand-signal from Jones, they sling their rifles over their shoulders. Warily, the men and woman attempt to absorb their surroundings, here in a dimension completely removed from the entire universe of their birth.

They appear to be standing atop a large flat mesa. Beyond this table-top stretches a landscape of canyons and arroyos, wind-carved buttes and pinnacles, titanic blocks and spires, precarious arches and natural ziggurats, red, yellow, sandy beige, brown and gray. The quiet vista is unbroken by tokens of civilization from horizon to horizon. The air is dry, the sun vibrant. Of animal life there is no sign.

"We might have popped out in a more convenient place," says Jones. "We certainly won't be able to get down off this mesa and back up in two hours. It seems our exploration will be limited to these few acres."

"That's true," says Montreaux. "Still, we're protected up here."

Kent says, "Looks kinda like Arizona."

"Yeah," says Blount, "'round Coconino County,"

"Why is that name so familiar?" asks Benson.

Blount laughs. "You're showing your age, kiddo. That's where—"

"Look!" shouts Montreaux suddenly.

The others follow his outstretched finger skyward with their eyes.

A daytime moon hangs low. It is shaped like a ball of Gouda cheese with an irregular slice taken out of its dorsal side. It is as yellow as a butternut squash.

Everyone is shocked into silence, until Jones speaks.

"It must be an illusion, a trick of the atmosphere. The refractive index of the air, perhaps. No natural astronomical object could be shaped like that. Remember, Carr warned us to be alert for small differences in the physical makeup of this place."

"Whatever the explanation is," says Kent irritably, "I don't like it. Either we can't trust our senses, or the natural laws here are screwed up bad. Either way, we could be in for trouble."

"Just get a grip on yourself, Tom," admonishes Jones. "We'll be fine as long as we step carefully and hang together. Okay, let's check out the periphery of this mesa, and see if there's not an easy way down."

Adopting a patrol formation, the five move off, Jones is pointman, Blount and Benson are in second rank, and Kent and Montreaux bring up the rear.

As they move toward the edge, Jones wonders briefly if he should rearrange the pairings. Kent—always a touchy type—has had spats in the past with Montreaux, and his nervousness might trigger more today. The team cannot afford any such arguments or dissension now. However, Blount and Benson are an efficient duo. The pudgy Blount seems to have a crush on the aloof but tolerant Benson, which makes him extremely solicitous of her welfare. It would be a shame to split them up. No, to shuffle things around might be worse, cause trepidation and nerves, decides Jones. Best to leave the assignments as they are—for now.

Reaching the eastern edge of the mesa, the five halt and peer cautiously down.

The ground is hundreds and hundreds of feet below. A thin thread of blue defines a snaky river. The sides of the formation are absolutely vertical. Here, at least, there are no obvious means of safe descent.

"Okay," says Jones. "We'll circle south and inspect the whole perimeter. We might have better luck elsewhere."

They don't. A half-hour's hike around the circumference reveals that they are efficiently bottled up on this desolate mesa, with only a few large cacti for company.

Jones assembles his squad at the original spot of arrival. During the recon, the two pairs of teammates have been conversing quietly between themselves, so that Jones could not overhear. Now everyone falls silent. Overhead, the moon has impossibly crossed a full fifty degrees of the heavens in the short time they have been here.

"Well," begins Jones, "it seems we'll have a boring report to make, but sometimes that's for the best—"

"Fuck you!" shouts Kent.

Jones goggles at Kent until he realizes that Kent's expletive is directed at his partner, Montreaux, and not at Jones himself.

"Tom, get ahold of yourself. What's wrong?"

"It's this bastard Montreaux. He's been bugging me, saying stupid things, trying to burn my ass."

"George, is that true?"

"No way. It's Tom who's the instigator. He's been spouting crazy talk about how we're all gonna die here. I've been trying to calm him down."

Jones tries to ascertain which man is telling the truth, and fails. He looks for help to Doctor Benson, his second-in-command. Jones is grateful when Benson speaks up.

"All right, listen up now. This must be the onset of the psychic abnormalities the test-animals exhibited. Everyone break out their mood-stabilizers."

Following Benson's example, the four men soon hold their individually tailored neurotropin pills in one hand, unstoppered canteens in the other. At a nod from Benson, all five swallow the doses down, Kent grudgingly.

"There," says Jones gratefully, "that should do it. Now, let's split up in pairs—I'll remain here by the drop—and take some sensor readings and samples. See if you can find any traces of animal life, however simple."

His subordinates obey his orders. Jones watches them disperse, then falls to his own sampling of the ground around the poles.

A yell brings Jones out of his concentration.

Montreaux is flat on his back, Kent astride him and choking him. The really odd thing about this scene—the sight that Jones cannot initially accept—is that Montreaux's tongue extends a full twelve inches out of his mouth and is vibrating like a New Year's Eve favor, while his eyes have popped out on stalks. In addition, the victim's face is turning an unnatural royal blue.

Jones rushes toward the pair, sensing Blount and Benson close behind him.

Wrestling Kent off Montreaux, Jones drags the insane assailant to his feet and begins to shake him. When Kent seems a trifle more in possession of himself, Jones releases him.

"What the hell is the explanation for this, Tom? Why would you want to hurt George?"

Kent passes a hand across his brow. "I—I don't know. It seems I just can't stand the sight of him."

Blount and Benson have helped Montreaux up. As inexplicably as it altered, his face has returned to normal, and he seems okay. Jones moves over to examine him.

No one notices that Kent has a grenade in his hand until the pin is pulled.

Jones has time only to shout: "Down, down—!" before it lands in their midst and explodes with a roar.

The smoke clears to reveal four standing figures, centered in a carbonized sunburst of cracked ground. Their white Kevlar armor is streaked with long black trailers of soot. Their hair stands up on end. Otherwise, they are unharmed.

"I can't believe it," says Jones with utter bewilderment. "We should all be in little piece…" Suddenly, their survival a given, an insupportable rage overtakes him, at the sight of the unrepentant Kent.

Without conscious decision, Jones makes a fist of his right hand. Gripping this fist with his left hand, he begins to screw his arm into a rubbery coil, armor and all, until it's entirely compressed at shoulder level. He advances on Kent, who quivers but does not flee. Once in proximity, Jones unleashes his fist.

The mighty blow catches Kent on the jaw. Little multicolored five-pointed stars spray out from the site of impact. Kent's head rockets back, stretching his elastic neck a full four feet. There is a BOI-OI-OI-NG noise. Kent's body finally catches up with his head. His feet leave the ground and he arrows twenty yards through the air. He lands in the arms of a large cactus. The arms close on him, spikes piercing through his armor. Kent screams: "Yeeee-oooow!" He shoots straight up into the air, reverses at the zenith, so that his head is pointing down, then plummets. When he hits, he piledrives into the mesa up to his waist.

Jones turns in astonishment to the other three. He barely notices that all effects of the blast have disappeared from their persons, as from his own. "I didn't mean to— I didn't know I could—"

No one pays any attention to their leader. Blount is solicitously inquiring after Benson's postgrenade condition. Montreaux, meanwhile, is laughing at Kent's fate, doubled up in hysterics, slapping his knees. He falls to the ground, kicking his legs in the air. He rolls onto his belly, pounding the dust, wetting it with his tears, until there is a large puddle around him. He does not notice Kent's return.

Kent is dirty and full of cactus spikes, but otherwise unhurt. He unshoulders his rifle. Montreaux seems to sense his presence. He ceases laughing, looks up, makes an instant transition to his feet and starts running. Kent lets him go, flicking his rifle to single-shot action. He draws a careful bead on Montreaux's fleeing ass and squeezes off a round. The bullet hits with a noise like a bell being rung in a sideshow shooting gallery. Montreaux jumps straight up—"Yikes!"—then resumes running. Kent begins to chase him around the mesa, stopping now and then take another potshot at his tail.

Jones does not attempt to stop them. He's scared of what he might do to them. Instead, he turns to Benson and Blount. At least they've stayed sane...

Blount is holding Benson's hand. He has somehow progressed from inquiries about the effect of the grenade on her health to fervent protestations of love, made in an atrocious Maurice Chevalier accent.

"Mah leetle pee-geon, you feel mah heart wiz love. Mwa-mwa-mwa-mwa-mwa."

This last noise accompanies Blount's kisses, which he is planting hotly up and down Benson's arm.

"Stop that! Stop that, you—you skunk! Quit it!"

Blount does not heed Benson's wishes. He grabs her waist, tips her backwards so that she is balanced on one foot, the other leg extending out in the air, and begins kissing her neck.

Benson oozes out of Blount's grip as if oiled.

His arms remain in a circle, and he continues to kiss the air for several seconds after she is gone. When he notices her absence, he straightens up.

Benson has her rifle aimed at Blount's midsection. Jones notes with despair that it's on automatic.

"Don't take one step closer—" warns Benson.

"Surely you do not mean zat, ma cherie," says Blount, and takes the fatal step.

Benson lets loose with about two hundred rounds of large-caliber ammo. Jones closes his eyes.

He opens them to see Blount pierced with holes. He is solid through and through, like a potato.

"You have caused a thirst een mah stomach, mah leetle lovebug," says Blount. He drinks from his canteen. Water spouts from all his bullet-holes like a fountain. "Now zat I am refreshed, let us resume our battle of love."

Benson tosses her rifle into the air in fright and runs off. Blount drops his knuckles to the ground and pogoes unconcernedly off on all fours after her, bouncing impossibly high into the air with each "step," stopping once to sniff a cactusflower in mid-pursuit.

Jones is left standing alone. From across the mesa drift sounds of gunfire and explosions, shrieks and shouts of triumph, interspersed with weird sound-effects: slidewhistles, crashes, echoes, reverb, racheting...

Dazed and broken-spirited, Jones trudges off.

He finds himself at the mesa's edge. He sits despondently down, legs dangling over the abyss. Reflexively, he checks his chronometer. Less than an hour until pickup. He supposes he should be returning to the rendezvous-point, but hasn't the heart. The mission is a complete failure, a total bust. How can he face Carr and the others and report what he has allowed to occur? Jones grips his head dejectedly and shakes it. There is a rattle as of marbles in a can from inside his cranium.

"BEEP-BEEP!"

Jones is hanging in midair, having made an instantaneous transition from being seated on the cliff-edge to hovering above the abyss. He has just enough time to see an impossible creature standing on the mesa behind him, fluttering its impudent tongue at him, before he realizes that there is nothing below him. He pokes the air tentatively. Yup, that's plain old air, all right... He tries to run in the air, his legs windmilling, his arms outstretched, but gets nowhere. Then he plummets.

The fall is long.

Jones has plenty of time to anticipate the impact.

When it happens, it knocks him senseless for a while. When he comes to, he realizes he's still alive, lying at the bottom of a Jones-shaped hole. So, there is no escape from humiliation and failure here, even in death...

Jones climbs wearily out. The inviting river lies a few feet away. He walks to it for a drink. Bending down, he cups his hand and scoops up some water.

A grinning shark zips out and swallows Jones' head and neck. Jones stands up, bearing the shark aloft like a hat, its tail flapping. He gropes around until his hand lands on a petrified stick. With the stick, he begins belaboring the shark with meaty thumps, until it finally releases him and flops back indignantly into the river.

"Yipe-yipe-yipe-yipe!"

This incident has convinced Jones that he must get back to his own universe. His despair has been replaced by renewed ambition. But the portal-locus is far above. He cranes his neck backwards, examining the vertiginous wall. There is nothing for it but to climb.

Jones, utilizing cracks and crevices, begins the ascent.

Such a climb should be impossible. But it is not. It takes nearly half an hour, though.

As he lays his first hand over the rim, he hears a cracking and crumbling. He realizes with a sinking feeling that this portion of the rim is giving way. A mass of rock detaches, carrying Jones back down with it.

Jones lands first. This time he unexplainably does not make a hole. A shadow grows around him. Jones removes his Emergency Umbrella from his belt and opens it over his head. The giant boulder lands on him.

He emerges from beneath it, flat as a pancake, hairy on top, with feet protruding on the bottom. With a SPROING he accordions out, resuming his normal shape.

Wearily, he makes the climb again.

This time he gains the surface of the mesa successfully.

It is almost pickup time.

Jones rushes back to the markers.

He has only one minute to spare. He wishes he could somehow re-cover the others, but there is no sign of their whereabouts, and no time to search. A better-equipped force can return for them later. Jones stands hopefully between the poles.

Idly, impulsively, using the tip of his boot, Jones draws two parallel lines in the thin dirt, then connects them with crossbars.

The sketch immediately becomes twin gleaming iron rails lying on tarry sleepers. An enormous express train materializes a few yards away, travelling one hundred miles an hour straight for Jones. The impossible creature is driving it. Before Jones can move, he finds himself riding the cowcatcher across the mesa. When the train reaches the edge it continues onward across a heretofore-nonexistent bridge.

Jones' wails doppler off into the distance.

* * * *

Back at Mission Control, nerves are tightened to the breaking point. A large clock sweeps out the seconds till retrieval with a thin red hand. Carr wishes there were some switch, however symbolic, which he could throw, so he'd feel as if he were instrumental in bringing the team home. But the whole return process, like the dispatch, is under the control of the machines.

Carr checks his watch, then the clock, then his watch again. The other members of the Mission Control stand at their stations, watching their readouts, alert for any significant fluctuations in the fabric of the dimensions. The assembled members of the intelligence community exchange glances only they can interpret.

The whine of the generator is rising, rising—

Zero hour arrives.

No one is breathing.

The generators unleash their snap, like the cracking of some hunter-god's whip.

No explorers reappear. The stage is empty.

Initially, everyone is stunned by the failure of the explorers to return. There is absolute silence for a time. Then, two things happen simultaneously.

Carr notes that although the generator has been automatically shut down, the connection between the dimensions remains open. At the far end of the cornucopia is a tiny circle, bright with sun and sand and a small crazy Herriman moon.

At the same time, the technicians begin nervously calling out their reports.

"Planck's Constant dropping!"

"Boltzmann's Constant increasing—up to one point three eight zero four two—"

"Avogadro's Constant falling. Down by point zero zero zero zero zero zero three!"

A phone rings; someone answers. She listens, then drops the receiver, white-faced.

"That was Cerro Tololo Observatory. Hubble's Constant is changing!"

A hot wind blows out of the ring, smiting Carr. He grows dizzy, puts a hand to his head. It seems he can see the distant single headlight of a train approaching out of the tiny circle, hear its mad whistle. A set of railroad tracks suddenly snaps into being, leading out of the concentric rings of the annulus, across the floor, where they sever cables and pipes, and through the wall of the soundstage, which has opened in a train-shaped hole.

Carr feels at last that he has to speak, all the enormous responsibility devolving on him. Everyone's shocked faces are imploring him. But what to say? What words can possibly sum up the utter finality of the disastrous mission?

At last it comes to him, the phrase tripping over his unwieldy tongue: "Tha—tha—that's all, folks!"

If I had to pick one perfect rock 'n' roll song out of the sixty years worth of that artform, I would hesitate over the Beatles and Neil Young, the Hollies and Joni Mitchell, the Pixies and Talking Heads, and then inevitably settle on "Waterloo Sunset." My regret with this tributary story is that it does not caputre the ineffable sweetness of that Kinks song, but focuses on the melancholy vibes. I'd like to try again some day, if only just to confuse any bibliographers, who would have to annotate two stories with the exact same title.

I also seem to recall that part of the inspiration for this story was the opening scene in Philip Jose Farmer's first Riverworld novel.

WATERLOO SUNSET

"Where the christ are we going? I mean, just tell me that, and I'll shut up, okay?"

Terry was turned in his seat to face Julie. His outburst had caused her to start crying silently. Her blue eyes welled with tears, her blonde pageboy-cut hair flew as she violently shook her head, her breasts beneath her short-sleeved flowered blouse heaved.

Terry turned away, feeling sick. He rested his head on the steering wheel of his green '65 Mustang, the lavish gift his parents had given him upon his college graduation last month. He hadn't meant to make Julie cry. They were in too deep a fix now to start hating each other. He supposed he had been talking wildly, nonstop, and it must have gotten on her nerves. But she shouldn't have told him to shut up. That was not the attitude to take. Being quiet was not going to cause the mess they were in to disappear.

Oh no, indeed, not a situation as bizarre as this one.

The engine of the Mustang convertible was off, its gears in neutral, yet the vehicle moved along at roughly four miles an hour. Its impetus came from the crush of people surrounding it, pressing against its fenders and sides, carrying it along with their blind forward surge.

The people extended in all directions, as far as Terry had been able to see by standing up in his seat. Their faces were stony, unresponsive to his attempts at communication. Although he could have touched the closest ones, he refrained, feeling a deep repugnance for their zombielike state.

Terry and Julie had been travelling this way for such a long, if indeterminate time that they had come to ignore the human sea, speaking and acting as if alone in the open car.

The landscape they traversed was desolate, conducive only to despair. The patches of ground Terry could discern beneath the feet of the mob appeared to be a gritty, filthy ice. Overhead, the sky was a sunless grey pall seemingly composed of soot and ash. It darkened and lightened in what seemed to be a twenty-foot-hour day. Regardless of the natural cycle, the vast, single-minded mass of people moved continuously, unresting.

Neither did Terry or Julie feel the need for sleep. They existed in some sort of timeless suspension of their natural function. They did not grow hungry or fatigued, and despite the frigid environment, felt no cold. Yet they could not say they were warm either.

"Terry." Julie's subsiding sniffles indicated she was trying to reassert control, master her quavery voice. "Terry, I'm sorry."

Terry raised his head from the steering wheel. Its knurled plastic had left an are of dents in his brow. He regarded Julie sadly, all his anger gone.

"It's all right, Jule. It's just, you know—what else are we gonna do but talk?"

Julie rubbed her reddened eyes and essayed a brave smile that quickly shattered.

"Oh, Terry, I'm so scared. I think I know where we are. We've d— died and gone to Hell." She began to wail this time, interspersed with a broken sentence that Terry interpreted as remorse for their ever having slept together before marriage.

"Goddamn it, Julie," Terry shouted. "We're not dead yet! We can't be! We have too much to do yet, too much life to live. I'm joining the Peace Corps, remember. And you're gonna wait for me and work for your dad, and then we're gonna get married." Terry switched from emotion to logic. "Listen, do you remember dying?"

Julie managed to shake her head no.

"Of course not, 'cause we didn't. If this was Hell or Limbo or something, you'd have to remember your whole life up until dying, just so you could be sorry for it. Doesn't that make sense?"

Julie nodded yes.

"All right, then. That's settled. We're not dead. Which means we have to do something, even if it's only find out where we're heading."

Julie had composed herself, and Terry felt proud that he had asserted himself and provided a rationale—however tenuous—for their existence.

On a roll, he continued. "Maybe we've been kidnapped by aliens, and this is their way of testing our initiative. Stranger things have happened, Julie. Or maybe we're really at one of those wild parties Ken throws, and some hippie put acid in the punch. Could happen, couldn't it? Okay, then. Whether this is a bad trip or whatever, let's get in control of the situation. We've drifted long enough. Buckle your seatbelt, Jule. We're taking off."

Julie did as he said, asking, "But where, Terry?"

"To the head of this parade," he said, and turned the key in the ignition. The Mustang's motor coughed once, then caught with a full-throated growl.

"We're going left," Terry said arbitrarily, but with a false confidence. "We'll get out of this pack of no-minds, and then race ahead of them."

"Whatever you say, Terry." Julie's smile stayed a little longer this time, and she even felt good enough to retouch her mascara in the rearview mirror, using the tube from her purse.

Terry shifted into drive and cut the wheel slowly to the left. The people against that fender slowed mindlessly down, allowing the car to gradually turn until it was perpendicular to the flow, which immediately began to exert a noticeable pressure. Terry inched the car forward, careful not to hurt the automatons, just in case the hidden Ethicals were judging his compassion. Terry noted with satisfaction that his fuel gauge was on full. That always gave him such a good feeling that he began to hum tunelessly.

Like an icecutter cleaving through 'berg-filled water, the car made its slow progress across the human traffic.

Terry studied the people who filled the frosty plain beneath the dead sky. They look just like regular folks, he thought. American faces and clothes that wouldn't appear out of place in his hometown. But their familiar looks only made their grim concentration all the more eerie.

"Hey, Julie, let's see if we can get some music."

Terry switched the dashboard radio on, not really expecting music, just to cheer Julie up with timeworn rituals. Instead, to his amazement, a sweet melody filled the gelid air.

"Whadda ya know? It's our song, Julie. *Waterloo Sunset*."

The near-falsetto of Ray Davies of the Kinks carried the tale of the love of Terry and Julie mellifluously across the wastes. When they had first heard the song, they had been startled by the fact that its characters bore their names. Then they had come to adopt it wholeheartedly as their anthem.

Now, though, Terry noticed the underlying sadness to the tale. Why had he never heard Davies sing, "Chilly, chilly is the city outside my window? "

Terry snapped the radio off with an angry twist.

"Why'd you do that, Terry?" Julie petulantly asked. "I was feeling happy for the first time in a long while."

Terry didn't reply. Instead, he gave the car a little more gas, nudging the individuals who clogged the way with a little more violence.

After a timeless interval, Julie, sitting recklessly atop the back of her seat, shouted, "I see the fringes, Terry! We're almost out!"

The remaining distance seemed to take as long to cover as all the previous stretch.

Finally, they broke through. Terry spun the car parallel to the flood, braked to a stop and shut off the engine. The gas gauge still read full.

To the right, for limitless miles, the horde of trudging people stretched, silent, determined, incessant, laboring ever onward under the ashen sky.

"Hot damn!" Terry yelled, hitting the unpadded dash. "We did it, Julie." He pulled her to him and kissed her deeply. When they broke apart, Terry twisted the key savagely in the ignition, floored the accelerator without concern for his tires for once, and let out a war-whoop as they shot forward.

"Now we'll learn what's at the end of this little outing," he said. Julie smiled and gripped his right bicep with both hands.

Their course was parallel with the edge of the ranks of people. Maneuvering over the obstacle-free icy sheet was easy, and Terry had plenty of time to study the faces on his right. Juiie supplemented his observations with things he missed.

After what the odometer claimed was three hundred miles, they noticed two things.

The first was a hulking range of mountains low on the horizon, lit from behind by a subdued glow. The second was that the moving clot of humanity was now composed almost entirely of Chinese. Their Oriental faces and grey-jacketed forms were recognizable to Terry and Julie from occasional newscasts of them, usually in some connection with the war in Vietnam.

"How many Chinese are there in the world, Julie?"

"Almost a billion, I think."

After another hundred miles, Terry said, "I guess they're all here, Jule."

"I guess so," she replied.

Now they were almost upon the mountains, which lowered ahead and above them like sullen gods. Terry gazed intently at the outline of one peak in particular, way off to their right, on the far side of the crowd, which was narrowing due to the funnel nature of the terrain.

"You know, Julie, if it wasn't for all these glaciers, I'd swear that's Pike's Peak."

Julie followed his outstretched finger with her eyes. "It could be," she said hesitantly, as if it hurt her to admit it.

The mass of Chinese had begun to ascend the mountains through a narrow pass which they filled completely, leaving no room for the car. Terry stopped perforce at the mouth of the canyon.

"What now?" Julie said. "Should we wedge ourselves back in with them?"

Terry thought a moment. "No—I don't think so. We might hit an impassable spot, and we'd never be able to back out against their momentum. We'll just have to find another way over."

Not wanting to cut across the river of souls again, he turned left—south, if that really was Pike's Peak—and began casting about for another pass through the Rockies.

Beyond the mountains, the sky fulminated in one spot like a livid bruise against the leaden heavens.

Some time later, they came upon a likely pass. Its walls exhibited the drill marks of highway construction, although its floor was the same speckled ice as the rest of the world.

They ascended at top speed, recklessly impatient.

As they crested a final ridge, they saw far below them the straggling line of people and their ultimate goal, the source of the infernal light.

Terry stopped the car.

At the end of the line towered a massive atomic fireball, like a cancerous red-orange mushroom, or the spinal stem and brain of a malignant entity. Although it roiled and churned internally, it neither grew nor climaxed and faded. Instead, it remained in eternal ripeness, and seemed to be moving across the icy plain non-destructively, like a film-loop of itself, pulling the tail of people along with it.

"Jesus Christ," Terry said softly.

"What does it mean?" Julie asked.

"I don't know. I just can't figure it out." He laughed harshly, a bark of pain. "It's our Waterloo. Our Waterloo Sunset."

They watched the procession for over an hour, holding each other, but it never changed.

At last Julie said, "What now?"

Terry didn't know. He hugged Julie tighter, feeling her breasts against him. Suddenly he noticed the floor-mounted shift keeping them apart. Wordlessly, he half pushed, half dragged her into the back seat. When she realized what he wanted, she complied eagerly.

With their jeans around their ankles, their car open to the bruised sky above, they made love. Whatever they were, whatever was happening, they could still do that.

After they were finished, Terry said, "We're going back."

"Back?"

"If we can't make any sense of where we were going, maybe we can understand where we came from."

Terry got the car heading east, and they descended the range.

They picked up the line of people at the original pass. Then they began to follow it backwards.

By rough guesswork involving the speed of the people on foot, how long they themselves had been travelling independently, and the odometer readings, Terry could tell when they were abreast of their home position in the line. The passive American faces of the men and women and children failed to reassure them.

Below this point, everything was new.

It didn't take long for Terry and Julie to realize that they were, in a way, travelling in time.

The composition of the line changed every hundred miles or so, while they were still among their contemporaries, and even more frequently the further they went, as if the nations of people grew smaller, and more different types could be compressed in the same space.

The first change they really noticed was the Victorians. They marked a clear line between the people from the modern era and those from the previous century. The men in frock coats and top hats, the women in corsets and full skirts looked just like the illustrations in Terry's college history text.

After the Victorians, the changes grew overwhelming, too much to absorb.

There were Indians, Old World and New; Africans, Arabs, Japanese and Polynesians, all from the nineteenth century. There were miles and miles of Imperial Chinese, Tartars and Mongols too. Then the diversity really increased, as they left the relatively homogenized periods behind.

There were Spaniards from Isabella's time, Renaissance Italians and royalty from France, all recognizable by their unique costumes. Citizens of the Holy Roman Empire and medieval Englishmen trooped side by side. Further on, Goths and Vandals marched dispiritedly. Then came Classical Romans and Greeks, Dynastic Egyptians and the citizens of Ur. Millennia flashed by with the miles.

Past the cavalcade of history, Terry drove like a demon, intent only on reaching the unknown beginning. Only when Julie gasped did he look up.

They had left homo sapiens behind. Terry had missed the Neanderthals. Now they were among the distant ancestors, Australopithecus and their ilk.

The hominids had never swarmed over the earth like *homo sapiens*. But there were four million years' worth of them.

* * * *

It took hours and hours to get by them.

Following the upright hominids was a scampering mass of small, lemur-like animals. They were so close to the ground that they did not obscure the building in the twilit distance.

Terry willed the Mustang to further speed.

At last they came to a stop beside the building. Terry could see that it was the top floor of a multistory structure protruding above the ice. As they eyed it, a single lemuroid scuttled from a glassless window and scurried after the rest.

Terry swung open his door, noting with a fraction of his mind that the fuel gauge still pointed to F. He didn't even wait for Julie, who had to hurry after him.

Together, they ducked through the twisted frame.

A portion of the roof was missing, allowing some of the dim light to filter down. When their eyes adapted, they could make out a recumbent figure lying in the roofed corner of the debris-filled room. They advanced.

The man was clad in a dozen layers of rags and fur, against the cold. His eyes were glued shut with mucus, his bearded face rimmed with frost. Yet he still breathed, imperfectly and irregularly.

Obviously he had been living—surviving—here for some time. Empty cans of food were strewn around him. A wooden chair lay half-consumed by fire amid dead coals.

As Terry and Julie watched, a wisp of white ectoplasm formed above the man's midriff. It billowed and contorted, eventually assuming the form of a lemuroid, its left hind foot still connected to the man. It pulled and struggled, eventually popping free. Then it scuttled off, to rejoin the rest.

"He's the last," Terry said without prelude. "Don't ask me how I know, but I do. He's the last living person."

Julie took it calmly. "Then we're—"

"Just extrusions of him, like that little weasel. The whole fucking thing is just his hallucinations."

"More than that," Julie said.

Her words touched a chord in Terry. "The racial memory, the collective unconsciousness. We learned about it in school. It all focused down into him, like water collecting behind a dam. Then he dumped it, like a flood."

"But why us, Terry? Why are we the only ones who seem truly alive?"

Julie squatted down beside the barely breathing form, as if to ask him. Then she gasped.

"It's you, Terry. He's you."

Terry stared hard. Beneath the sunken flesh and ragged beard, he saw his own face, transmogrified by age and suffering.

"You're right," he said. He knelt by his doppelganger and sought to touch him. Terry's hand disappeared into his chest, ectoplasm returning to its source. As if the intrusion had energized the man, his eyes twitched beneath the gummed lids, but failed to open. Terry withdrew.

And then the man died.

Terry and Julie remained.

They stood up.

"Terry, look," Julie said. She held up a tattered photo she had found beside the man. It was her face, older too.

"I guess he remembered us from when we were happiest, huh, Terry?"

"I guess," Terry said.

Silence reigned. And then Julie said:

"Where are we going now, Terry? Where now?"

This one's pretty simple: it's my homage to Harlan Ellison's "Pretty Maggie Moneyeyes." If I were writing it today, of course, iPads, iPhones and various other gadgets would assume the dominant metaphorical role.

But really: from Harlan's 1960s tale to my 1980s tale, to a hypothetical version set in 2013, so little about human nature changes. It's only the transient trappings cloaking the thoughtless vapidity of our wired, virtual lives that mutate.

The disaffected, Martian-narrator style of the story, however, is eternal, and probably owes a debt to Brian Aldiss's *Report on Probability A*, one of my favorite novels ever.

MODERN CONVENIENCES

The concierge was holding a package for Patti when she got home from work that evening. It was a small parcel about the size of a book, wrapped in brown kraft paper and bearing a typed label with her name and address on it. The return address was a post office box. The item had come through the mail. It had ten cancelled stamps with T. S. Eliot's face on each one in the upper right hand corner. The transformation into an image, and subsequent duplication, had obviously not agreed with the dead poet, for he looked sourer than ever.

Patti took the package from the hand of the uniformed man. He sat behind a console. The console had a built-in black-and-white monitor which showed a continuously changing panorama of closed-circuit views of Patti's apartment complex. The images shifted automatically: the stairs, the entrances, the garage — the bedrooms?

"Thank you," said Patti as she took the package.

She uttered the phrase reflexively. She didn't mean it at all. The concierge was a nonentity to her. She passed him at least twice each day, yet if, on pain of losing her life, she had been pressed for a description of him, she could not have delivered it. For all she knew, the concierge could have been a different person each day.

"You're welcome," said the concierge.

Patti knew he didn't mean it either. But at least he had a motive for his superficial politeness, which was the hope of cadging a tip.

Patti didn't oblige. The small Louis Vuitton purse slung over her shoulder remained unopened. She walked with her package in one hand and her slim leather satchel in the other over to the bank of elevators.

There was no one else waiting for an elevator. When one came, Patti got on alone.

The inside of the elevator was painted a muted pink and grey. Its lights were concealed in etched and fluted glass sconces. There was maroon carpeting on the floor.

Patti pressed the button for her level. The elevator doors closed silently, with a hint of power in reserve. The car began to ascend.

When it reached Patti's floor, the elevator spoke. It had a woman's voice, It was the same voice featured in many talking cars, and in the recitation of phone numbers when one dialed Information. The voice had been modeled on that of a real woman. This woman had been paid a small sum to allow her voice to be copied and digitized. She had received no residuals for it. Now, as she went about her daily mundane life she regretted allowing the endless duplication of her voice. Whenever she got into a car or elevator, or dialled Information, she was forced to listen to her own subtly distorted tones, saying utterly banal things that meant nothing to her.

The elevator's thank-you sounded neither more nor less sincere than Patti's.

Patti got off and walked down the hall and around a corner. She passed many doors. She didn't know who lived behind any of them. Her door was the first one after the turn, on the left. She unlocked it and went in.

The assorted table lamps in Patti's apartment were already shining cheerfuly when she opened the door, welcoming her home. Each light seemed to be grinning sunnily. The lamps were controlled by a timing system. Each lamp had a module intervening between itself and the wall outlet from which it pulled life-giving electricity. These individual modules were slaved to a master controller, which sat imperiously on a shelf. The master controller was very intelligent , and could be programmed to do an astonishing number of things.

Patti's apartment consisted mainly of a single large room with windows at one end that gave an enchanting view of the nighttime city. On the floor of the room was an oriental carpet, neither cheap nor ostentatiously pricey. Part of the room functioned as a dining area, with glass-topped table and and cane-bottomed chairs; part as an entertainment center, with couch, coffee-table, television and stereo. A final section, delineated by a folding Chinese screen, served as Patti's bedroom. Additionally, there was a galley kitchen and a small bathroom.

Patti walked over to the television set and placed her package down atop the large, simulated-woodgrain console, intending to open it later. She tossed her satchel and purse on the couch. Then she took off her tailored suitjacket and draped it over the back of a chair. Patti's suit came from Saint Laurie's and cost nearly a thousand dollars. She had two identical ones which she alternately wore—with identical white blouses—like a uniform. The one not being worn at the time could go to the cleaners.

At the waistband of Patti's skirt was clipped a beeper. The device was as big as a pack of cigarettes. Unlike the elevator, it did not speak, but instead had a small LED display just big enough to flash a phone number. Patti's job required her to be on call twenty-four hours a day. The beeper had a range of five hundred miles. Even at home, Patti was never more than ten feet from it.

Patti took off the beeper and laid it next to the telephone. Beside the telephone, connected to it, was an answering machine. The machine was a very expensive model, chock-full of features. Patti could retrieve her messages from remote locations, if necessary, and even reprogram the machine with the aid of a special control she carried in her satchel.

She listened for messages now. There were none. She shut off the recorder.

Patti kicked off her low-heeled shoes and stood in her nyloned feet. She curled her toes gratefully. Then she walked to the kitchen.

From the freezer she took a package containing a solid block of variegated ice. Once, this had been food. Soon, after the proper treatment, it would be food again. Patti ripped the cardboard covering from the meal, revealing a white plastic oval lidded container. She put this container into her microwave. Patti loved her microwave. She couldn't live without it. If anyone had forced her to choose between her microwave and, say, her VCR, she would have hesitated like a donkey tethered between two equally attractive pile sof hay. Like the donkey, she probably would have died of frustration.

Inside the microwave was a little carousel that would spin the meal so it heated evenly. Patti set the oval dish on it. While the machine irradiated the varicolored ice, Patti began to unbutton her blouse, revealing a white slip beneath. A lace frill on the slip covered her prominent collarbones. When she had removed her blouse, Patti went to a tiny washing machine cunningly concealed beneath the kitchen counter. She put her blouse into the machine, added some detergent, and started the wash cycle.

Patti always tried to stay on top of her dirty clothes. Her life was too busy not to. They could quickly get out of control if not attended to. Luckily, one of the conveniences her building offered was individual-sized washer and dryer in every apartment.

The microwave beeped, not unpleasantly, signalling that it was finished thawing her meal. (Patti understood there were now talking models available. But she couldn't bring herself to trade in her old model, which had served faithfully for so long.)

Patti removed the meal and got herself a napkin and fork. These she deposited at the glass-topped table. She removed a trade magazine from her satchel and brought that to the table too. She read it while she ate, sitting in her slip and skirt, her legs crossed at the ankles beneath her chair. Just as she was finishing her meal, her beeper sounded, flashing its red digits across the room. Patti stood and crossed to the phone. The phone was a cordless model. It had a range of five hundred feet. In this feature it was inferior to the beeper. Otherwise, it was a very efficient machine. Patti lifted the receiver from the base station and punched in the number dictated by the beeper. She walked about the room, holding the phone to her ear as it rang on the other end. Someone picked it up.

"Hello," said Patti. "Yes, yes, no, that's what I told you earlier. Yes, that's right, sell. They need it tonight? Okay, I'll get right to it."

Patti put the phone back on its base. The crimson digits disappeared from the beeper's display panel. It seemed quiescent. Patti hoped it wouldn't be activated again tonight. She had other things than work which she wanted to attend to this evening.

She looked for a moment at the parcel atop the television. It would have to wait.

In one corner of the room was a desk that bore several shrouded forms. Patti went to the desk and snapped on a light above it. She pulled the dust-covers off, disclosing the components of a computer, and also a small personal xerox machine. She turned these items on. Their power-lights glowed reassuringly. Sitting down, Patti got quickly to work.

Several hours later she had finished. The relevant information had been transmitted over the phone wires, and also printed off. Patti had made xeroxes of the report. Each copy had been stuffed into a Federal Express envelope, which she had then addressed and sealed.

On the desk at Patti's elbow was an innocuous cube with a pressure plate on top and a speaker-grille on its side. Patti pressed the plate and the clock spoke the time.

"Nine-fifty-nine."

There was a Federal Express office nearby that would accept packages for intracity delivery until midnight. Patti decided she had a little time to spend on herself.

Patti stood up and powered down the machines. She replaced their dust-covers protectively. Remembering the blouse in the washer, she went and transferred it to the dryer. Retrieving her jacket from the back of the chair, she moved to her bedroom, behind the lacquered divider. There, she undid her skirt and stepped out of it. She carefully hung up her suit in a closet. She took off her slip and hung that up also.

Now Patti was clothed in white bra and panties. Her nylons were upheld by a garter belt. (No one at Patti's office would have said that she was the kind of woman who might, on occasion, wear such an item of clothing. She had a reputation as a hard, unfrivolous sort.)

On the night-table beside her bed was a surf-sound generator. Patti switched it on. A gentle, reassuring sussuration filled the apartment.

Patti emerged from behind the Chinese screen and walked to the windows, where she drew the drapes. Leaning in the corner was a video-camera on a tripod. Patti set the camera up so that its lens was focused on the couch. She put a blank videotape in it and made sure it was recording correctly. Then she took the package the concierge had given her and removed the wrapping.

Inside was an unlabeled videotape. Patti inserted this into her VCR. She picked up the remote control for the unit. Then she turned the camera on and walked around into its field of view.

"Hello," she said to the camera, which did not reply. "I've just gotten your tape and I'm going to enjoy it now."

Patti lay down luxuriously on the couch. With her left foot on the floor, she threw her right leg up over the back of the couch. She rubbed the remote control over her crotch, outside her undergarments. Then she turned on the player.

On the screen of the television appeared a handsome naked man— whom Patti had never actually met—seated in a leather chair. He greeted Patti by name. Then he began to masturbate, while telling Patti all the things he'd like to do to her.

While she watched, Patti began to masturbate also, her free hand beneath her panties. Soon her undergarments wear around her ankles. She let the camera enjoy the sight. After a few minutes, when her sensations began to intensify, she dropped the remote control and began to squeeze her breasts.

Patti and the man on the television climaxed together.

For several minutes Patti lay with her eyes closed. The tape had reached its end, and now only static filled the screen.

Patti stood up. She shut off all the devices. She put the man's tape on a pile of similar tapes next to the television. She removed the one she had made from the camera and set it on the coffee-table. In the morning she would wrap it up and drop it in the mail.

In the bedroom, Patti changed into jeans and a sweater and sneakers. She still had the Federal Express packages to drop off.

"Lobby," said the elevator. "Thank you."

Patti's lips formed a silent "You're welcome."

The concierge watched her leave the building with a look of boredom in his eyes. He might have been the same man who had handed her the tape. Possibly not. In either case, there was no connection.

The streets and sidewalks were still busy at this hour. Couples emerged from theaters and restaurants. Patti did not see anyone she knew.

It was not until she was several blocks from home that she realized she had forgotten her beeper. She put her hand to her waist in disbelief. A sudden feeling of nakedness overtook her. She picked up her pace.

After she dropped off the reports she felt a little better. Even without her beeper she was attending to business. Efficiency. Achievement. Prioritizing of goals. It amazed her how much she was able to do in a single day. Of course, none of it would be possible without timesaving devices. Modern conveniences. How had anyone ever lived without them?

Patti's efficient orgasm had left her with an appetite. She wanted an ice-cream cone. But she had left the house without any cash. Luckily, though, she had her instant-teller card in her purse.

Patti walked to a nearby branch of her bank. Its antelobby was brightly lit. Patti had her card in her hand, ready to enter, when she noticed that there was a woman already using the space.

With the advent of these useful machines had developed a new etiquette. Late at night, one did not breach the security of the antelobby when someone else was using the machine. It was improper. Therefore, she did not trigger the door latch, but stood waiting on the sidewalk for the other woman to finish.

Patti soon noticed that the woman was a novice user. She didn't seem to have the faintest idea of how to interface with the machine. She hesitatingly picked out her security code, then dithered over which instruction to enter next.

Patti began to grow impatient. She tapped her foot. The woman inside ventured to strike a key. Patti, from long experience, could see even at this remove that it was the wrong one. The machine cycled back to give the woman another try.

She botched the second try too. Feeling Patti's eyes on her, she looked back over her shoulder. Her face was nervous. Patti glowered.

The woman began to try for the third time. If possible, she went even more slowly.

Patti couldn't stand it any longer. She tapped irritatedly with her nails on the glass.

The woman failed for a third and final time, perhaps due to Patti's annoying tapping. The machine, as programmed, ate her card.

The woman looked on in disbelief, at an utter loss. Patti, considering the transaction over, entered.

"It kept my card," the woman said sadly.

"You can get it back in the morning. Now, if you don't mind—"

The woman left despondently.

Patti had her money in thirty seconds flat.

Tucking it in her wallet, she pressed the panic bar on the door.

The door refused to open.

Patti pressed harder. The bar was rigid as the continental shelf.

Perhaps this was a new security measure, thought Patti. She tried to remember if the other woman had had any trouble exiting, but failed to recall. The other woman's presence and actions hadn't really registered, after she had ceased to be an inconvenience to Patti. Was there a card-slot on the inside to trigger the door, as there was on the outside? No, there was none. A button, perhaps? No, no button.

Patti went back to the console Would the control be there? No, there was only the standard array of keys.

This was ridiculous. Was she to be trapped here all night, or until someone else came by? Damn, the bank would surely hear of this in the morning!

Patti went to stand by the door, awaiting the next customer.

Half an hour passed. No one came. Patti felt humiliated, caged like an animal on display behind the glass, alhough in fact no one seemed to pay much attention to her. Perhaps they thought she was a homeless crazy, holed up for the night. Surely her dress and demeanor would indicate otherwise…

Finally, a man and a woman approached the door. The man took out his card, the door buzzed, and Patti moved to catch it before it could close. No sense in the three of them getting stuck in here…

Her arm swung out to intercept the door, incidentally blocking the couple's entrance.

"Thank God—" began Patti.

The couple walked right through her arm, oblivious to her presence. The door clicked shut. Patti was too shocked to utter a word. It had to have been a hallucination. Fatigue, nerves… She worked too hard…

Before Patti knew it, the couple was ready to leave. They still seemed not to have seen her. She fell in behind them, intending to walk out with them.

An invisible barrier stopped her. It was as if the doorway were closed with an invisible sheet of plastic. She met resistance that proved insurmountable.

When Patti was alone again, hysteria overtook her. She began to pound on the glass and shout. No one outside paid her any attention, not even the policeman who passed, whistling.

After a while she fell exhausted to the floor. There she sat for a time, hanging her head.

At last she stood. For reasons she couldn't explain, she went again to the instant-teller. She took out her card and inserted it.

The machine came alive. It, at least, had not rejected her, still responded to the reality of her existence. Patti felt a little better.

Until the machine's screen altered.

The little black-and-white CRT flared into full color. Patti watched, transfixed, as the tape she had just made at home began to play. There she lay on the couch, hands roaming her body, making love to the videocamera, being made love to by the television.

"No," said Patti weakly. She placed her hands over the screen—vivid colors, the unmistakable tones of flesh, leaking from between her spread fingers—and looked over her shoulder, dreading to find a crowd gathered there for the spectacle. But, as before, the passersby seemed oblivious to her plight.

Patti took her hands from the screen. The tape reached the climax, then began to play again.

She stepped back in horror.

At that moment the two slots on the machine—the small one that took in envelopes of money and the larger one that dispensed cash—opened.

A lurid red light streamed forth, impaling Patti.

She felt drawn to the machine. Without volition she stepped forward. Forearms braced against the wall, she pressed her breasts against it. Her protruding bank card jutted into her midriff like a plastic tongue. Her loins were level with the small shelf of the machine. She ground her pubis into the metal ledge. Just as the colors on the screen had leaked through her fingers, so now the red light from the interior of the machine seemed to be filtering through her body, emerging a deeper, blood-red hue.

The light flared. In the next moment, Patti went incandescent, becoming a skeletal negative of herself. She was atomized and vaporized, simultaneously dispersed and compressed, transfigured and transposed, pulled body and soul inside the machine like an illegitimate magnetic card.

The machine shut its doors. It spat Patti's card out on the floor. Its sreen went blank. The next person to use the machine found Patti's card. A Good Samaritan, he slid it under the locked doors of the bank.

When he used the machine, marvelling as he always did at its convenience, he encountered nothing unusual, from his perspective.

But his fingers on the keys gave Patti the first of many wonderful, inescapable orgasms.

Every once in a while a story title arrives out of the blue, like a goddess springing from a sweaty forehead, but bearing no sense of what any substance behind it might be. This was one such instance. Luckily, thanks to college memories of some Philosophy 101, a fondness for Jung's autobiography, and a reliance on the original Ghostbusters movie for ambiance, I was able to cobble together a comedic accompaniment to the original inspiration. But it was pretty much tail wagging the dog all the way.

If only I had seen, back in 1989, the 1952 Howard Hawks film *Monkey Business*, in which Cary Grant play a scientist whose experiments provoke similar chaos, I would have had an even more reliable model for my story. But I only encountered that gem a year or two ago.

I KANT CUZ I'M TOO JUNG

"Do you remember," asked Pennypacker, "the thumbless children?"

"Indeed I do," Jearl replied. "And a good thing we ditched them before the University found out."

Sitting in Pennypacker's office, drinking something noxious and green from bell-shaped flasks, the two men presented a glaring contrast: Pennypacker tall and cadaverous, looking like a puppet assembled from the bones of a dozen species; Jearl thick and lumpy, as if constructed from poorly mashed potatoes. Each man wore a white labcoat on front to rear, the buttons in back misdone, causing the garments to ride up crazily.

"I can't forget what high hopes we had for that one," Pennypacker continued. He seemed nostalgic today, as if contemplating past glories that would never come again. "We were going to settle once and for all the role of an opposable thumb in the development of man's intelligence. We set up the orphanage with some of our grant money, and you hired the staff from the Salvation Army residence halls."

"Very tractable they were, too," Jearl said. "As long as they got their daily shots."

"A few discreet whispers among the indigent members of the city, and the children began pouring in. I feel it's a shame, by the way, this lack of morality among the young today, thinking nothing of rutting like guinea pigs, and relying on science to handle the consequences."

Jearl burped agreement.

"In any case, we had our subjects. Once we reached a critical mass, so to speak, of infants, it was the work of only a day to dethumb them. Then, it would have been a simple matter of sitting back and observing our little community, to see whether they developed intelligence as we define it."

"But the police came," Jearl said morosely.

Pennypacker pounded a knobby fist on his desk. "How were we to anticipate one of those hysterical young women might want her baby back? What nerve! Laymen have no conception of what true science demands. Luckily, our hands were clean in the whole affair. Imagine if we hadn't taken those precautions I insisted upon— Where would our careers be today? As it was, they came damnably close to catching us. The newspapers didn't let the story fade for a whole year. Reporters sniffing even around the campus."

Jearl shifted his lumpy bulk uncomfortably in the visitor's chair. Pennypacker's mood had infected him now too. "It seems that the era of great science is past, Pennypacker. Imagine Pavlov or Mengele struggling under these conditions. Begging for funds, complying with the EPA and genetic-engineering watchdog committees, lecturing pointy-headed proto-yuppies, whose vision extends no further than a six-figure income. How are men of our insight and daring supposed to advance the cause of science with such petty restrictions?"

The two men sat silently for a time, contemplating injustice and the fickleness of the world.

At last Pennypacker slammed his desk again. "We can't despair, Jearl! The future stretches before us, beckoning. Don't we have our minds, our hopes? Surely there's territory left to conquer. Let's reason about this."

"You know my feelings about reason, Pennypacker. It's never gotten us anywhere. It's our instincts we have to rely on. As Jung said, 'The great decisions of human life have as a rule more to do with the instincts and other mysterious unconscious factors than with conscious will and well-meaning reasonableness.'"

"Don't quote that charlatan in my office, Jearl. My thoughts on the subject are fixed. Reason and logic are what separate man from the animals. Take a supreme rationalist such as Kant—whom you would do well to study, Jearl. What did he recommend? Intensive scrutiny of one's every action, to determine all its consequences. 'Act only on that maxim through which you can at the same time will that it should become a universal law.' A fine mess we'd be in if I had let you rely on your instincts with the orphanage. 'We should appear on television,' you said. 'Publicize ourselves.' Hah! We would have publicized ourselves right into a jailcell."

Jearl composed his crevassed face into lineaments of hurt and distress. "Get in touch with your shadowside, Pennypacker, and you won't be so miserable to be around."

"Bah! Rubbish! Look at your actions in the light of the Categorical Imperative, Jearl, and recognize your flaws."

"I'm sick of this argument," Jearl said petulantly. "We always have it when we're in between experiments. I wish there was some method to settle it, one way or the other."

Pennypacker shot to his feet, as if his strings had been pulled. "Jearl, you've hit upon it! Our next conquest! We'll answer the question that has plagued mankind since it crawled from the slime. Which approach to life is more beneficial? Brain or heart, thought or feelings, rationality or instincts!"

Like pudding, Jearl rumbled up excitedly out of the chair. "Classical or jazz, Asimov or Vonnegut, PBS or ABC!"

"Exactly!"

Jearl's smile faded then, and he asked, "But how?"

Pennypacker advanced to his friend and put a bony arm around a suety shoulder. "The brain is an open book today, Jearl. Out of a hundred neurotransmitters, surely we can adjust a few to achieve a person who relies solely on either rationality or instincts. Then, we monitor his life, and objectively determine which way brings more success."

Jearl looked skeptical. Pennypacker bent low and whispered, "Dopamine."

Wistfully, Jearl said, "You hope o' mine."

"Serotonin."

"Got me moanin'."

The two joined hands and began to dance around the office, knocking furniture and files.

"Norepinephrine."

"Causes such a scene."

"Acetylcholine."

"Gets you nice and mean."

"GABA."

"Makes me jabber."

"Glycine."

"Could turn *me* lean!"

Laughing, the two collapsed into their seats.

First to recover, Pennypacker said, "Let's get busy."

Three weeks later, they sat once more in the office. On the desk between them stood two vials filled with clear fluid. One was marked with a black label, the other white.

"That didn't take too long, did it?" Pennypacker said. "Without the computer simulations and molecule modeling, we'd still be at it. I suppose this decadent age has a few benefits. Now, we need to decide who runs the first trial. I nominate your serum for the initial test."

"Not so fast," Jearl said. "You're hoping something goes wrong, and I have to discount my results. No, you go first."

Pennypacker shrugged. "You wound me, Jearl. That was not my intention at all. I have faith in my chemistry, even if you don't. There's no advantage to going last. I'll be proud to begin this experiment."

"Aren't we forgetting something?" said Jearl.

"What's that?"

"The subject."

Pennypacker waved his hand. "Not to worry. Remember the words of one of the greatest science popularizers of all times, Jearl."

"Which are?"

"There's a subject born every minute."

* * * *

Kirsten James walked briskly across the campus, her mind beset by problems. If her problems could have been objectively ranked—always a doubtful proposition—the top three might have been:

1) Arthur.
2) Money.
3) Grades.

But not necessarily in that order.

At least, she thought gratefully, as she reached the steps of the biology building, money won't be a problem much longer.

After all, the ad in the campus paper had promised a thousand dollars for just two weeks work.

She hoped fervently that she would get the position. They only needed one subject, though. But a friend on the staff of the paper had tipped her off in advance, and she was certain to be the first applicant.

Tripping lightly up the stairs, Kirsten wondered what the nature of the work would be.

On the third floor, she came to the office mentioned in the ad. Two silhouettes—one tall and skinny, the other short and lumpish—moved on the frosted glass as if in a dance. Kirsten supposed it was a trick of the late afternoon sunlight. She knocked. The shadows stopped abruptly, separated and disappeared. A shuffling of chairs sounded. A voice came:

"Enter, please."

Kirsten opened the door and went in.

Behind a standard professorial desk sat the man who had obviously cast the elongated shadow. His labcoat was all disordered, rucked up somehow around his neck. To the side, barely fitting in a big chair, a second man sat, identically dressed.

"Ah, my dear, come in, come in," the tall man said. "My name is Pennypacker, and my esteemed associate here is Jearl. I assume you are responding to our solicitation for a subject to aid us in our latest work."

"Yes, I am," Kirsten said. Were they wearing their coats backwards?

"Wonderful. You're the first, and hence undoubtedly the best quali-fied. We merely have to ask you a single question concerning your epis-temology, before making a final decision."

"My what?"

Jearl spoke up. "Don't take offense, Miss. We refer merely to your philosophy regarding knowledge. Do you favor rational thought over intuition, or vice versa?"

Kirsten pondered the question for trick implications, could discern none, and thought it best to answer honestly.

"Well, I try to apply both in my life. I mean, if you don't listen to your heart, where are you? But on the other hand, it pays to look before you leap."

Pennypacker clapped his hands together. "Marvelous! I could hardly have found two cliches more suited to express the attitude we are seeking in our subject. You're hired! Here is five hundred dollars up front, for the first trial."

Advancing around the desk, Pennypacker stuffed the bills in Kirsten's purse.

"Hey, wait a minute. I need to know a little bit more about this ex-periment before I agree. Don't you want my name, at least, and some references?"

"Nonsense. We trust you implicitly. Your word is your bond, we are sure."

"But I haven't agreed yet! What are my responsibilities? Is this gonna cut into my free time a lot? I'm carrying a full course-load this semester."

"Your duties are minimal. We wish you to live your life exactly as you have been doing, merely keeping a diary for us of your inner reac-tions to the drug and how it alters your decision-making faculties."

"Drug! Hey now, the ad didn't say anything about drugs. I don't smoke, drink or do dope. This isn't the sixties anymore, you know."

Pennypacker dismissed Kirsten's fear with a suave gesture. "The so-lution you will receive is simply a mix of chemicals already present in your brain. It's one hundred percent natural. Just like NutraSweet. Now if you will kindly submit to Jearl for a moment—"

Somehow, Jearl had come up behind her with impossible stealth. Now he pinioned her arms. She watched as Pennypacker took out a hypoder-mic and filled it from a glass vial bearing a white label. He advanced on Kirsten with an odd smile.

"You should be grateful," Jearl said from behind her. "Before we solved the problem of getting past the blood-brain barrier, we used to have to drip the solution directly onto the cortex."

Kirsten fainted.

* * * *

"—two tickets."

His speech concluded, Arthur Hennepin stared longingly at Kirsten, his moony face nearly bisected by his broad smile. The couple sat at a food-speckled table in the cafeteria. Arthur was rather pudgy, with thin blond wisps of hair straggling across a spot of premature baldness. His major was accounting, his minor subject ornithology. Kirsten's girl-friends frequently demanded to know what a beauty of her caliber saw in Arthur. She would patiently explain that they had known each other since elementary school, that Arthur was "sweet and devoted" and that he would someday make a good salary, at his longed-for job: keeping the books for the Audubon Society.

But her girlfriends would always persist: "Isn't he dull as dust, though?"

And Kirsten, honestly forced to reply "Yes," was lately beginning to have her doubts about Arthur.

However, at this minute she had much more on her mind than Arthur's lack of stimulating qualities.

Those two screwy guys—exactly what had they done to her, and what was she going to do about it? Imagine their nerve, injecting her with some untested drug without her permission! Yet, hadn't she tacitly agreed to participate when she hadn't immediately rejected their money? It was all very confusing. Why not give them the benefit of the doubt? Perhaps they were just eager to come up with some new wonder drug that would benefit all mankind. She suspected scientists got carried away occasionally with their enthusiasms. Take that Sagan fellow, for instance. Why, sometimes he seemed almost frothing— And the drug seemed to have no adverse effects—yet.

Kirsten opened her pocketbook, verified that the money was indeed there, and decided to go along.

"Kirsten," Arthur said with an impatient whine, "I don't think you've heard a word I've said."

"Of course I have, Arthur," she replied, although truthfully, she hadn't. In fact, the whole trip across campus to the cafeteria was somewhat hazy in her mind, and she seemed to be having trouble concentrating. Perhaps she had been a little hasty in discounting the effects of the drug.

Kirsten took Arthur's hand and squeezed it. His smile threatened to wrap around his ears. "I'm sorry, Arthur. Maybe I was a little distracted. Would you mind running things by me once again?"

"Well, since you've been saying lately that we don't do anything exciting, I gave it some thought, and decided, what the hell, let's splurge.

So I managed to buy two tickets to the concert tonight. You know, that guy you like." Arthur made a face. "Davey Zowie, or whatever his name is."

Kirsten squealed. "David Bowie! You managed to get tickets! Oh, Arthur, how did you do it? That concert was sold-out weeks ago."

Arthur looked smug. "Oh, I just found a scalper—"

Suddenly Kirsten's brain shifted into hyperdrive. The room seemed to collapse into a pinpoint of light and disappear, while her thoughts raced with nanosecond precision and silicon clarity.

Scalper. Tickets bought unethically in blocks. Eager consumers deprived of their fair chance. Prices jacked up. Unhappiness. Unfair. What if everyone scalped? Chaos, despair, young girls slitting their wrists, Bowie finding out and feeling responsible, becoming too distracted to sing. Patronize a scalper? No!

The whole process took less than a second. Kirsten came out of the intensely rational state, back to the noisy room. Wow, what had all that been about? She had never experienced anything like that before. She shook her head. Maybe she could just ignore it.

Arthur studied her with puzzlement. "Aren't you excited, Kirsten? Don't you want to go?"

Kirsten opened her mouth to say how glad she was, when a new sensation struck. It felt rather similar to constipation, only it was located directly behind the bridge of her nose.

All at once, she found herself speaking without control.

"Arthur, such behavior is reprehensible and not to be taken as a guide to universal conduct. You will return those tickets immediately. I want nothing to do with them."

Kirsten stood and began to stalk out of the cafeteria.

After half a minute, Arthur recovered enough to pursue.

"Kirsten, hey, wait a minute. I never thought you'd take it like this. I was just trying to make you happy. Those tickets cost fifty bucks apiece. Slow down a second, will you! Let's talk."

"There's nothing to talk about. Get rid of those unethically purchased items at once."

"The scalper's not gonna take them back, Kirsten. What should I do with them?"

Stopping at a random table, Kirsten said, "Give them to these people. Your charity will nullify the original unethical act."

With trembling hands, Arthur took out the tickets. He looked as if he might cry. He eyed Kirsten imploringly, but her unrelenting face gave him no hope. He handed the tickets to the seated students, who had been watching the whole affair with amazement.

"Hey, thanks, man," one said. "Is this a promotion or something? Are you guys from a radio station? Will you say my name on the air?"

"Just shut up," Arthur said, then hurried after Kirsten, who was already outside.

On the walk, Arthur caught her by the arm. "Okay, I did just like you said. Let's forget I ever brought it up. Boy, a hundred dollars down the drain."

Kirsten halted. What had come over her? She put a hand to her forehead. It seemed to be over now.

"I'm so sorry, Arthur. I—I can't explain it."

"It's all right. We'll just have a quiet dinner at my place, like we do every Friday."

Arthur began to guide Kirsten home.

By the wrought-iron campus gate, they came upon Johnny Z. Johnny was a bedraggled, burnt-out hipster who had been a fixture on campus for twenty years. He cadged loose change and beers from each passing generation.

"Spare cha—" Johnny began.

Before Arthur could stop her, Kirsten delivered a vicious kick to Johnny's stomach, whereupon he promptly folded and collapsed.

Arthur regarded Kirsten with fright.

"People," she said sternly, "should work for a living."

* * * *

The lights were low in Arthur's off-campus apartment. He and Kirsten sat side by side on the couch. During the evening, Kirsten had suffered no more of the strange attacks. Both she and Arthur felt relieved. Arthur, however, wanted to discuss the incidents. Nervous and feeling contaminated, Kirsten had not told him of the injection, and so his theories were hopelessly off the mark.

"Could it be that PMS thing…?"

"Oh, Arthur, just be quiet and kiss me."

Arthur knew when to comply.

After a time even under Arthur's inexpert caresses, Kirsten began to grow excited. She felt happy and relaxed, all the troubles of the day receding in the wake of a mellow sexual warmth. Surely no troublesome decision could lurk in this encounter—

Without warning, Kirsten sat up straight and stiff as a frozen fish. Arthur fell back, arms folded across his stomach as if to ward off a foot.

"Whatever it was, I didn't mean it!"

"Arthur," Kirsten intoned like an automaton, "this issue of sex is one of the most complicated to objectively judge. On the one hand, intercourse outside of societal structures such as marriage is non-productive and not to be sanctioned, insofar as it tends to undermine the necessary social matrix. On the other hand, coitus remains a natural function, tending to contribute to both the mental and physical well-being of the individual, especially among males of your age-group. Therefore, I have decided that I will now proceed to have sex with you, but under no circumstance will I allow myself to enjoy it."

With this statement, Kirsten lay back, arms rigid by her side, her face a mask. "You may now undress me and continue what you were doing."

For just ten seconds, Arthur considered the matter.

He made the sidewalk before the inner door even slammed.

* * * *

Kirsten stood in front of the door to Pennypacker's office. A week had passed, and she was expected now to report.

She hoped she had the strength.

It had been quite a week.

Kirsten had managed to alienate everyone she knew, teachers and friends, strangers and relatives, shopclerks and waiters, and, most of all, Arthur.

She shuddered now to recall everything that had happened.

A termpaper had arrived in the mail, ordered from one of the mills. She had been so happy, confident that now she would pass Chaucer. In amazement she had watched her willful hands rip it into shreds. Needless to say, her own efforts netted an F.

Shopping with her best friend, Carol, she had been startled to see the other girl pocket a scarf in the department store, although only days ago, Kirsten might have done the same thing. The floorwalker was very eager to press charges, and Kirsten volunteered to testify. Carol had stopped crying long enough to swear at Kirsten, using words Kirsten would have sworn Carol didn't know.

And that awful altercation with the fat girl eating an extra-large pizza— Who could say why the girl had reacted so intemperately to a spontaneous lecture on the evils of gluttony, delivered in the packed restaurant? Kirsten was still removing mozarella from her hair.

These events constituted merely the tip of the iceberg of embarrassment. She had done things that would never be forgotten. There were people now who fled from her on sight. And all because she had wanted a little extra cash.

Kirsten sighed. She had thought long and hard about how she was going to extricate herself from this mess. Eventually, she had rejected the idea of turning in the two scientists to the authorities. They were the only ones who could restore her to herself. In the end, there seemed nothing to do but play along.

Kirsten knocked, turned the handle and entered.

Jearl and Pennypacker occupied the same positions as on that fateful day a week ago. They seemed to have been waiting patiently here for her, like fungus on a log. For a minute, she actually believed they lived in the office.

Pennypacker rose eagerly to his feet. "Ah, Miss James. Word of your exploits have filtered back to us. It seems as if you have become living proof of the immortal Kant's wisdom. No doubt your life has been revolutionized for the better, and you see no need to try Jearl's serum."

"Wait just a minute now," Jearl rumbled. "Let the girl speak her mind."

"It's been revolutionized all right," Kirsten said ruefully. "I don't know about the better part. Anyway, it's all in here." Kirsten rummaged in her purse and found a small diary with clasp, which she tossed on Pennypacker's desk. "I hope you don't mind it's not written real scientific like. I had a lot on my mind. And just skip over the first few pages. They're private."

Pennypacker seemed disappointed at Kirsten's lack of enthusiasm for his point of view. "We are engaged in a scientific trial here, Miss James. You may rest assured that we will hold everything in the strictest confidence."

"Okay, you'd just better. I don't want Arthur or anyone else finding out my innermost secrets—if they still even care about me. Now, let's get the second part of this over with."

Pennypacker spoke with resignation. "Jearl, I suppose you may administer your little cocktail now."

Jearl drew off some liquid from the black-labeled bottle. Kirsten closed her eyes.

She felt the needle go in. Then something inside her sucked her consciousness down into a bottomless pool.

* * * *

Arthur sat in the cafeteria, moodily regarding his cup of Sanka. (Too much caffeine normally upset him, and lately, with Kirsten acting so bizarre, even one cup seemed like too much.) What could be wrong with Kirsten? She had changed so drastically in such a short time. This stern morality was so unlike her. Previously, her entire code of ethics had consisted of misquoting the Golden Rule. Was it something he had done? Perhaps it was a subtle comment on his own behavior. He supposed he could be something of a prig at times.

Abandoning his unprofitable speculations, Arthur raised his cup, tilted back his head to sip, and—

My God, what was that commotion by the door—?

Kirsten burst in, trailed by a crowd of whooping students. Her blouse was ripped, hanging off one white shoulder. Somewhere she had lost her shoes. Her hair seemed charged with electricity, her eyes feverish. Breasts heaving, she moved like an animal. Lifting her face to the ceiling, she bellowed, "I am the Anima!"

Arthur sprayed out a mouthful of coffee.

Kirsten continued to address the sky. "Where is my soulmate? I must have him. He is the strong horse I will ride to ecstasy!" Kirsten scanned the cafeteria. Her eyes lit on Arthur. She regally raised a long arm to point. "He awaits me on his throne." She began to advance, with a sinuous gait the likes of which Arthur had never seen.

Arthur hastily scraped back in his chair, got to his feet. His knees felt weak and his stomach churned.

"Uh, hi, K—K—Kirsten. What a surprise."

"Discard words," she said. "I am going to melt your spine with love."

The crowd's hoots redoubled.

Kirsten was almost upon him.

"W—wait just a minute," Arthur stammered desperately.

Too late. Kirsten leapt.

Somehow Arthur found himself off his feet. Kirsten had lifted him in a grip of steel. Now her feral face hovered inches from his. Her breath was hot, and she smelled of musk.

"Prepare to know heaven," she growled.

Arthur fainted.

* * * *

Who would have ever thought the unconscious held so many archetypes? Certainly not the innocent Kirsten of old.

What a varied lot they were!

And so prone to surface with the slightest prompting.

Take, for instance, the time the Wily Trickster persona had possessed her. That had been while she was trying to explain to campus security about the scene in the cafeteria. She had never evidenced any talent for ventriloquism before then. Despite her lack of practice, however, she had convincingly projected her voice so as to simulate a riot outside. When the rent-a-cops turned their backs, she had split out the window.

After that, time seemed to pass confusingly, in a frenzy of events.

Somehow, the Eternal Virgin had convinced an entire fraternity house of horny males to shelter her for two days, without laying a finger on her. When the police inexplicably learned of her whereabouts, the Noble Savage had helped her escape over the rooftops. After that, she had lived in the city's parks for a week, stealing food from the concession stands and once even catching and roasting a squirrel. At last, the Naive Waif had enlisted the aid of an elderly couple, who had disguised her as their twelve-year-old grand-daughter and delivered her safely back to the campus. (Amazing how each persona seemed to mold her body accordingly!)

Now she stood for the third time outside the office where she had met so much grief and trouble. Surely Pennypacker and Jearl could ask no more of her. She had co-operated to the max. Let them restore her old self now.

Bruised, weary, cynical, she went inside.

As before, two familiar figures confronted her.

This time, it was Jearl who rose to greet her.

"My dear, how wonderful to see you. You rather slipped out of view there for a few days. We thought our experiment might have to end prematurely. How good to know you still survive. And evidently, you've flourished!"

Jearl sat, as if the greeting had fatigued him.

Kirsten looked down at herself. Although clean and wearing whole clothes, she was marked with scratches, contusions, and poison-ivy rash. Her fingernails were broken and she knew her cheeks were gaunt. Flourished?

She shrugged. "Whatever you say, Mister. I'm tired now. We can discuss the results of part two later. Just give me the antidote and let me get back to my old self."

Jearl and Pennypacker regarded each other nervously. Neither seemed to want to tell her certain bad news. Finally, Pennypacker spoke, his skeletal fingers intertwining uneasily.

"Ah, Miss James, it seems we neglected something crucial at the beginning of this experiment. We made no record of your original unique mix of brain chemicals, and so are unsure of precisely what to restore you to. We could, however, experiment further—"

Kirsten felt tears fill her eyes. This was beyond belief. Surely she didn't deserve this much torment for such a simple transgression as a little greed. Her mind began to whirl under the pressure. The leftover drugs from Pennypacker's shot began to battle the remnants of Jearl's. Ultimate rationality surged against primal instinctual drives. Kirsten thought her head was going to crack wide open.

Peace descended without warning. She probed internally, as if touching a sore tooth with tongue. Which was the victor?

With wonderment, she realized what had happened.

Integration had occurred.

Something of her unique wholeness must have shown on her face. Pennypacker and Jearl made motions as if to stand.

Using her new powers, Kirsten paralyzed them both in an awkward crouch. At the same time she controlled them, she levitated two hypodermics from their shelf. One filled itself from the vial with the white label, the other from the black.

Sweat started from the brows of the two men. Kirsten smiled. Then she sent Jearl's serum into Pennypacker's buttock, and vice versa.

She let the two collapse back into their seats. Their faces were starting to mirror an inner discontent.

As she turned to go, she said:

"Be sure to record the results, gentlemen."

One thing that amazes me about my younger self was how short I wrote. This tale is a mere 4000 words or so, complete. Nowadays, I'm lucky if the typical story idea I have fits into twice that space. But does this change in scope bespeak increased sophistication, or merely increased verbosity? Only the ages will reveal my decline or ascent! In any case, this slightly Sturgeonesque examination of a certain fetish is probably just long enough. It seems now, in the light of the internet's merciless exposure of all kinks, as antique and innocent as a lady's bustle.

This story appeared in a little modest printzine called Boing-Boing. What's that? You say you've heard of such a venue, but it's one of the internet's most famous websites? Yes, they are one and the same creature, the latter evolving from the former. My writing life has now encompassed entire geological eras.

HEAVEN SENT ME AN ANGEL, C.O.D.

Peter Skelly pulled carefully up to the curb, directly opposite the fire hydrant. His right rims squeegeed against the granite coping as he neatly aligned his unwashed red Chevy with the inoffensive fireplug. He shut off his engine. He removed his sunglasses, folded their stems, and slipped them inside his jacket pocket. (Skelly always felt faintly foolish wearing shades. They reminded him too much of a goggle-eyed insect perched on his nose, with its cricket legs clinging to his ears.) He rolled down his window, allowing the monoxide-laden summer breezes to waft in. He commenced to wait.

City traffic surged by, a medley of horns and screeching brakes. It was a busy hour. Skelly did not expect to wait long.

After fifteen minutes a small three-wheeled vehicle, its doors curtained with plastic, arrived, stopping in front of Skelly's car. Skelly pretended not to notice the traffic-buggy, all the while maintaining a close scrutiny of it. The once-transparent plastic of its doors was scratched and dirty, and concealed its occupant from Skelly's eyes. Skelly waited, ready to flee, but hoping there would be reason enough to stay. His stomach was knotted like an Incan string message. His hands, he suddenly realized, were clenched so tightly on the knurled steering wheel that they ached. Forcing his hands to uncurl, he removed them. They left patches of moisture on the wheel that immediately began to fade.

The plastic flap of the cart stirred ominously. A hand with chipped crimson nails pushed it aside. The driver emerged.

Skelly released his breath.

The driver was a young black woman. Skelly barely noticed her face, although he had a quick impression of prettiness.

He was more interested in her uniform.

The meter maid was dressed entirely in shades of brown that complimented her complexion. A stiff-brimmed chocolate cap decorated with gold braid sat lightly atop her short tight afro. A cocoa-colored short-sleeved shirt with Oxford collar buttoned tightly was neatly bisected by a man's mocha tie. A badge denoted the location of her left breast, like the X on some pirate's map. Her brown pants, masculine in cut, were sharply creased and hung loosely on her legs, although they followed the contours of her rump in a beguiling manner. Piping of a contrasting shade ran down the outer seams of her pants. Highly polished clunky brown work shoes—like those a conscientious janitor might wear— completed her outfit.

Skelly had never seen her till that moment.

But she was everything he had been waiting for.

He knew he was in love.

The meter-maid approached Skelly's car. Skelly fumbled with the door-handle, finally managed to manipulate it, and emerged to stand on jellied legs.

"Mister," said the woman, "do you know you're blocking that hydrant?" She waved her pad of tickets at the wronged object.

"A—a—am I?" was all Skelly could reply.

"Yes, you are, and I'm gonna have to give you a ticket unless you move."

"Could we just talk a minute?" implored Skelly.

"Not about where your parked, Mister. It's against the law."

"Good. I mean, that's okay, because that wasn't what I wanted to talk about."

The woman regarded Skelly suspiciously. She pulled the brim of her cap lower, shading her eyes in an intimidating manner. "What then?"

"Ah, you're not married are you?"

The meter-maid stiffened. "What's it to you?"

"Would you go out with me? On a date? I mean, I know it's unusual to ask under such circumstances, but I'm not a bad guy, really."

Relaxing a trifle, the woman surveyed Skelly for a few seconds. He tried to project normality and sweetness. It seemed he was succeeding, for the woman smiled.

"Well, it's kinda weird—but why not? You're sorta cute."

Oh, Lord, thank you! At least he had gotten this far. But now came the tough part. God grant him strength and cunning…

"Great. I'll pick you up right after work. When do you get off?"

"Oh, no," said the meter-maid, "I'd want to go home and freshen up first, change out of this uniform. You could pick me up at my apartment."

"Christ, no— I mean, you don't have to bother."

The woman's suspicions seemed aroused again. "What're you talking about? Of course I'd want to change. You don't think I'd go out dressed like this, do you?"

Skelly said nothing. For this was of course exactly what he hoped.

Seeming to divine his thoughts, the woman grew angered. "Mister, I've got a hunch you're some kind of pervert."

Skelly knew his chances of swaying this woman were rapidly evaporating, but desperation made him continue to try. "I'm not, really I'm not. It's just that you look so fine in that uniform. Really, it's tailored quite nicely. If you took off your badge and cap, no one would ever realize it was a meter-maid's get-up." Skelly's tongue was running away with him, but he couldn't control it. With the situation so obviously unsalvageable, he blurted out his deepest hopes. "Although of course in the privacy of one's home—if we were alone, and you felt so inclined—you could put the badge back on—"

The woman's eyes widened and her nostrils flared as she scowled. "Mister, you're really fucked up. I sure as hell ain't going out with you, and you're sure as hell getting a ticket."

Skelly said nothing to this. Only silence could preserve the pitiful fragments of his dignity.

The woman put one foot on the fender in order to write the ticket. This pose drew her pants tighter, defining her buttocks with anguishing clarity. Skelly nearly fainted.

Handing him the ticket, the mater-maid walked toward her cart. At the doorflap she paused, fixing Skelly with an angry glare.

"Fucked-up. That's what you are, Mister." She got in and drove off.

Skelly, left standing, ticket in hand, supposed she was right.

* * * *

The cause was untraceable.

The roots of Skelly's fixation or fetish (God, how he hated that latter word, with its connotations of loathsome deviance so alien to his otherwise mundane and conservative lifestyle) was lost in the jumbled moraine of his past, which Time had first scraped together, then pushed and polished as a glacier noses boulders along. The source of his compulsions was buried beneath the detritus of a hundred thousand insults and injuries, negative and positive reinforcements, and exciting or disgusting stimuli whose general outline was shared by all individuals. This was assuming, naturally, that Skelly's particular needs and fantasies were attributable to a single incident or string of incidents. Maybe it was genetic. Lost and despairing, he had frequently thought so.

There was that one time though...

Pete Skelly, six years old, is walking to school. It is a cellophane-crisp fall day in the city. Children kick through drifs of leaves and shout excitedly. Young Skelly, always somewhat reserved, hangs back from the crowd, apart, daydreaming. Gradually his peers pull away, until he is left alone.

Ahead, an intersection looms. On the far side, the crossing-guard stands with her back to Skelly.

Mrs. Besarabian. As an adult, Skelly realized she was probably still in her early thirties. Now, she seems impossibly old and mature, a parental figure, an immutable fixture of Skelly's circumscribed youthful existence.

Lost in forgotten thoughts, Skelly steps out into the street without looking.

A shrill police whistle, the shriek of brakes and tires, the screams of other children, impact—

Skelly opens his eyes to find Mrs. Besarabian bending over him, crying and cradling him. He learns that he has been struck by a car, but surprisingly, nothing hurts. Mrs Besarabian helps him up. Nothing seems broken. Mrs Besarabian's quick actions must have caused the driver to stop just in time, with only enough force to knock him down.

Skelly looks up at the crossing-guard. To think that anything that happened to him could make her cry— It seems an awful responsibility, yet somehow thrilling at the same time, conferring a sense of unusual power on him. Suddenly, with eyes made more acute by his near-demise, Skelly really sees Mrs. Besarabian. She's wearing a little black pillbox cap with stubby wings, a white shirt with a black bow knotted at the neck, a fluorescent-orange bandolier, a black skirt, thick stockings and black shoes.

Without warning, Mrs. Besarabian gathers Skelly to her bosom, squeezing and nearly smothering him. Her starchy blouse smells like cotton dried outdoors. Skelly faints away...

Was this it? A whole lifetime of frustration emanating from a senseless accident, a tangle with fate? Surely it couldn't be so simple... It was all so, so Freudian. Hadn't that old humbug been discredited long ago?

Whatever the answer to Skelly's questions, one thing was certain:

The only way he could derive real satisfaction from sex was to make it with a woman in uniform.

There. For the first time, stung by the insults of the meter-maid, he had admined it to himself as curtly and simply as possible.

Was it really such an awful hangup, though? Should he really be vilified for what amounted to little more than a fashion preference?

As far as Skelly could see, it wasn't something creepy or humiliating like dominance or submission he was after. The uniformed women whom he was attracted to occupied positions both of minimal authority (policewomen, firewomen, nurses, doctors, security guards) and of subservience (McDonald's workers, waitresses, UPS truck-drivers, bellhops), and Skelly expected neither pampering nor abuse from his nonexistent lovers, but only a tender mutuality. No, it was strictly an essential aesthetic experience, a visual titillation that he sought.

Why didn't everyone share his appreciation of women clothed in the accoutrements of their official positions? Couldn't they see how stimulating it was, what an incredible turn-on?

Thank God he lived in the age he did...

All across this glorious emancipated nation, every day of every year, millions of women young and old rolled out of bed, sleepy-eyed or peppy, naked or gowned, wearing men's pajama-tops or Hanro tee-shirts and panties, and began to dress for their day's work. What an incredible assortment of standardized clothing they would don! Tunics with brass buttons and epaulets; coveralls with names embroidered above the breast; ivory stockings and chalky white shoes; rounded and flat-topped and crested caps; lab-coats; combat boots and camouflage pants and shirts; long black waterproof coats smelling of smoke; the white jackets of delicatessen help, doomed to be smeared with egg-salad and gravy; bus-driver greys and blues; Forest Ranger greens, with Smokey-the-Bear hats; subway-conductor tans and khakis; abbreviated doughnut-shop-girl dresses tied in the back with pink bows; cosmeticians' dusters; beauticians smocks; the blazers and slacks of Senate pages; Federal Express skirts and jackets and ties; the dresses of stewardesses; pilot's wings; the finery of concierges; the elegance of wine-stewards with keys to their cellars hung at their waists; the tall hats and white blouses and pants of chefs; hard hats and climbing spikes of telephone-linewomen; the thigh-high rubber boots and slickers of female mariners...

It wasn't the clothes themselves that so excited Skelly, of course, but what they implied about their wearers. Competence, ability, hard work, sweat, sweet exhaustion at day's end being dispelled by arousal and segue into passionate, disuniformed lovemaking...

God, this was Skelly's vision of heaven.

But he just couldn't seem to meet a woman who felt the same.

And so he was left begging at the locked gates of his Paradise, where all the angels were dressed as crossing-guards and danced tantalizingly just out of reach.

* * * *

There came a curt, professional knock at the door of Skelly's modest hotel room. Swinging his feet to the floor, he sat up nervously in bed, fully clothed atop the rumpled covers.

"Come in."

The door opened. An attractive woman walked confidently in, the click of her heels muffled by the thick carpet. She carried a large zippered garment bag by its hook. Skelly did not notice what she was wearing nor what she really looked like. He was too perturbed by the fact that she was someone different.

Whenever Skelly's sexual frustration built to an unsupportable level he would call Classy Chassis Escort Service and arrange for a meeting with his usual "escort." The whole procedure was vastly humiliating to Skelly, and he always put it off for as long as he possibly could. Besides, it was quite expensive, what with renting the room and all...

To suddenly discover that his usual partner—whom he had taken so long to feel comfortable with—had been inexplicably replaced by a stranger was too much for Skelly's already taut nerves.

"Where's Mona?" said Skelly.

"Mona's sick," replied the woman. She hooked the garment bag on the ledge above the closer door. She took her purse off her shoulder, doffed her cotton jacket, and began to unbutton her blouse.

Skelly got to his feet, alarmed. "Hey, listen, I don't know about this. Mona would do certain special things—"

The woman continued to calmly undress. "No sweat. I know all about it."

This startling assertion gave Skelly pause. "You do?"

"Sure. Mona told all the girls."

Oh my Christ— His embarrassing affliction was common knowledge among the entire Classy Chassis Callgirl Corps. How could he continue living—?

The woman seemed to sense his uneasiness. "Don't worry, Petey, it's not the worst I've seen or heard about. Pretty tame, in fact. Kinda innocent. You never hurt a girl or nothing. So what's the harm?"

"I just don't know ......

The woman finished with her buttons and removed her top, revealing a lacy white bra. "Aw, c'mon, Petey, I'm here now, aren't I? Look, you don't want to lose out on your fun, and I want to earn my money."

"I suppose... Did you bring the, ah, uniform?"

Reaching down to one foot to remove her shoe, the woman looked up at Skelly. "Gee, all you guys are blind. I'm about twice Mona's size, how the hell could I ever fit in that schoolgirl outfit?"

Mona, a petite woman, dressed for Skelly each time as a parochial-school student: starched white shirt, blue blazer with a gold school crest, short blue-and-green tartan skirt, navy tights and brown Oxfords with flaps concealing their laces.

"Just stop undressing then," said Skelly. "If you don't have the uniform, it's useless."

"Another one wouldn't do as good?"

"Another one?" This was something Skelly hadn't anticipated.

"Sure. You think I don't prepare for a job? And believe me, I really had to run around to find something that would fit."

"It's not from a costume shop, is it? I can tell a fake. "

The woman had removed both her shoes and was unzipping her skirt. "Nope. I borrowed it from my brother." She looked momentarily nervous. "We can't rip it or anything. He needs it this weekend."

Skelly was becoming aroused. "I guess after you went to all that trouble... Say, what's your name?"

"Kimberly."

"Well, uh, Kimberly—what is it?"

Now clad only in panties and bra, Kimberly stepped to where the garment bag hung. "You'll see soon enough. Just turn around now."

"All right."

Skelly waited with his back toward Kimberly.

He heard zippers zipping, cloth rustling, and briefly, the bite of metal against metal. He grew more and more excited. Time seemed to stretch.

At last Kimberly spoke. "Okay, you can look."

Skelly turned.

Kimberly wore the uniform of an NFL referee: white cap, black-and-white-striped shirt, white pants, black-ringed white socks, cleated shoes. A size or so too small in the hips and bust, the uniform fit with a delineation of her anatomy bordering on the obscene.

Skelly was astonished. He had never in his life imagined such an apparition. One thing troubled him though. "Are there really women refs in the NFL?"

Kimberly walked toward him, cleats digging into the carpet. "Does it matter?"

"Yes, it has to be real."

Kimberly embraced Skelly and began to kiss him. The uniform smelt of sweat. Skelly hoped Kimberly's brother would get a chance to clean it before the game this weekend.

Between kisses, Kimberly whispered, "Well then, if it matters, sure, there are women refs."

Skelly took her at her word. He slid his hands down to her buttocks.

"Uh-oh," said Kimberly, "that's a foul."

"Wrong sport."

"Oh, sorry. Um, offside?"

"Good enough," said Skelly.

Later, she remembered enough to shout, "Touchdown!"

* * * *

For several weeks after Kimberly's inspired impersonation, Skelly was as happy as he ever got, living off memories and hopes. He dreamed of the day when he would have saved up enough money to call the offices of C.C.E.S. and request Kimberly's services once more. (Skelly was not entirely fickle: Mona still occupied a fond niche in his heart, and in his wildest dreams he even dared to speculate about being able to afford her and Kimberly together, although what plausible script could be constructed for the meeting of a Catholic-school girl and an NFL official eluded him. Perhaps a field trip…?)

In the meantime, all Skelly could do was go on with his rather insipid and frustrating existence—and pray that Kimberly's brother did not contemplate a change in jobs.

Skelly's own job was a source of discontent, although of a mild and tolerable sort. He worked in an office in a huge multistory glass-sided building, shuffling papers, as did everyone else he knew. The people were nice enough the men companionable, the woman ranging from smart and pretty all the way up to brilliant and beautiful—but in terms of Skelly's peculiar fixations, there was little stimulation. About the only thing that might liven up his day was the arrival of a female messenger, or, in his lunch hour, the sight of a flock of hairdessers-in-training from the beauty school next door, which required its students to dress alike in white, like doves.

At those moments when it seemed as if he could not tolerate his job any longer, Skelly would daydream about joining a branch of the United States Armed Forces. (Such episodes were usually provoked by watching a surfeit of *M*A*S*H* reruns.) He could waste hours envisioning being surrounded by women dressed in Navy blue and Army khaki, Air Force white and Marine olive. Uniforms of every kind, twenty-four hours a day… Oak leaves, stripes, brass, muddy boots. Access to Paradise, just for signing on the dotted line? Skelly's common sense always persuaded him otherwise. He knew he would be signing away his independence, and that the kind of fooling around he dreamed of would be severely frowned upon. No, that was not a solution to his fix. It appeared that his best bet was to stick with his familiar life and hope that someday he would meet the woman of his dreams, however improbable that often seemed.

One lunch hour Skelly was idling in the plaza outside his building, watching the strolling crowd go by. It was a warm autumn day as goldenly transparent as the cellophane on a butterscotch candy. Skelly was soon treated to an awe-inspiring sight. There materialized, just a few yards down the sidewalk, all lolita-limbed, giggling, and wide-eyed, a troop of adolescent suburban Girl Scouts, under the watchful tutelage of their leader, who, like the girls, was uniformed in a thrilling forest-green wool skirt and top, complete with neckerchief held by a brass slide.

Skelly fell in love with the older woman at once. He watched her deft competence as she she herded her charges safely across the street. Was there official Girl Scout underwear also? Perhaps imprinted with the Sacred Trefoil just above the mons…?

As the troop halted for a second on the sidewalk, pandemonium broke out nearby.

"Help, help!" shrilled a woman. "My chain!"

From the crowd of lunchers dashed a scared-looking youth clutching a gold chain. He sprinted through the stunned watchers, making good his escape.

Approaching the street, he took his eyes off his path, looking instinctively for traffic.

He collided with the Girl Scouts.

Snatcher and shrieking Scouts went tumbling.

In a second the boy was up again and running. The girls who had been knocked down were slower to recover.

Skelly was shocked. Leaving the apprehension of the snatcher to others, he hastened to help the fallen Scouts.

Skelly had his hands under the armpits of one Scout, helping her to stand, when some vague apprehension made him look over his shoulder.

Behind him stood the meter-maid whom he had propositioned months ago.

"So," she said, "it's the pervert. Get your hands off that girl."

"No," said Skelly, "you don't understand—"

Specatators had clumped around the scene.

"Oh, yeah, I know what's going on, you creep. You couldn't control yourself any longer."

The girl whom Skelly had helped up now stepped cautiously away from him. He could feel the massed gaze of the watchers boring into him. "You're crazy lady. That's not what happened at all…"

"Yeah, well I think I'll just keep you here until the cops come."

The woman grabbed Skelly's arm.

Skelly jerked away. "The hell with you. I'm leaving."

The meter-maid turned toward the audience, as if to implore their help. Several of the men stirred tentatively. Skelly got frightened.

He turned without looking and took three steps into the street.

Shouts, screams, brakes, and life was looping back, a fleeting impression of a speeding white bulk tinged with red and blue, Christ, he was being run over by America—

This time there was no soft crossing-guard's lap to awaken in.

"Mister Skelly," said the nurse, "you have a visitor." Skelly wondered who it could possibly be. Although in traction, he could still nod, after a fashion.

"Fine, send him in."

"It's a she," said the nurse.

"Oh. Well, send her in."

The nurse departed. Skelly admired her immaculate uniform. There were compensations for everything...

Steps sounded. Skelly laboriously turned his head.

A short, dark-haired woman stood tentatively in the doorway.

She was dressed as a United States Postal Employee.

"Mister Skelly?" said the mailwoman.

"Yes?"

"I'm Angelica Mason. I was driving the truck that hit you."

"Oh, Miss Mason, I'm so sorry—"

"You're sorry? That's supposed to be my line."

"Oh, no, it was all my fault. I stepped right out in front of you. There was no way you could have anticipated it, or stopped in time."

Angelica seemed to relax. "It was kinda stupid. I was sure I had killed you. And then, when I found out you had survived, I was so afraid you'd hate me."

"Hate you? I couldn't hate anyone."

"I can't tell you how glad I am you feel that way, Mister Skelly."

"Peter, please."

"Angie.

Silence.

"Uh, won't you have a seat, Angie?"

"Oh, no, I'm sorry, I couldn't stay. I'm on my break. I just wanted to stop by and see how you were doing."

"Not bad. I'll be up and around before you know it."

"That's wonderful. Well, I guess I'll be going then. If I can, I'll visit again."

"That would be great, Angie."

Skelly coughed as the postwoman was halfway out the door. She stopped and looked back.

"Could I ask you one question, Angie?"

"Why, sure, I guess."

"Do you enjoy your job?"

In the late 1980s, I had occasion to spend a fair amount of time in New York City, with nothing to do but walk the streets in search of knowledge and adventure. I was accompanying my partner Deborah Newton on her assignments as a freelance editor at *Vogue Knitting*. During her office hours, I occupied myself with these expeditions, till I had traced my paths in ballpoint ink on a sweat-wrinkled map to the point of tattering the document. The knowledge gained from these pleasant peregrinations was invaluable and omnipresent. Adventures such as the one in this story were less easily found, and so had to be contrived on the page.

PS: Another period alert: people once actually could smoke in public establishments! And Times Square really *was* exceedingly seedy.

A NIGHT IN THE THIRTEENTH AVENUE MISSION

Bright cutlery lay on clean white linen. The tines of the large and small forks curved with wordless elegance. The spatulate butter knives with pistol handles promised perfect heft. Serrated steak knives seemed eager to slice and cut. The polished bowls of the soup spoons captured the perfect interior of the restaurant in unattainable miniature.

Pastel-pink cloth napkins stood folded at the top of each sparkling plate, beside gleaming crystal wine glasses, half-full of blood-dark wine.

"So in the end," Harry Scoon said to his dining companion, "they sold the place for twice what they paid, after holding on to it for less than eight months."

Scoon sat back in his padded chair, evidently exhausted from rendering his complicated tale of high-finance intrigue. He rested one hand across his vest-covered paunch, as if to appease a stomach that had gone untended for more than four hours. With the other hand he reached for his glass, lifted it to overripe lips, and drank.

Mark Chambliss smiled with an insincere show of appreciation. At times, Harry could be so boring—especially when talking of these legendary big deals made by people Mark never knew—that he was painful to be with. If they hadn't attended law school together, and formed a kind of businesslike, forced friendship under the pressures of the place, Mark doubted they would have had anything in common. And look at that gut Harry was developing— It was eating in places like this every day that did it. Mark reflexively placed a hand on his own trim waist, calculating how much extra workout time this meal would cost him later tonight.

The two men sat amid the supper crowd at Streets of Gold, a popular spot in the renovated South Street Seaport, not far from the east end of Wall Street. Waiters dressed nearly as expensively as the customers moved with grace and precision among the close-packed tables. Overloud laughter, the clink of glass and silver, and the almost palpable tension generated by a frenzied scramble for conversational points created an atmosphere that made rational thought impossible. Outside the restaurant's windows, immaculate, purposeful men and women crossed the quaint cobblestones.

Scoon set down his glass, now nearly empty. He motioned toward Mark's. "What's the matter? My taste in vintages no good? Drink up, boy. We're not in our offices now."

"No, we're not," Mark agreed. "But I do have to return later and get some work done."

"Ah, I forgot," Scoon said melodramatically. "The probity of a public servant. How is life under the eye of our illustrious DA these days? Prosecuted any good sex offenders lately?"

Hot bile filled Mark's throat. What right did Harry have to make fun of his work? Sure, it wasn't so glamorous or so lucrative as working for a national firm with four hundred sixty-two other unscrupulous threepiece-suited sharks. But didn't conviction and a desire to do good count for something?

"As a matter of fact," Mark said with restraint, "we're handling a very interesting corruption case now. Some big names are going to take a fall on this one."

Scoon perked up, sensing blood. "Among whom are—?"

Mark briefly enjoyed the uncommon feeling of power, then immediately felt guilty over even such an innocent bit of boasting. "I can't say. You know that. I couldn't risk jeopardizing the investigation."

Smiling superciliously, Scoon relaxed his alertness, toyed idly with a knife. "Still the Boy Scout, I see. Well, perhaps one day you'll learn. Altruism is a dead-end, Mark. No payback from it. Eventually, you'll stop wasting all your energy in futile do-gooding and make something of yourself. You know that with my recommendation, Wharton, Kline and Lambert would take you on anytime."

Mark was stopped from spilling out a scathing dissertation on the pedigree of Messrs. Wharton, Kline and Lambert—which wouldn't have really damaged his friendship with Scoon, who frequently said worse things about his employers, in a way that revealed pride and envy in their perfidy—by the approach of the waiter with their meal.

The polite silence which ensued allowed time for Mark's anger to bleed away, and afterwards Scoon was too busy eating to respond to talk.

At meal's end, Scoon sat back with a suppressed belch followed by a deep sigh. He took a pack of Dunhills from his inside jacket pocket, searched for matches and came up empty.

Mark, who didn't smoke, nonetheless patted his pockets automatically. Before he could disappoint Scoon even in such a small way, their observant waiter had come forward with a lighter. But the unintended search of his coat had turned up a folded piece of paper, and Mark recalled that he had meant to show it to Harry.

Taking out the grimy sheet of paper, Mark said to Scoon, "Here's a curiosity for you. A cop I know found it on a poor bum who died of exposure. He was going to throw it away, but it caught my interest, and I asked him if I could keep it."

Mark unfolded the quartered sheet and proferred it to Scoon, who took it with evident reluctance between two fingertips. He read it quickly, then tossed it to the tabletop, where it lay like a macroscopic piece of New York soot. The paper bore this message:

HOMELESS IN MANHATTAN?

COLD? TIRED?

NO PLACE TO SLEEP?

COME TO THE

THIRTEENTH AVENUE MISSION

FOOD—CARE—SAFETY

NO CATCHES

NO QUALIFICATIONS

NO DEMANDS

"So what?" Scoon demanded. "Just another soup-kitchen of some sort. Evidently the bum who had this paper never made it there. Why'd you even bother to save it?"

"You don't see anything strange about it? For instance, where's the address?"

"All right, so there's no address. These things spread by word of mouth. I'm sure every baglady and wino in the city knows where this place is."

"What about the name?"

"What about it?"

"There is no Thirteenth Avenue in Manhattan."

Scoon paused a moment, as if checking the internal map of the city that every resident possessed. "Okay. There's no Thirteenth Avenue. I repeat: so what? It's a fanciful name, dreamed up by some preacher or social-worker. You know, like Stone Soup or something."

Mark shook his head. "I don't think so. There's been no publicity about this place that I've seen. Isn't news coverage the first thing a mission like this would go after, to get funding and volunteers? No, I get a feeling there's more to this than what we see on the surface."

Scoon laughed like a sick crow. "Don't you have anything better to occupy your mind? Don't waste your time thinking about it. Listen, this city is full of unexplainable things that could drive you nuts if you let them. Try concentrating on the important issues: women, money, real estate."

As Scoon sucked in an enormous lungful of smoke and immediately released it in a noxious cloud, Mark took up the paper, refolded it and stowed it away.

If he had ever considered leaving the mystery of the creased and spotted broadside unsolved, Scoon's words and tone had irrevocably committed him to finding the answer.

Outside, the happy, well-fed, clean-clothed citizens strolled.

* * * *

Forty-second Street exuded a tawdriness more clammily repellent than the cheapest carnival that had ever crept into town under the cover of dusk. The once-grand theaters reduced to showing sex-films and karate-flicks; the peep-shows and live-sex acts; the filthy fried-chicken restaurants with their shapeless batter-crusted lumps cooling on grease-stained paper. And the people who thronged it: shuffling old men wearing two or three shabby overcoats apiece; kids offering "coke-hash-smoke" as if it were one item; epicene dollboys and fat black whores in torn nylons and vinyl miniskirts; the disaffected, the abandoned, the unloved.

The very sidewalks seemed stained with the oily perspiration of human suffering. Pairs of cops patrolled with hardened intensity.

Mark strode quickly down the Deuce, a member of the suited and shoe-shined minority. Work was over, and he was determined to spend some time investigating the curious paper he had shown Scoon at supper.

Why he should be so intrigued by the puzzle, he couldn't say. Scoon's scorn had been only the catalyst that had firmed up a resolve that had been steadily growing since the message came into his hands.

He had always been a sucker for lost causes, though. Even his unconscious choice of Forty-second Street as his path west, he realized, reflected his fascination with the down-and-out in society, the losers and hard-luck cases. And his choice of careers—well, there was material for a year's worth of psychoanalysis. Why did anyone chose to labor in the masochistic vineyards of public prosecution, after spending all that money and time and energy on an education in law? Was he really still guilty about his parents' wealth? Must every summer spent in Martha's Vineyard be repaid by a season in hell?

Who could say? Certainly not the man most closely involved.

Shrugging his shoulders, Mark continued down the strip.

Once he crossed Ninth Avenue, he left the worst of the sleaze behind. Now he was surrounded only by raw poverty and desperate entrepreneurial struggles to stay afloat: mom-and-pop groceries, furniture stores where all the goods looked excavated from Ur, resale clothing shops. Here too, human misery was evident in the people: homeless crones shouting obscenities at the uncaring sky; bored teenagers feeding videogames; sidewalk vendors peddling secondhand household trash spread on dirty blankets.

After three more long blocks, he found himself down by the Hudson, on Twelfth.

The last avenue before the water.

Mark stopped.

Where was Thirteenth Avenue, and its mission?

Before him the Hudson surged, an oil-slicked, litter-flecked moat separating the relative greenery of Jersey from the grey of Manhattan. A couple of blocks north, to his right, the West Side Elevated Highway began, running north above Twelfth like a concrete canopy. Nowhere, however, was there sign of an avenue on the far side of Twelfth.

Where should he turn now? He knew that south of his position, Twelfth petered out and Eleventh became the westernmost street. Surely the mysterious Thirteenth could not be there. No, if it existed at all, it must be north of him.

Mark crossed Twelfth, putting himself on the far side of the Elevated, to be as close to the waterfront as possible, and headed uptown. He passed the *USS Intrepid*, looming at its museum dock like a steel bird of war. He idled by the Pier Exposition center, where a trade-show had attracted buses and crowds of jewelry salespeople. He watched the tourists lined up to ride the Circle Line boats around the island. Before burned-out and devastated warehouses he paused, wondering at the secret wars of commerce, the shifting tides of trade, responsible for wreaking such casualties . The Sanitation Department garages hummed with activity, huge garbage trucks lumbering in and out of the gates like scabrous white elephants.

All along his route, the Hudson slopped among its piers and pilings like an uneasy beast.

Eventually, at Fifty-ninth Street, he reached a dead-end. A tall chain-link fence, topped by barb- and razor-wire, surrounded the Conrail yards, a vast desolate weedy tract slated to become housing and stores at some indefinite future date. Mark knew the geography north of these yards: Riverside Park, the Cloisters, Fort Tryon, Inwood Hill Park… No Thirteenth Avenue lurked there.

Baffled, he turned up Fifty-ninth, which ran under an arch supporting the Elevated. The arch was the elaborate product of another era, proclaiming itself with cement inscriptions and decorative motifs as if it were still a proud portal to a bustling waterfront, instead of a dismal gate to nowhere.

Mark felt it mocked him somehow with its witless pride.

* * * *

It was going to be a hard autumn and winter for the homeless. Already, in October, a cold snap had caused the various private and public shelters around the city to become overloaded, forcing them to turn people away. Every morning, during his jog in Central Park, Mark saw men and women lying on benches, rolled up in ragged sheets of foam, like that used underneath wall-to-wall carpeting, only their heads and feet protruding. On the way to work, he saw more of the destitute huddled in his subway stop, glad for the warm stenchy air. On the streets at lunchtime, he noticed them in plazas and parks, soaking up the pale autumnal sunlight as if to hold it through the long night to come.

Of course, all this was nothing new. There had been unhoused souls in the city as long as the city had existed. One could not help but be confronted with them every day. The fellow shaving himself with a disposable razor, a shard of mirror and a coffee can of dirty water; the woman pushing her shopping-cart full of worthless possessions and rehearsing affronts she had suffered; the old man without shoes scavenging cans from the trash for a nickel apiece.

Institutions and charities struggled valiantly but futilely to help the tide of wanderers. But it was like trying to drain the sea with a straw. More surged in than could be handled. And the average taxpayer cared too little about them to be bothered funding institutions at the necessary level.

Mark, with his particular bent of mind, had always had more of an eye for these hapless men and women than most people did. He carried pocketsful of change for handouts, kicked in sizable amounts to the United Way, and had spent a month of weekends helping renovate a church hall to dormitory housing. But even so, since he had chanced upon the flyer for the elusive Thirteenth Avenue Mission, his attention had focused on the homeless to an unnatural degree. Unable to find the Mission, and its attractive promise of FOOD—CARE—SAFETY (and why did this promise seduce him so; did he not have these things in abundance already?), he had fastened on those who surely must patronize the Mission regularly, assuming that it even existed.

Which assumption he made with an unwavering force that was beginning to border, he feared, on monomania.

So far, Mark had not found the nerve to actually question any of the homeless as to the whereabouts of the Mission. Used as they were to being harassed and ripped-off, they would be suspicious and reticent. Instead, he mulled over vague plans of following one of them at the start of chilly dusk to the hidden Mission. But which of the many shambling figures would lead him there? Surely not everyone ended up on Thirteenth Avenue. The full-capacity load of the other places told him that. And what would he do when he got there? Ask to be admitted? Why? Had his identification with the luckless progressed so far?

Only when the second Mission flyer was thrust upon him by the dying bum did Mark realize he had to act shortly, or simply fail to ever solve the mystery.

* * * *

Early morning in the fresh-smelling Park. Gravel crunched beneath Mark's sneakers and his breath came hard. Soon sunlight would slant through the colored leaves, fall in cool lozenges upon the path. Mark rounded a curve and saw the Carousel, closed at this hour and season. Its gaily painted doors with horse bas-reliefs were a welcome sight, halfway point of his run.

A gaunt apparition appeared from nowhere, stumbling into Mark's path. Unable to stop in time, Mark ran into him, and both crashed to the ground.

Mark recovered quickly, and came to his knees. The other man lay still, as if afraid to move. His wild eyes were open, staring into the leafy canopy. His bristled face was emaciated. He wore a ragged assortment of castoff clothing, caked with streetgrime, twigs and soil. The soles of his shoes flapped open with unintended comicality. He smelled of urine and wine.

"Are you okay?" Mark asked. The question seemed to free the man from his bondage. His limbs flapped around in an ungainly fashion, but failed to aid him to rise. His thick tongue protruded and wet his cracked lips.

"Gotta get there," he croaked. "Gotta get there, just found out, gotta get there, can't miss it—" His broken litany suddenly ceased. A grimy hand came up and clutched Mark's sweatshirt. The other sought to push a crumpled paper into his face.

"Take me there—" the man urged. Before Mark could reply, the man stiffened, then began to thrash in an epileptic fit. His wild buckings tossed Mark off. When he finally stopped, Mark sought with trembling fingers inside his mouth to insure he hadn't swallowed his tongue, then went to find an emergency phone. The man's breathing was shallow and rapid.

By the time the rescue squad came, the man was dead.

Mark had pried the paper from his fist before the medicos could find it. The message read:

ANNOUNCING THE CLOSING

OF THE

THIRTEENTH AVENUE MISSION

LAST FIVE DAYS

NOVEMBER 8-12

* * * *

Mark finished relating the disturbing event in the Park to Harry Scoon. His mouth was excessively dry, and he drained his glass of water, waiting for Scoon to give his opinion.

Scoon's expression was unusually solemn. Hardly a trace of his natural cynicism showed through. He regarded Mark quietly for a moment before he spoke.

"Listen, what's the matter with you?" he finally asked. "I don't like what's happening to you lately. You're letting this whole foolish matter assume more importance than it deserves. It's unhealthy to pay so much attention to these dregs and scumbags. Who cares what's happening at some crummy flophouse?"

Mark said nothing, and Scoon leaned forward, elbows on the table, as if to fix Mark with his intensity.

"Did you take my remarks last time as some sort of challenge? I never meant them as such. You know my way of talking better than that."

"No, it's nothing you said," Mark admitted reluctantly. "It's something that's been building up in me for a long time. I don't particularly like my job, or my life. I feel guilty all the time, like an impostor or hoaxer. Why do I deserve what I have, when others are so bad off? I can't explain it, Harry. It's just what I feel. Maybe it's what all these other people wandering the streets went through before they hit the skids."

Scoon sat back and lit a cigarette, puffed and considered. "This is what you do. Take a vacation somewhere out of this fucking city. Having that bum die on you was enough to shake anyone up. When you come back, I promise I'll have the answer to this place. I'll use all my connections to find out about it. When you see that's it's nothing but another Salvation-Army-type setup, you can dismiss it from your mind. You'll see there's nothing there for you."

"But it's closing," Mark said. "It'll be too late."

"Just do what I say," Scoon said.

Mark suddenly deflated, all energy gone from his shaking frame. He nodded in submission.

But he and Scoon both knew he lied.

* * * *

In front of the Plaza Hotel, limos pulled up and disgorged men in tuxes and women in furs. The Park's horse-drawn carriages clattered by, bearing tourists to snapshot immortality. Late-shoppers poured from Bergdorf-Goodman bearing boxes and bags.

Mark walked through the night along Central Park South, heading west. Wearing jeans and a leather jacket, he felt out of place among the well-dressed crowds pouring from the hotels and restaurants along the street. Had he come down here any other night, he too would have been costumed as they were. But not tonight.

Tonight he had another destination, impossibly further than any they could conceive.

Cutting into the Park, Mark wandered down paths ill-lit by the stray unbroken lamp until he came to a cluster of benches that held a serried rank of slumped shadowy shapes.

He flopped down at the end of one bench, prayed that his day's worth of stubble and ratty running sneakers looked convincingly streetwise.

No one spoke to him, or took overt notice of his presence. Mark sat in unconscious imitation of the others, legs extended into the path, shoulders hunched against the cold.

For six hours or more, no one spoke. There sounded only the wracking phlegmy coughs indicative of untended ills, and the rumble of empty guts.

Mark had plenty of time to think.

He found he had no thoughts.

At last, around two in the morning, the forms on the benches began to move. One by one they came to their feet and shuffled off toward the west, never bunching or clumping, which would have attracted undue notice.

When Mark's turn to rise came, he found his legs stiff as bowling pins. Somehow, he endured the pain and stood. Hurrying to keep the man ahead of him in view, he moved on his awkward legs through the deserted Park.

At Columbus Circle, his guide went south, around the Coliseum, then picked up Fifty-ninth at Ninth.

Gradually, they left all mundane crowds behind, moving with agonizing slowness down meaner and meaner streets.

Now the number of people all heading in the same direction became apparent.

When they reached the huge dirty grey brick ConEd generating station at Fifty-ninth and West End Avenue, its tall stack like a prophet's finger pointing to a just heaven, the multiple threads of streetpeople from all over the city had gathered into a writhing knot of unwashed flesh.

Mark couldn't tear his eyes from the crowd ready to submerge him. There was a giant black man wearing only vest and running pants, his hair in matted dreadlocks. There were bagladies toting tattered shopping bags from designer boutiques. A teenager in ripped Army jacket and camouflage pants leaned against an old man with rheumy eyes and a hacking cough.

And still they poured into the intersection, swarming, Mark knew, from all over the city which had turned its back on them. From the restrooms in Penn and Grand Central Stations they came. From Central Park and Morningside Heights, from the Lower East Side, the Bowery, Bryant Park and Washington Square. From Grand Army Plaza, beneath the Brooklyn Bridge, Chelsea Park, Union Square and the Port Authority Terminal. Every rough grating moist with life-giving steam and rubble-filled doorway that cut the cruel wind had given up its inhabitants for the night.

For a fraction of a second, Mark hesitated before plunging into the reeking, shivering mass. Then he abandoned all conceits of difference and surrendered himself to their herd-warmth.

How long, he wondered, would it be before a police-cruiser came by, and the riot started?

Movement surged through the crowd, and Mark was borne along with it. Straining on tiptoe, he saw that he was being carried toward the fence enclosing the Conrail yards. Surely they didn't intend to scale that vicious razored barrier—

When Mark reached the fence, a portion of it simply wasn't there. An irregular opening gaped, its edges melted as if by heat.

The crowd surged through the portal, fanned out across the grassy acreage, heading toward the river.

The Hudson. Thirteenth Avenue.

Mark followed, his will no longer his own.

Behind, the last of the homeless had come through. Silently the fence reformed in a blast of light.

Not a car had come by during the whole time, as if the traffic lights had conspired to hold them back.

Stumbling blindly across the unlighted, rock- and rubbish-strewn lot, Mark knew he liad to reach the river, although he couldn't have said why.

He crossed with the others a maze of tracks, cinders whispering unintelligible truths beneath his feet.

By the weedy riverbank he stopped, a line of his fellows extending to left and right. As he watched, each of them was enveloped in a scintillating golden nimbus. Looking down at his own limbs, he saw himself similarly encased.

Then they entered the river.

Their new skins gave them negative buoyancy, and they walked out along the sloping riverfloor to the center of the Hudson. They turned north, forming a line like an amber necklace threaded with black water, and continued walking.

Their glowing integuments allowed them to see for some distance around them. Wrecked and weed-wrapped cars, some with skeletal occupants, littered the bottom. Trash of every description—girders, washing machines, slabs of concrete—impeded their progress, caused them to scramble and weave. Still they wended their way upstream, human fish heading for ancient spawning grounds.

Mark felt neither happy nor sad. All emotions had been temporarily denied him.

In the distance, a grouping of lights appeared. As Mark neared it, it assumed the form of a fiery castle or arcane vessel, mired in the riverbottom muck. Its myriad windows glowed with radiance unlike any he had ever seen before.

The line entered through a seemingly solid wall, their bubbles merging through the side of the building-ship.

Once he was in, a sense of wellfed healthiness pervaded him, a suffusion of good spirits that banished all cares. He felt sane for the first time in his life, as if all his mad past had been cut away by an invisible knife. It struck him as such a wonderful thing—him, who knew lesser comforts as a matter of course—that he wondered how the miserable streetpeople could stand the joy. At the same time, he felt his body dissolving, his corporeal self melting away with the bodies of all the rest. All his senses fled: vision, touch, hearing. He was a disembodied presence floating in a primordial soup, having surrendered his constituents, his carbon and water and trace elements, to the needs of his new benefactors.

How his self still existed, he couldn't imagine.

After a period without measure, he came to sense the selfhood of all the others. They began to blend with his in a spontaneous meld, each one giving up his loneliness to share in the general happiness.

Mark's senses returned, but now they were located in the skin and interior of the castle-ship. He felt the cold water of the Hudson brush his sides, saw through the murky waters right up to the stars that glowed above. Access to an inner clock informed him, impossibly, that it was still the same night he had entered.

A glorious piping music began to fill his new ears. The communal voice of the human meld began to soar in song. From some former part of their new self came the thought: *Hamelin, and the rats.*

Mark thought back agreement as he felt the ship begin to lift from the riverbed, ascend toward the sky.

Right. But this time the rats are being left behind.

Since I wrote this story, archaeologists continue to find evidence of the centrality of beer to man's development and continued existence. Of course, they could have just asked Homer Simpson.

PS: You can tell this is a very old story because in it academics actually communicate by snailmail.

STRANGE BREW

Jerzy sneezed, and almost blew apart the papyrus.

This is not good, he thought, reaching for a kleenex with white-gloved hands. I've been working too hard, getting sloppy. And this cold—I need a break.

Standing, Jerzy carefully lifted the fragile papyrus, which rested loosely on white acid-free museum board, and slid the whole assemblage gently back into its protective slipcase.

The reference librarian who guarded the reading room Jerzy liked to use said, "Done for now, Professor?"

"For now. Could you watch my stuff while I put this back in the vault?"

"Sure."

The reading room was in the basement of the Beinecke. Its eastern glass wall gave a view of an open-aired sunken courtyard. The slant of light revealed the hour to be around four. In the middle of the courtyard, like a monument to some anonymous Neolithic inventor, stood a sculpture of an enormous stone wheel. Late at night, after hours of concentration and eyestrain, Jerzy had more than once sworn the wheel had rolled.

Only a fraction of a foot. But still.

The elevator took him down a level. He signed into the climate-controlled vault that held the rest of the Yale Papyrus Collection. He went straight to the proper drawer in the correct case and replaced the fragment he had been examining. Then he paused.

As always, the rows of cases and their contents oppressed him. Over half of the Collection had never been examined in the century of its existence.

Just last year, a doctoral student had found a missing portion of the Nag Hammadi Codex III. Who knew what else lurked buried in the stacks? And he was the only fulltime researcher currently assigned to the Collection. Never in his lifetime would he even make a dent in the unread material. The realization depressed him. When it did not drive him to extremes of scholarly exertion.

He signed out of the vault and rode the elevator back up a level. In the reading room he placed his magnifying glass, notes and Coptic dictionary inside his briefcase. He stripped his gloves off and dropped them in too.

The gloves protected the papyrus from his sweat, which contained microbes and chemicals harmful to the ancient manuscript.

But sometimes Jerzy wondered if the gloves didn't also serve to protect him from the papyrus.

Once on the ground level, he left the white tessellated marble cube of the Beinecke and walked across the quad to his office.

Setting his case down on his desk he opened a drawer and took out a pack of Sudafed. He removed a capsule and went to the men's room. He swallowed the pill with a handful of water, took a long-delayed leak, and turned to leave. Then he noticed something new.

The University had installed a condom dispenser on the wall.

Was this a Viennese whorehouse? Were the faculty being officially encouraged to indulge in wild office sex? Jerzy vaguely remembered something in the *Herald* about new anti-AIDS measures. What an age to live in—

But still.

He stepped back to the sink and washed his hands.

After leaving the restroom, Jerzy recalled that he had not checked his mailbox today. So he went to the department offices.

There was a letter in his box from Doctor al-Banna of the Coptic Museum in Cairo. Excitedly ripping open the garishly stamped envelope, Jerzy forgot his cold and his fatigue.

Doctor al-Banna had succeeded in tracking down the meanings of more than two dozen highly obscure Coptic words and phrases which a puzzled Jerzy had submitted to him. The sleuthing—as detailed in a tedious preface by the voluble Doctor—had involved visiting the library of a Coptic monastery whose monks had specialized for nearly two millennia in brewing beer.

As soon as Jerzy read this, he knew that success was in his grasp.

He rushed back to the Beinecke. Like a film run in reverse, he went backwards through his recent actions, until he was finally seated once more with the papyrus in front of him.

This scrap, although relatively young (circa 400 AD), announced itself to be a copy of a much older Pharaonic manuscript, which in its turn claimed to be a transcription of a pre-Dynastic tablet, thus making the actual text over five thousand years old.

The papyrus itself had come to America, as so many had, as wrappings on a mummy, roughly around 1833. After decades of hard use as an exhibit in various sideshows, the nameless mummy and its cerement had ended up in Barnum's circus. Finally, on the point of disintegration, it had been donated by Barnum himself (ever-alert to make something out of nothing) to the University closest to his Bridgeport home.

Beyond its standard introduction, the papyrus's contents had been far more elusive than its physical history. With words missing and others unknown to him, Jerzy had been stumped. All he had been able to deduce was that the text was a recipe and invocation of some sort.

Now, with al-Banna's letter spread out before him, Jerzy determined to solve this mystery.

Hours fled. Jerzy was lost somewhere fine. When he came back, the courtyard was in darkness, and he had a working translation.

"...beautiful Ninkasi, mistress of men, breeder of bubbles, easer of pains, grant this...success. From out of the air...small, invisible...here forever. We men...your vessels...slim-necked [the vessels, or Ninkasi? wondered Jerzy]...bread part-baked, wheat, water, and juice of dates ... stand...gases separate from the air... Celebrate...with straws. We become Ninkasi. We carry...we excrete...Ninkasi breeds in us, we live... her. The cycle is complete..."

Beer. It was a recipe for making beer. Jerzy recalled the work of Solomon Katz, an anthropologist at the University of Pennsylvania. Katz had theorized that brewing was the primeval technology that had induced mankind to leave behind the hunter-gatherer style of existence and settle down as agriculturalists. In Katz's view, all of civilization, the whole vast ten-thousand-year-old edifice, was reared on a foundation of beer.

Well, thought Jerzy, sitting back wearily in his chair, Katz and a few others would be pleased to see this. But still. It was hardly, as Jerzy had been secretly hoping, another find equivalent to the Nag Hammadi Codex. So much work, for so little. Perhaps the next fragment...

All this talk of beer had made Jerzy thirsty. He decided to visit Toad's Place for a drink.

When the papyrus had been restored to its modern crypt, he assembled his materials and left.

Out in the courtyard, the stone wheel seemed innocent of motion.

High Street ran behind the Beinecke. Jerzy crossed it, and cut through the block-long Sterling Memorial Library, Gothic and brooding, to York Street. He turned left, and soon stood before Toad's.

Toad's was a rock club. Jerzy found the atmosphere puerile, but it was one of the few places in New Haven that maintained his favorite beer on tap. If one left before the so-called live music began, it was just acceptable.

Looking at his watch, Jerzy saw that he had an hour or so to enjoy his drink in relative quiet.

Inside, he was surprised to see a colleague sitting alone. It was young Summers, from the biology department. They had taught an interdisciplinary course together a few semesters ago.

Jerzy went to sit with him.

Three empty steins and a fourth half full already occupied the table. Summers looked blearily up at Jerzy's arrival. "Oh, hullo, Jerze. Long time no see. Pull up a chair."

"Thank you," said Jerzy, regretting his decision even as he found himself unable gracefully to escape.

"How's everything been?" asked Summers. "Discovered the name of Jesus's main squeeze yet?"

Jerzy chided himself for ever attempting to explain the Nag Hammadi fragment to Summers. "No, Stephen, I have not, However—"

The arrival of a mini-skirted waitress interrupted Jerzy's intended announcement.

"What'll it be, Prof?"

"A draft of the usual."

Summers grabbed the waitress's hand and began to nuzzle it sloppily. "Bue'ful, bue'ful Nan. Nan Casey, so bue'ful. Why won't you screw me again? Do you still have that yeast infection?"

The waitress yanked her hand away "You're a pig, Steve," she said, and left.

Summers turned to Jerzy mournfully "Lookit that body. Hard to believe it's just a collection of colonies."

"What do you mean?"

"Don't you keep up with the latest theories, Jerze? Try to broaden your mind, for Christ's sake! Sagan. Dorion, not Carl. Helluva gal, Thinks our bodies are really just composites of different independent microscopic units. 'Animals are the result of multigene—I mean multigenome evolution.' You and me and Nan, Jerze, jus' walking cities of cells. Big bug democracies. Hey, remember what that beetle guy said when someone asked him what he's learned all these years? 'The Good Lord must be inordinately fond of beetles, for he made so many of them.'"

The waitress returned with Jerzy's beer and set it down, keeping carefully out of Summers's reach.

The first quarter of a glass, combined with the long hours and the Sudafed, set Jerzy's head spinning. He did not even protest when Summers got up to play the jukebox.

"Cream," said Summers enigmatically when he returned.

Jerzy heard a deep rumbling from York Street, as of a passing truck with stone wheels.

"I beg your pardon—?"

And then the music reached him.
"Strange brew, feel what's inside of you—"

As with "The Jones Continuum," real-world events rendered this story instantly obsolete after its publication—at least as far as representing cutting-edge technology went. The fax machine had a brief pre-internet moment when it ruled supreme as the hip mode of communications. Then suddenly one day it was as au courant as Morse code. (Although Japan still boasts a huge use of this antique technology, for cultural reasons. See "In High-Tech Japan, the Fax Machines Roll On," from *The New York Times* for February 13, 2013.) But with luck, the characters and their doings will still appeal. Maybe it's finally time for "faxpunk" SF! Especially since I seem to have incidentally invented "sexting" and "going viral" in this tale.

FAX

Garth Barth weighed ninety-eight and one-half pounds. And that was counting a dozen pens in a plastic pocket protector, a pair of Hush Puppies and eyeglasses with lenses thick as geological strata. He wore chinos and madras shirts buttoned to the neck. His hair sported a cowlick that resembled the ass-plumage of a certain species of South American quetzal. In short, Garth looked like a quintessential member of that much-maligned class known far and wide across the nation, a class which boasted members in every high school, college, and large corporation.

A techno-dweeb-hacker-nerd-bookworm-poindexter-putz.

The only difference between Garth and other members of his class—and a large difference it was—was that his look was a conscious effort, a deliberate disguise. Protective camouflage, if you will.

At age thirteen, just as he was preparing to enter the violent Darwinian social arena of high school, Garth had come to the conclusion that there was no one in his peer group who could share his particular interests and concerns, these ranging from the history of altered states of consciousness to artificial intelligence, from comix to industrial music, from biology to theology.

Moreover, there existed certain individuals who were downright inimical and hostile to his point of view, people who actively resented his opinions and would defend to Garth's death his right to be beaten up for trying to use his freedom of speech.

Having reached this conclusion, based solidly on the facts available to him, Garth decided he would strive to become as invisible as possible, hiding his true subversive nature beneath a mask of acceptable weirdness. Making a survey of all possible sociocultural roles, Garth settled upon his current disguise as providing the best cover. Not only did most parental adults look approvingly on such inbred scholastic types, but to Garth's peers the nerd somatype had become almost transparent, due to overexposure in the media. Even the most brutish jock nowadays could hardly be bothered to torment such a nonentity—especially if the nerd in question could be counted on to supply written-to-order term papers.

Three years after coming to this decision, Garth was still somewhat surprised at how well his scheme had worked. No one had ever noticed that his Hush Puppies were cleverly crafted foam shells concealing

Adidas, nor that the tee-shirt under his madras advertised a Captain Beefheart album, nor that his lenses were plain glass, nor that half of his breastpocket pens concealed tightly twisted joints in their barrels.

Still, despite the success of Garth's disguise and the freedom it gave him to pursue his own interests, it was a lonely life Garth led. Sometimes he wished there was at least one person he could open up to and be himself...

One fine spring day during gym period Garth found himself sneaking off the playing field of Xerox Inc. High. (The school had renamed itself in gratitude after receiving a large corporate grant.) A coed field hockey game was in progress, and Garth had no desire to have his shins bashed to flinders. Some of those girls were really vicious... No, such sublimi-nated warfare was not for him. Instead, he would sit peacefully in his usual hiding place until it was time to get dressed. He would peacefully smoke a joint and contemplate his latest experiments.

Around the side of the building, a set of wide concrete stairs led from the ground to a second-floor emergency exit. The stairs were open on ei-ther side. Beneath the cement structure, set back in the thickest shadows, was an old plastic milk crate someone had lifted from the cafeteria. Here Garth could sit and, by occasionally craning his neck, still maintain a view of the game, so that he would know when to rejoin his classmates.

The bare dirt beneath the steps smelled of urine from a hundred drunken extracurricular pissings. Garth was anxious to light up and dispel the aroma. He had just taken his seat and removed a pen from his pocket (he still wore his buttoned-tight madras with his gym shorts) when he became aware of a subdued sobbing directly at his elbow.

"Uh, who's that?" asked Garth warily.

The sobbing stopped. Through sniffles, an accented voice said, "It's me, Reba. Who're you?"

Reba Amoeba was a recent arrival to Xerox Inc. High. Her family had moved here from Texas, fleeing that state's economic depression. Reba's real last name was Tupple. Everyone called her Reba Amoeba cuz she was kinda fat. She probably weighted twice as much as Garth, but she was tall too. Garth didn't think she looked so bad. She had a sweet, albeit blotchy face and dressed nice. In addition, she had the biggest, most awesome tits Garth had ever seen. He suspected that half of the enmity she incurred from other girls stemmed from unacknowledged jealousy. Garth also thought her accent was charming.

"It's Garth. From math class."

Reba snorted. "Humph. Mister Brain."

Garth felt hurt. His self-devised image and reputation had never seemed so cumbersome. Perhaps he could let it drop just this once.

"Maybe," Garth replied mysteriously. "And maybe not. What're you doing here anyway?"

"I hate all those smug dudes and bitches and they hate me. I don't need to get whopped upside the head with a stick to make it sink in."

Garth nodded in the darkness. His eyes had adjusted, and he could make out the silhouette of Reba sitting on the grungy dirt. Her hunched shoulders made her look pretty miserable. Garth felt bad for her. "That's more or less my situation too. But listen, I got something to make you feel better. Here, hold this a second."

Passing the pen to Reba, Garth fumbled for some matches.

"Oh, great, a pen. What're we gonna do—write some equations?"

Garth just smiled. "Let us not prejudge things, shall we?" Garth took back the pen, unscrewed the barrel and removed a fine joint. He held it toward Reba so she could see.

"Wow," she exclaimed appreciatively. "I haven't smoked anything since I left home."

"Uh, care to share my seat ... ?"

Garth shifted, and Reba quickly settled half her large butt onto the milk crate, leaving a little corner for Garth. It was enough. Her big old warm hip felt like heaven. Garth lit up, and passed the joint to Reba. In between tokes, they soon began dissing representative local shitheads. Before they knew it, they were laughing and hanging on each other like forever best friends. When they stumbled out from beneath the steps at the end of the period to head back to the locker-rooms, they saw that each had one bare thigh whose back was imprinted with a waffle pattern. This really cracked them up, and they could barely walk.

Meeting afterwards in the corridor outside the gym, Reba and Garth looked somewhat shyly at each other. Things seemed a little different in the light of day, on the downside of their shared high.

"Uh, you won't tell anyone about my pens, will you?"

"Not if you don't tell 'bout how you found me crying."

"Oh, no, not a word, I promise."

"Me too."

They were silent a moment. Then Garth said, "Wanna come home with me after school and see what I've got in my basement?"

"Why, sure."

Garth smiled broadly up into Reba's face. She lit up too. He tried to think of something suitably impressive to say, but nothing came to him. Finally, he took off his glasses and whispered, "They're fake."

"Oh," said Reba. she seemed to understand. At least Garth hoped so.

After school Garth found Reba waiting with a fatalistic look that betokened many previous disappointments. When she saw Garth, she broke into a huge smile. He had been half hoping she wouldn't be there. This sharing stuff was tricky, and took more thought and work than being alone all the time. He hoped he was up to it, after such a long solitary existence.

At the door of Garth's house, Reba paused.

"Won't your Mom think it's funny, you bringing me down the basement?"

Funny? Garth felt a quiver. What did this girl have in mind? God, she was big… He tentatively took Reba's hand. She squeezed it. Garth was moved. "I don't know. I never had anyone over before. Let's see."

Mrs. Barth was skiing. Dressed in Rossignol boots, red spandex tights and a leotard, she shuffled on a Nordic trainer in front of a wall-sized rear-projection television screen which Garth had constructed from scratch. Synched with the trainer, the visuals on the screen zipped through Alpine slopes glistening with fresh powder.

"Hi, Ma. Listen, I've got a friend with me. We're gonna look at my hardware, okay?"

Mrs. Barth was intent on her cross-country pilgrimage, and didn't look up. "Uh-uh, fine, dear. Oh, could you turn up the heat before you go? It's a little chilly in here."

"Sure, Ma."

After notching up the thermostat, Garth brought Reba to the cellar door. He flipped on the basement light and they went downstairs.

"Your mother seems nice," said Reba.

"She's heavily into fitness."

"I thought so."

Garth unlocked the door of his basement headquarters and motioned for Reba to enter first.

Half of Garth's secret hideaway looked like an electronics retailer's. There were racks of stereo equipment, VCR's and monitors, and computers. Piles of CD's and tapes spilled from shelves. The other half looked like James Watson's wet dream. There were pocket gene-sequencers and peptide-linkers, ribosomal simulators and enzymatic baths. There was also a couch and a dorm-sized fridge.

"This place is so cool!" Reba said. Garth felt proud. "Where did you get all this stuff? And how did you ever afford it?"

"Oh, I do a little work for a few companies. Programming and stuff. It pays pretty good."

"Don't they mind how young you are?"

"They never see me. It's all done over the net."

By the way of illustration, Garth powered up a Pentium machine. Then, remembering his manners, he went to the fridge and removed a beaker containing a yellow liquid. "Want a drink?"

Reba looked slightly suspicious. "What is it?"

"It's just a mildly psychoactive relaxant and stimulant that will uncoil your DNA, ream out your cholesterol and refresh your long-term memory. And best of all, it doesn't taste like anything gross. I usually cut in with orange juice."

"In that case, I don't mind if I do."

Garth poured the drinks, and they toasted, then sipped.

"Mind if I get our of this stupid disguise?" asked Garth.

"Go right ahead."

Garth took off his glasses and combed his cowlick down. He stripped off his button-down to reveal a John Zorn tee-shirt. He unlaced his foam Hush Puppies and cast them aside. He put on a CD and turned around. Reba was sitting on the couch.

"This DNA stuff is great. I feel like I'm floating above all my problems."

"I thought you'd like it."

"Come sit down with me."

"Okay."

They sat quietly for a while, listening to the music. It was Talking Heads.

> I got a girlfriend that's better than that
> She has the smoke in her eyes
> She's moving up, going right through my heart
> She's gonna give me surprise

Reba had finished her drink. Her eyes were full of smoke.

"Do you want to see my tits? I noticed you're always looking at them."

Garth nodded wordlessly.

Reba peeled off her shirt.

She wasn't even wearing a bra. She didn't need one. Reba's boobs were the largest unsupported domes this side of Saint Peter's in Rome.

Garth jumped up. "I-I've got to digitize those."

"Say what?"

Garth was already scanning Reba's chest with a videocamera. In thirty-seconds, her magnificent equipment had been transferred as pixels to the screen of Garth's computer.

"Is that all you want to do with them?"

Garth mentally kicked himself. Where was his head at? He had been pretending to be a nerd for too long.

"No. I mean yes. I mean—oh, you know."

It was time to stop making sense. Garth threw himself on Reba.

Pretty soon they were making flippy-floppy.

* * * *

Garth stared at the full-color image of Reba's tits on his monitor. Thank God for high resolution!

It was the next afternoon. Reba had to help her mother with grocery shopping, and couldn't come to Garth's house. In a way, beneath his disappointment, Garth had been grateful. He needed a little time alone to collect his thoughts and try to figure out what he was feeling.

Basically, he guessed, he was very proud to have Reba as his girl-friend. They had talked a lot yesterday, and she seemed like a really smart and sensible person. Plus she was really sexy. At least Garth thought so. And who wouldn't, looking at those breasts…?

Studying Reba's digitized physiology, Garth was overcome by a sudden feeling of benevolent pride. He wanted the whole world to realize what a great body Reba had. He wanted to broadcast this picture to every television in the country…

Garth's thoughts jarred to a stop. Wait just one second. He could do something almost as good.

Garth's computer had a fax board in it, effectively transforming it into a fax machine. It also had a database containing thousands of public-access fax-machine numbers. Garth had obtained these from a paper-back book sold in any well-stocked bookstore. They were the numbers of many major corporations, retailers and government organizations. In addition, Garth had added any further fax numbers he had happened to run across, from local delis to foreign embassies.

These numbers, he supposed, represented a sufficient cross-section of the populace to appreciate Reba's tits.

Garth brought up the fax program. He instructed it to send a fax of Reba's tits to every number in the database, first routing the messages through a circuitous path that would prevent it being traced back to him.

Garth hit the ENTER key and sat back. The first black-and-white fax was already on its way.

Twenty-four hours later, as Garth opened the door of his den and ushered Reba in, the last fax was just going out.

Garth proudly explained to Reba what he had done.

She was silent for a moment. Then, very calmly, she said, "You sent a picture of my boobs to every bank, every newspaper, every television station you could find?"

"Yup."

"Every realtor, every architect, every lawyer?"

"Uh-huh."

Reba's lips were compressed to a thin line. Garth began to grow a bit nervous.

"Every Kinko's, every Staples, every Seven-Eleven with a three-hundred-dollar fax machine?"

"Well, I didn't—in fact, that's exactly—"

Garth was on his back on the floor. Reba was kneeling and choking him and screaming.

"If you wanted to ruin me, why didn't you just drag me naked through the town behind a bus! I've heard of guys who kiss and tell, but you're a monster! This is the worst thing I've ever been involved in!"

Garth croaked pitifully. Reba slightly relaxed her hold on his throat.

"Your face wasn't in the shot! And no one will ever trace it back here. I swear it! I'd never do anything to intentionally hurt you, Reba. Never!"

Reba started to cry. Garth got painfully up and put his arms around her. After a while she stopped.

"You know what I should do?" said Reba.

"What?"

"I should digitize your stupid willy and send it out after my boobs."

"Well, go ahead, I deserve it. But the disparity in size will make for a big anticlimax."

Reba managed to laugh. "Well, you know, I can see what appealed to you about this idea. It's kinda neat to think you can hit all these people with any message you want, and they just have to take it."

Grateful for an exit to the incident and also intrigued by where Reba was leading, Garth said, "Oh yeah? What kind of faxes would you send?"

"Well now, I don't rightly know offhand. Let's have a drink of that DNA stuff and talk about it."

* * * *

Reba entered Garth's basement workroom. She was such a fixture around the Barth household now that she let herself in and out.

"Your Mom yelled from the living room to me as I was going through the kitchen. She wanted me to turn on the water in the kitchen sink and splash it a little. I did, but I didn't ask why."

"She's got a rowing machine now."

Garth spotted a rolled-up magazine in Reba's hand. "More visual fodder?"

Reba grew excited. "You bet. Look at this. Can you believe it?"

She opened up the magazine, which was a copy of TIME. Inside was a picture of Vice President Gore holding a little girl on his lap. The caption said she was this year's Easter Seals poster child.

Garth eagerly grabbed the magazine. "If we had asked him to pose for us, it couldn't be better! You're obviously thinking of that image we were wondering what to do with last week—"

"Exactly."

"Okay, let's see how they fit."

Garth digitized the Vice President. He erased the little girl from his lap. Then he loaded an image previously extracted from a recent hit movie: a naked woman in a sitting position. He pasted her into Gore's lap. The Vice President's face remained plainly visible; his hands now rested in the woman's snatch. His wooden expression assumed new dimensions. A little fill concealed the seams between the two images.

"Perfect," said Reba.

Garth switched to typing mode and signed the image:

THE MAX PLANCK-MAX ERNST BRIGADE.

Then he sent it out over the phone lines.

"I wonder if this one will get as much publicity as the one we did about the Pope?" speculated Reba.

"It would be hard to top the Pope bowling with Mother Teresa. But this one might do it."

"I'm already thinking about the next one."

"Me too."

It hadn't taken Reba long that day a month ago to convince Garth that he was missing out on the true potential of his fax scheme. Sure, sending out an image of her boobs had been a cute start. But he could hardly continue in that mode. If he was going to go to the trouble of flooding the unsuspecting public with images, he should make sure they were suitably subversive ones. The spontaneously formed, unplanned and unregulated network of fax machines around the world had the potential to function as a kind of guerrilla anti-media. And Garth and Reba could be the schedulers.

Since that decision, they had sent out one fax daily.

They had rudely abused dozens of public figures, but realized they had still merely scratched the surface. They had portrayed Yeltsin screwing Maggie Thatcher. They had depicted Billy Graham rolling for high stakes in Vegas, surrounded by chorus girls. They had shown Jesse Jackson shaking hands with the head of the Aryan Nations. They had rigged improbable couplings of various stars: Cher and James Earl Jones, Eddie Murphy and Meryl Streep, Mick Jagger and Dolly Parton. They had done collages without human figures illustrative of various world problems. Tractors emptying grain into missile silos, an anthropomorphic mosque duking it out with an animated cathedral, an elephant drowning in a sea of human junk.

The reaction among the recipients of these images had been bigger and better than Garth and Reba could ever had hoped. For the most part, of course, the collages had not been taken as "real," whatever that meant. (Although there had been one small Midwestern paper which had run the image of the Pope bowling with the caption: POINTIFF ENJOYS DAY OFF.) Instead, the images had entered that amorphous netherworld of office humor and rumor, previously populated with crudely drawn sketches of outhouses with funny signs, bigbusted secretaries fending off the advances of their bosses, and vaguely anti-authoritarian or cynical slogans. The quality of the work done by Garth and Reba was so superior, the conceptions so funny and radical, that their images drove the weaker ones out of the urban mythological ecosystem.

The output from Garth and Reba was xeroxed and circulated far beyond its initial outlets. Within hours of its initial dissemination, it was multiplied hundred fold and disbursed across miles.

The two kids found out about all this a week or two after starting the transmissions. Feeling down about the apparent lack of response to their work, they had been hanging around watching television. The six-o'clock news came on. There on the screen was that day's image: Tipper Gore attending a drag queen's ball, looking right at home.

Garth and Reba perked up and listened.

"The President has vowed to bring to justice the perpetrators of what he called 'this libelous and scurrilous semi-scandal-type aggravation.' He added, 'Not that I feel that so-called gay or homosexual individuals necessarily de-connote a less-than-positive image in my administration.'"

After that, things really took off. Several alternative weekly newspapers began running a week's worth of faxes on their comix pages. Anarchistic individuals began blowing them up to poster size and hanging them around their neighborhoods. Anti-American foreign governments began using certain images as propaganda. The CIA printed up millions of the fax that depicted Qadaffi humping a camel and showered them over Libya.

When other unknown co-conspirators began issuing similar faxes, Garth and Reba decided to label theirs, to distinguish them from inferior imitations.

www.ingramcontent.com/pod-product-compliance
Lightning Source LLC
Chambersburg PA
CBHW031358250626
47155CB00004B/1322